Dear Reader:

We are especially proud to be bringing you this book, which is an iPublish.com original publication.

What that means is this book was discovered and endorsed for publication by other readers like you.

The author submitted the manuscript to iPublish.com, where it received ratings and reviews from other writers and readers. Their overwhelming enthusiasm for the submission brought it to the attention of the iPublish.com editors. We agreed this is a book that deserves to be enjoyed by many readers.

And one of them is you! We hope you agree it's a real find.

Sincerely,
The iPublish Editors

P.S. If you're interested in submitting your own work for publication consideration, visit us at www.ipublish.com to find out how!

Readers' Choice

"I wanted to write a contemporary romantic comedy, in particular, a romance between two lawyers. (I'm an attorney who fell in love with and married an attorney, so I know how romantic that can be!) This story practically wrote itself. I hope you love it."

KATE DONOVAN is an attorney in Elk Grove, California. She loves writing offbeat romance of every sort, from paranormal to historical to romantic suspense. Her first published novel was a time-travel historical romance, and more recently she has been writing mail-order bride stories set in post–Gold Rush California. *Harmless Error* is her first single-title contemporary romantic comedy.

HARMLESS

ERROR

KATE DONOVAN

For information address iPublish.com, 135 West 50th Street, New York, NY 10020.

An AOL Time Warner Company

ISBN 0-7595-5023-9

First edition: October 2001

Visit our website at www.iPublish.com

PROLOGUE

Seven men and five women filed slowly into the jury box, their expressionless faces giving no hint of the verdict to come despite the buzz of curiosity and anticipation that their return had created. Not that the verdict mattered to the tall, dark-haired attorney who was watching from the back of the crowded courtroom. Derek Grainger hadn't come to the courthouse to learn the fate of the defendant. After all, he wasn't the guy's lawyer, just an extremely interested observer.

Still, Derek had no doubt as to the outcome. If half of what he'd read in the newspapers was true, and if that information had been competently presented during the six-day trial, this jury really had no choice but to find George Perry guilty of the kidnapping and murder of his five-year-old daughter. Derek's ten years as a successful criminal defense attorney qualified him to confidently make this assessment. The question wasn't whether Perry would be convicted, but whether Perry *knew* it.

Because George Perry's expression, unlike that of the jurors, was eminently readable, and the optimism therein caused even a hardened legal warrior like Derek to sympathize. Hadn't the guy's lawyers prepared him? If not, it was an insidiously cruel variation on malpractice. George Perry had been through too much, these last harrowing six years, to be burdened now with false hope, yet there it was, lighting his thin face, evident in the set of his slender shoulders, reflected even in the relaxed hands that should have been clenched tightly into fists, bracing this artist-turned-murderer for the worst.

Forget about Perry, Derek advised himself grimly. *He's been doomed since the day he married Veronica. This just makes it official. There's nothing you or anyone else can do for him now. She's made sure of that.*

The observation reminded him of his reason for coming to court that day: to see *her.* Not her hapless ex-husband. Not the jury. *Her.* He had to see her, after all these years.

As he scanned the room for a glimpse of her, he prayed she wouldn't glance up or over at that moment. If she did, she'd recognize him despite the tinted glasses he was wearing in order to disguise himself, both from her and from the reporters who had thronged to hear the verdict. Any journalist who covered criminal proceedings in San Francisco would know Derek Grainger's face, and even those who didn't would be likely to spot him, thanks to the publicity about a recent movie based on his performance in a high-profile murder case. They'd clamor to learn his involvement with this case and wouldn't believe him if he said he'd never met George Perry and had no interest in these particular proceedings. They'd sense the makings of another movie, never guessing that that particular film would be too hot for any legitimate filmmaker to handle. Any accurate depiction of Veronica Keyes Perry would be both sordid and X-rated, given the woman's spellbinding proportions and degenerate pastimes.

Finally, he spotted her—the pseudo-perfect victim, dressed in black silk, her pouty pink lips and exotic green eyes so vividly sensuous that, despite old lessons learned, Derek felt a twinge of awe at the sight of them. She was sitting down and thus did not seem quite the Amazon he knew her to be. She had clearly attempted to appear wounded and heartbroken, and Derek wondered if she had succeeded. He could hardly be expected to be objective, given the nature of his former association with her. He knew the truth—that she was a cold, passionless woman, despite the heat her features and machinations could provoke.

As he watched from his anonymous vantage point, Veronica Keyes Perry brushed a platinum curl from her sculpted cheekbone and openly fixed her emerald stare on the hapless jury foreman, willing him to speak. And because men inevitably bent to her will, at least initially, the foreman cleared his throat and announced, too loudly, that the defendant was indeed guilty of the kidnapping and murder of his child.

Reactions, from gasped protests to muted cheers, filled the room, but it was *her* reaction Derek had come to see, and he wasn't disappointed. As he watched in morbid fascination, her bloodred mouth curled upward in a Cheshire-cat smirk that signaled complete and utter satisfaction.

He had seen that smile—in his office, when she had first

seduced him; in her bed, where she had further ensnared him; and last but not least, in his rearview mirror, when he had blessedly come to his senses and bolted out of her life.

If only George Perry had bolted. Instead, the poor fool had married a psychotic and would now spend the better part of his life in a prison cell atoning for that stupidity. At least in prison he'd be safe. And his daughter would be safe in her grave. Only a chosen few—perhaps only Derek Grainger and George Perry—could be expected to understand that the true crime would have been to allow an innocent child to grow up in Veronica Keyes Perry's twisted grasp.

◗ ● ◖

Two weeks later, circumstances forced Derek to rethink his cavalier attitude toward George Perry's fate. He was about to meet the man face to face, having been unable to delegate to his secretary the task of turning down an urgent request for appellate representation. Having also been unwilling to deal with Perry impersonally, by mail or telephone, Derek now found himself following a prison guard toward a conference room where, hopefully, the unpleasant task could be accomplished as quickly and mercifully as possible.

He had once viewed Perry as a victim—a man who had defied an ill-advised custody decree in order to save a sweet, innocent child from the clutches of a depraved woman. Now he needed to abandon that romanticized notion and to acknowledge the convicted man's crime spree, during which he had violated a lawful custody order concerning his daughter; *drugged* the custodial parent, his ex-wife, Veronica Keyes Perry; kidnapped their five-year-old child; crossed the state line into Nevada in order to hide the little girl in a remote cabin; and, last and most damning, he had left the girl alone with a defective propane stove, which had exploded into an inferno that had literally consumed her. Not exactly a folk hero, after all. In fact, despite his good intentions, George Perry was just what the jury had proclaimed him to be—a kidnapper and a murderer.

And there he was, sitting in a metal chair, waiting. Hope was once again shining in his huge brown eyes—this time because he believed that help had arrived in the person of Derek Grainger. It would be difficult to say no—but insane to say yes—so Derek reminded himself one last time to be tough, then extended his hand toward the prisoner. "Hello, Mr. Perry. I'm Derek Grainger."

"Thanks for coming," the gaunt young man replied. "I was afraid you wouldn't."

"I'm here to listen, Mr. Perry, but . . ." A wave of compassion interrupted Derek's carefully rehearsed speech and, as soon as the guard had left them alone, he murmured, "Do you need medical treatment, George? Your color isn't good, and—"

"I'm fine. I mean, it's a nightmare in here, but I'm not sick. I've just been . . ." He shrugged, then shook his head as though there was nothing left to say on the subject.

5

"Has anyone been bothering you?"

"No. Nothing like that. They leave me alone, pretty much."

"Good. Now, as I was saying, I agreed to come and listen, but—"

"But you don't want my case?" Perry's voice rang with innocent confidence. "I'm about to change your mind."

"I doubt that. But I have a referral for you. An excellent attorney with an impressive success rate on appeal. I'm sure he'll agree to take your case."

"I want *you*. You're the only one who can do this—the only one who can understand how I feel." The soft brown eyes narrowed slightly. "Whether you realize it or not, Grainger, you have as much at stake in this as I do."

"That's hardly true." Derek kept his face expressionless, although he was secretly delighted Perry had taken this distasteful route. It would be easy now to refuse him. Evidently, the man thought he could blackmail his prospective attorney by threatening to expose the sordid affair, so many years ago, with Veronica. He was mistaken. "I take it your ex-wife told you she and I were once lovers?"

Perry nodded. "Eight years ago, right? Two years before I met her. Three years before Amy was born."

The wistful mention of the lost child touched Derek despite his plan to be unmoved. "I'm sorry about your daughter, George. I know you were trying to do the right thing when you took her from Veronica. You may not have acted wisely, but you also could never have predicted that fire."

6

"That's not true." The young man leaned closer. "This is confidential, right?"

"Yes."

"I *planned* that fire."

Derek felt as though he'd been punched directly below the solar plexus. "What are you saying?"

"Do you remember last year, when that woman left her baby in the car on a hot day, down in San Jose, and the kid died of heatstroke?"

The attorney nodded, confused and wary.

"They prosecuted her for recklessness, or negligence, or something, and for murder. They even convicted her, but then"—his eyes filled with tears—"the judge said she'd been punished enough by losing her child, and shouldn't go to prison. When I heard that, I thought I'd found the answer to poor Amy's nightmare, and to mine, too. But instead I ended up here. It isn't fair!"

"Listen to me," Derek warned, his fists clenching at his sides. "If you're trying to tell me you planned your daughter's death—"

"I planned her escape from a nightmare, Grainger. I planned it perfectly. But that heartless judge gave me *twenty years!*"

"If that judge knew what you're telling me right now," Derek informed him icily as he reached for his briefcase, "you'd be on death row. Be grateful you got off so lightly."

"You don't understand yet," George countered. "I planned the kidnapping and the fire, so everyone would *think* Amy was dead. So they'd never search for her. They

7

found ashes in my cabin—ashes from my parents' mortuary that I planted for them to find. Amy was miles away when that stove exploded."

Derek's mouth and throat were instantly so dry that he could only croak, "Are you insane? Why haven't you told anyone until now? Did your trial attorneys know about— no! They couldn't have." He rose to his feet. "Tell me where she is. Is she safe? Is she with a responsible adult? Does anyone else know about this?"

"Sit down."

He stared at the man for a long, sobering moment, then explained quietly, "The attorney–client privilege doesn't cover ongoing crimes, especially the kidnapping of a child. As an officer of the court—"

"I said *sit down*! I'm not finished." When Derek continued to stand, the young man traded his anger for a more submissive approach and said, "If Veronica finds out Amy's still alive, the nightmare begins all over again. Can you accept that?"

"That's a separate issue," Derek objected, then he rested his hands on the table, leaned toward the prisoner, and tried for a soothing tone. "You're not alone in this anymore, George. I'll help you out, I promise. But first you have to tell me where Amy is. I simply have no choice but to insist."

"Only one person has the right to know where I hid Amy, and that's Amy's father. That's why I sent for *you*, Grainger."

This second psychological punch had landed even more forcefully than the first, but Derek told himself he had misunderstood and so managed to respond with a growl. "Listen, George—"

"Sit down and stop lecturing me," Perry growled in return. "I'm going to tell you what Veronica Keyes did, eight years ago, to immortalize your weekend of fun and games in Sausalito, and then"—his brown eyes challenged Derek confidently—"we're going to make some plans—for *my* release, and for *your* introduction to the sweetest, most precious little angel on earth."

ONE

"Ms. Banyon? Sorry to disturb you, but you have a visitor."

Laurel Banyon looked up from *People vs. Anderson* and smiled an appreciative smile. Her niece—*all* her nieces— were such good sports to play legal secretary for her whenever the need arose. This particular twenty-year-old drama major had been sitting in Laurel's outer office doing some schoolwork on a sadly outmoded computer but had obviously greeted an unexpected client with courtesy and professionalism. "Thanks, Jessie. Is it anyone I know?"

The girl glanced behind herself, then slipped into Laurel's office, closed the door to the outer room and blurted out, "He's gorgeous! Even more gorgeous than in the movie!" Clasping her hands to her heart, she pretended to swoon, then continued, "I can't believe you *know* him! Why's he here? Is it law stuff or acting stuff? Or"—her tone turned breathless—"are you *dating* him? Can I—"

"Jessie!"

"Huh?"

"Who is 'he'?"

"Oh!" The niece grinned sheepishly. "I thought you knew. It's the lawyer from *False Pretenses*."

Laurel arched an eyebrow in amused frustration. "Are

you saying Derek Grainger is in my waiting room? Or is it the actor who played him in the movie? Or just someone who looks like one of them? In any case," she added playfully, "he sounds promising. Did he give you his name?"

"He said, 'I'm Derek Grainger, and I'm here to see Laurel Banyon.' Then he *apologized* for not having an appointment—like *he* would need an appointment." Jessie rolled her huge blue eyes at the absurdity of such a thought.

Laurel nodded in sobered agreement. As much as she might have enjoyed meeting a famous movie star, a visit from Derek Grainger was, in many ways, more impressive. The man—a brilliant, highly principled defense attorney from San Francisco—was a legend at the age of thirty-three. While Laurel had never actually met him, she had read the book he'd co-authored on the subject of a celebrated case, and had seen the Hollywood interpretation of that same case, starring sex symbol Trevor Harris as a hunky, gutsy courtroom brawler. Despite her niece's admiring assessment, Laurel was fairly certain that the real Derek Grainger couldn't hold a candle to superstar Harris in the looks department. On the other hand, it was Grainger, not Harris, who had saved a doomed man's life and reputation by methodically reducing the prosecution's double-murder case to a pile of rubble and, to Laurel Banyon, *that* was the stuff from which true heroes were made.

"Laurel? Should I show him in?"

"I guess so. I just wish I wasn't wearing jeans. And"—she located a compact in her desk drawer and frowned into the mirror—"I wish I had my blue lenses with me."

"Why? I love your real eyes. We all do," Jessie insisted. "That's why Elaine's choosing violets for her bridal bouquet. As a tribute to you."

"There's a gruesome image. A bouquet of eyeballs? Anyway"—Laurel shrugged—"I like my eye color too. And I like my hair color, but put the two together and it's so melodramatic. On the other hand, I don't seem to have a choice at the moment, so . . ." She pulled an enameled clip from her auburn hair, allowing a tangle of waves to cascade around her shoulders. "Let's give him the full effect, shall we?"

"You look beautiful." Jessie's eyes were dancing. "Anyway, he's wearing jeans too. And a gorgeous heather gray polo shirt. Wait till you see him. You'll die."

"Assuming he's still out there."

The warning hit home, and Jessie quickly opened the door. "Mr. Grainger? Ms. Banyon will see you now."

Derek Grainger sidled past the wide-eyed niece, flashed a devastating smile, and extended his hand confidently. "Thanks for seeing me without an appointment, Ms. Banyon. Do you have a few minutes?"

Laurel gripped his hand as firmly as she dared, secretly grateful for its steadying influence. Jessie had been all too accurate—he *was* an extremely attractive man. Not flashy or bulked up like Trevor Harris, but tall, lean, and commanding, with deep blue eyes and wavy black hair. His hand was strong and warm, and just slightly callused, and there were laugh lines around his mouth—imperfections that made the overall effect even headier. The man obviously had charisma as well as a great build. And he was waiting for her to say something, so she said, "Hi."

"Hi." He grinned. "Nice to meet you. Nice office," he added, his gaze taking in the profusion of antiques, from her solid oak partners' desk to a row of salvaged filing cabinets, before returning to Laurel's face. He was waiting again, this time for her to release his hand, but she was too busy trying to formulate a coherent statement.

"Ms. Banyon?" Jessie prodded. "Do you want me to get some coffee or something?"

Laurel flushed and gave the visitor back his hand. "No thanks, Jessie. I'll call you if we need you."

"Do you want me to call the judge and check on that arrest warrant again?"

Laurel smiled at the sweet, illogical offer. The loyal drama major was giving this role her all, and her aunt loved her madly for it. "That's not necessary."

"Okay. Bye, Mr. Grainger."

Derek grinned again and waited for the girl to disappear before asking, "Call the judge and check on that warrant?"

"She's my niece. She wants to impress you."

"So far, I'm impressed by everything about you."

"I see." She tried to take offense at the remark—what did *he* know about *her*?—but his smile was so genuine she couldn't summon even token hostility. "How can I help you, Mr. Grainger?"

"You can call me Derek, for starters." He motioned toward an elegant green velvet settee. "Make yourself comfortable, Laurel."

She wanted to remind him this was *her* office, but her curiosity was outweighing her indignation, and so she perched instead on the corner of her desk. "What's this about?"

"I want to hire you."

"As your attorney?"

"*My* attorney?" He stared for a moment before succumbing to a deep, rumbling chuckle. "That's great! And very Laurel Banyon—esque, from all I hear," he said finally.

Annoyance, a little late but still welcome, flooded her, and she glared as she asked, "Didn't you just say you'd like to hire me? I'm a lawyer, Mr. Grainger. When people hire me, that's usually the reason. I may not be as famous as *you,* but—"

"Actually, I've found you're something of a mini-celebrity, at least around the Sacramento legal community."

"Is that so?" Laurel slipped off the desk and moved to the window, allowing the warmth and beauty of the spring day to soothe her ruffled pride. She had heard the gentle tease underlying Grainger's tone, and knew without asking that he hadn't heard the things about her that really counted. Laurel Banyon, straight-A student, high school valedictorian, Phi Beta Kappa, second in her law school class—and last but not least, up-and-coming young attorney who had never lost a case. Had he heard *those* stories? Undoubtedly not. He'd heard the other ones.

"Laurel?" He was standing behind her, his mouth uncomfortably close to her ear. "Did I offend you?"

"Why are you here?" she murmured.

"I want to hire you." His hands were on her shoulders, turning her to face him. "I'm putting a team together. A defense team, for a tough appeal. I think you'd be a perfect addition."

"Based on what?" Her voice was almost wistful as she added, "What is it you've heard? And from whom?"

"I spent last night with a couple of your biggest fans."

"Last night? Oh, no . . ." A knot had formed in the pit of her stomach. "Judge Seaton's retirement dinner?"

Derek nodded. "He and I are very close. He was my constitutional law professor, years ago, and we've kept in touch ever since. You could say he's my mentor."

"And somehow, last night, my name came up? Are you saying he dared to mention me in his retirement speech?"

Derek grinned. "I got the impression it's an established inside joke, right? That he retired to escape your antics in his courtroom."

"Antics?" She caught her temper and smiled icily. "Don't believe everything you hear."

"He produced a witness to corroborate the stories," Derek insisted mischievously. "Your ex-fiancé."

Laurel could feel her cheeks turning scarlet. "I'm glad you all had such a good time at my expense."

"They were singing your praises." His grin had become the sincerest of smiles. "Two years out of law school and you've already begun to make a name for yourself. That's impressive, Laurel."

She wasn't sure she wanted to know what "name" that was. Laughingstock? Kook? Failure? Joe Harrington adored

15

her, of course, but still saw her as a grandstander. And Judge Seaton! He had no respect for what he termed her "shenanigans," despite the fact that, like it or not, she'd been successful with each and every one.

Successful, but a failure nevertheless. Despite her triumphs, her clients had been unable to pay her anything approximating a living wage. Her criminal law practice was in trouble, and the jokes that constantly circulated weren't helping matters one bit. Now people were even coming from out of town to ridicule her! Eyeing her visitor grimly, she reminded him, "You mentioned wanting to hire me? Let me guess. Your next movie's going to be a comedy, and you dropped by for some pointers?"

The remark seemed to offend him. "I don't make movies, Ms. Banyon. I had nothing to do with—" He cleared his throat, then began again, visibly struggling to keep his tone even. "I co-authored the book, but the movie was strictly the client's circus. He's the one who benefited financially, and I had no involvement with it whatsoever. I haven't even seen it."

"You're kidding." She was enjoying the unexpected role reversal. Suddenly, Derek Grainger was the one feeling foolish, and she intended to milk it a bit. "You should rent the video, Derek. Really. It's very flattering. You came off as an incredibly virile guy."

"Virile?" He chuckled ruefully. "You wouldn't believe the rumors it's generated—about my stamina *and* my habits. I understand I routinely used the top of my desk as a sexual playground?"

"Your glass-topped desk," she confirmed with mock sincerity. "It was some of the best camera work I've ever seen. I'll never understand why it didn't win any Oscars."

"Are we even yet?"

"Pardon?"

"You're embarrassed over Seaton's stories, and so you're trying to embarrass me in return," he said with a shrug of his shoulders. "I've endured hundreds of hours of ribbing over that stupid movie, Laurel, but it hasn't hurt me professionally. If anything, the effect has been the opposite in that regard. That's what you need to do—take these stories about your creative lawyering and use them to help your image rather than hurt it."

"Creative lawyering?"

"You're creative. Imaginative. I admire that. That's why I want you on my team."

Laurel moistened her lips slightly, fascinated despite her better judgment. "Explain that."

"Sure." He drew her back to the desk, urged her onto her perch, then towered above her. "I want to mount an all-out defense for my client. No holds barred. We have an unlimited budget, and I've got the time, the skills, and the reputation. But *you've* got guts. You're willing to make a complete fool of yourself in order to win, and that's something I've never been able to do. I admire it. I *need* it."

She liked his use of the word "guts" almost as much as she despised "fool." "Don't *you* have guts?"

"Sure. I can be daring, but I can't be imaginative. I'm a technician," he explained quietly. "I know the law cold, I absorb facts like a sponge, and I inspire confidence in my listeners. Those are my strengths. But—" He paused to shrug. "There are times when those qualities aren't enough. That's where you come in."

"The fool?"

"Huh?"

"Never mind. Go on."

"You stood in Judge Seaton's courtroom and dared to argue that confidential communications between a woman and her hairdresser should be as privileged as those between a psychotherapist and his patient."

Laurel flushed. "Only under certain well-defined circumstances. Women *do* tell their hairdressers things, Derek. When someone's kneading your scalp and redesigning your appearance, you tend to let your guard down, and . . . well, never mind."

"It was brilliant," he assured her. "Irrational, but brilliant. I almost died laughing when Seaton told me the story."

"Did he tell you I *won* that case?"

"Absolutely. He said he threw out your client's confession because it was unreliable, but only after you dragged the whole court to the beauty salon to demonstrate how disorienting the odors from those chemical beauty treatments can be."

"They *are* disorienting. Two of the male jurors actually got nauseous from all those fumes. It was an unusually busy day at the salon," she added with a reluctant smile, remembering how her three oldest nieces had just "happened" to schedule appointments for permanents on that particular day.

"*That's* the kind of thing I'm talking about. Seaton admits no other attorney could have pulled it off. And your ex-fiancé claims you're a genius."

"Wait!" Laurel groaned. "Did Joe tell you that silly entrapment story?"

"Entrapment?"

"Never mind." She silently thanked Joseph Anthony Harrington, although she suspected it wasn't loyalty, but rather a bruised ego, that had kept him from telling that particular anecdote. After all, Joe had been the prosecutor in that case, and had been mortified by her successful theatrics. Maybe he was still smarting from the experience.

"In your own way, Laurel, you're as much of a quote-unquote legend as I am."

"With several obvious differences," Laurel reminded him. "You're the toast of San Francisco and I'm the laughingstock of Sacramento." Her eyes widened. "When you referred to my image earlier, that's what you were getting at, right?"

"Exactly. I think you need me as much as I need you. You'll bring a little inspiration to my case, and I'll lend a little dignity to your otherwise thriving career. It is thriving, isn't it?"

"I have a steady stream of clients, despite my tarnished image," she said wearily. "Unfortunately, I'm not handling the business end very well."

"Which explains why your niece is filling in as your secretary?"

19

"Worse. I can't even afford *her*," Laurel said with a laugh. "She's just out there working on an assignment. Luckily, I can type and I don't mind answering my own phone. When I get really swamped, there's a temporary secretarial service right across the street. I'm doing okay." Her chin came up defensively. "And I'm a damned good lawyer."

"I wouldn't be here if I didn't believe that."

"Well, then . . ." She took a deep breath. "What exactly would our arrangement be?"

"I'd hire you straight out. As an independent contractor. At a thousand dollars a day, for a minimum of two weeks, possibly longer. I'll set up an office here in town, and you'll work there, using my support staff and equipment. How does that sound?"

Laurel pretended to ponder the offer, but inside she was reeling. She had barely managed to pay her rent the previous month, and the thought of earning it in one day . . .

Derek seemed to read her mind. "I tried to come up with an attractive proposal. Have I succeeded?"

"I'm tempted," she admitted. "When's the final filing date for the brief?"

"In three weeks." Frustration had crept into his tone. "Assuming it'll take a full week for the actual writing, that leaves only two weeks to find reversible error."

"That sounds doable. Who else will be on the team?"

"I'm hoping we won't need anyone else. My plan is, I'll look for technical errors while you search for emotional ones."

"'Emotional'? Don't you mean 'irrational'?" She sifted

her fingers impatiently through her hair. "There's a tenor to this whole thing that frankly offends me, Derek. I happen to be a very competent technical lawyer. Those few notorious incidents you heard about last night only represent a tiny portion of my experience. I win my cases because I'm good, not because of stunts."

"And I win my cases because of hard work, not because of eloquence or style," he agreed confidently. "Still, we each have an ace in the hole, don't we? I'm suggesting we pool our talents and see what happens."

"For this one case only, right?"

"Right. I've got a couple of other matters pending, but I'm hoping to dedicate about ninety percent of my time over the next few weeks to this appeal."

"I've got some unavoidable commitments this week myself, but they shouldn't take much time." Laurel swiveled to study her desk calendar. "I can basically work around your schedule." She turned back to face him. "Tell me about our client. What kind of case is it?"

Derek's face became impassive. "I'm not at liberty to talk about the case. It's a sensitive one. Let's just say it's a challenge. When you're officially on board, next week, we'll go over the details."

His wooden demeanor alarmed her. "I'm not going into this blind, Derek. I already suffer from a damaged reputation, as you so ungallantly noted. I don't need to look any more foolish than I apparently already do."

"This man's situation is far from foolish, I guarantee you."

"He's a man? Okay." She took a deep breath. "Is he a rapist?"

"Is that a problem for you?"

"Yes. Rapists and child molesters are 'problems' for me, even at a thousand dollars a day."

"Even if the client claims he's innocent?"

"Yes. Even then."

Derek shook his head. "That's a lousy attitude for an up-and-coming defense counsel, but fortunately it's irrelevant. Our client wasn't convicted of rape or any other sex offense."

"And we're going to comb through the transcripts, find the errors, write the appellate brief, present the argument, and then that's it? Case closed?"

"Exactly. It'll be hard work, but the compensation is good and the experience, for both of us, should be invaluable."

"I suppose. You'll be the lead attorney . . ."

"And you'll be the well-paid flunky." He smiled to soften the possible insult. "I work long hours, Laurel. Ten or eleven a day, sometimes, and seven days a week when things get hot. You're working on Saturday now, so I assume that's not a problem?"

"I need one day off a week," Laurel corrected. "And I definitely can't work next Saturday. My niece is getting married."

"Her? She's just a kid!"

"She's hardly a kid, but she's also not the one getting married. I have *seven* nieces. You've met Jessie—the twenty-year-old. It's Elaine—a twenty-four-year-old—who's getting married. And I have to be there when she does."

"That's fine. I can spare you for a couple of hours."

Laurel grinned sympathetically. "The entire day, I'm afraid. This isn't a city hall wedding, it's a blow-out. But I can work next Sunday if you really think it's necessary."

"Great. We'll need every minute."

She studied him skeptically. "Are you so sure it's going to be this complicated?"

"I'm a detail nut," he explained with a smile. "When you said we'll comb through the transcripts, it wasn't an exaggeration. I want to discuss every word, every sneeze, every *everything*. We'll put it under my technical microscope and then we'll turn you loose on it, looking for the weak spot. I know it's in there."

Laurel slid to her feet and nodded. "It's *always* in there. And I agree, between the two of us, we're bound to find it."

He proffered his hand eagerly. "We have a deal?"

"Sure. One thousand dollars a day, six days a week. And strictly business. Right?"

He chuckled. "That goes without saying."

"Well, say it anyway," Laurel suggested. "I get enough pleasure from my business without mixing business with pleasure. Understand?"

"No, but I think I agree. When I'm working on a case, my social life goes on hold, so you can consider it an iron-clad part of our contract. One thousand a day, strictly business."

"Fine. You've got yourself a deal."

"And you've got yourself a ticket into the big leagues, where they appreciate creative genius."

This time she shook his hand with brisk confidence. If they were going to work together, it would have to be as equals, and she needed to establish that from the start. "I'm sure we'll make a good team, Derek."

"I've got a room at the Sutter Plaza now. I'll arrange for a suite instead, and we can work out of there. I'll lease any equipment we need, and transfer all the records up here."

"Wouldn't it be easier if I just commuted to San Francisco?"

"Actually, I think I need to be out of the city for this one," Derek confessed. "I want to concentrate. No distractions. My secretary can handle most of the calls and mail down there, and fax me whatever I need."

"The Plaza's good for me too." Laurel nodded as she spoke. "It's just three blocks from here, and within walking distance of the state law library."

"You won't need to use the library. I'll get a computer hook-up to one of the research services."

"That's a waste of money."

"It's also my decision. Plus, you'll need to have access to all the transcripts and records, and believe me, they're not portable. And by then I'll have copies of most of the major news stories, and bios on all the jurors."

"In other words, we're going to be buried alive under a ton of paper."

"We're going to eat, drink, and sleep this thing," he confirmed. "I want to cover all the bases on this one. I want this guy to go free."

"I can see that," she murmured, wondering if she'd just imagined the hint of vulnerability in his tone. "Don't worry, Derek. I've never lost a case. Not a single one."

"What?" His eyes widened. "Are you serious?"

"Completely." She flashed her most confident smile. "I'll see you bright and early Monday morning."

$$\bullet \quad \bullet \quad \bullet$$

When he'd left, Laurel flopped onto the settee and rehashed the encounter in her mind. Derek Grainger had tried to appear easygoing and upbeat, but beneath all that had lurked something grim and unsettling. She, in turn, had probably appeared defensive and off-balance, and she wondered if he'd been astute enough to guess she was actually a strong, confident woman. They would learn the truth about each other soon enough, she supposed. Working so intensely, in such close quarters and for such high stakes, would bring out the worst as well as the best. It made her grimace slightly—did she really want to see any man's worst?

"Laurel? Is everything okay?"

She motioned for her niece to enter. "Sit down and I'll tell you all about him."

"First things first: did he ask you out?"

"Hardly. It was all business, believe me." She laughed at the disappointment on Jessie's face. "The good news is, I'm going to work on a case with him. And I'm actually going to make decent money for a change. *And*," she nudged a stack of dusty books with her toe, "I can take these back to the library, for a while at least."

Jessie leaned down to examine the titles. "Wills, Trusts, Probate . . . This is what Grandpa and Uncle Bobby keep telling you to do?"

"They have lots of friends who'd hire me to do estate planning for them. Unfortunately, it doesn't interest me. But it pays well."

"But so does Derek Grainger?"

"Exactly."

"Is it another murder case, like the one in his movie?"

"I don't know," Laurel admitted, bristling slightly at her own ignorance. "He should have told me, but I think he's trying to establish who's boss by controlling the flow of information."

"He'll never control you, Laurel. Mom says even Grandpa couldn't."

"That's right," Laurel said with a grin. "Anyway, you and Lisa can still use this place during the week. I'll be spending most of my time at Derek's suite at the Sutter Plaza."

"The Plaza? Oohh, that sounds more like a date than work."

"Believe me, it's work. Ten hours a day, six days a week."

"It's *so* romantic."

Laurel grinned in defeat. "Have it your way, then. Just don't tell the rest of the family I'm having an affair."

"What about Uncle Joe? Will he be jealous?"

"Let's hope so. He apparently gossiped about me last night at a party, so I owe him some grief. In fact, I think I'll go see him right now and yell at him. With any luck, he'll have a hangover and be completely at my mercy."

Jessie sighed. "I wish you still loved him."

"I do. He's my best friend." She jumped to her feet and gave the girl a hug. "Want to go visit him with me?"

"I can't. Clay's taking me to the movies."

"Clay? Again? This is starting to sound serious."

"He's a loner," Jessie confided with a melodramatic sigh. "I'm just his latest conquest."

"Well, you seem to be taking it in stride." Laurel grinned. "Aren't you afraid he'll break your heart?"

"My drama coach says I need the experience, so . . ." Jessie pouted slyly. "I'm willing to suffer for the sake of my career, just like you."

Laurel smiled, enjoying both the performance and the sentiment. Of all her seven nieces, Jessie was the most like Laurel, from her flair for melodrama to her overactive and always optimistic imagination. They could have been twins, if it weren't for the six-year difference in their ages and the fact that Jessie was a tall, cool blond with huge blue eyes and porcelain skin. None of the nieces had the outrageous coloring that had been both a challenge and trademark for Laurel during her volatile career as an actress-turned-lawyer.

"Laurel?"

"Hmm?"

"What if you and Mr. Grainger lose the case?"

"As your drama coach would say, the experience would be good for me. On the other hand"—her flippant tone faded into cool determination—"I've never lost a case, and I'm not about to start with this one."

◗ ● ◖

"This is just great. You refuse to form a partnership with me, your best friend and the greatest lover you ever had, but some jerk from San Francisco walks into your office and you fall right into his arms."

"Does your head hurt, Joe?" Laurel rumpled her ex-lover's shaggy golden hair with mock concern. "Poor baby."

"Don't change the subject! This is nuts, Laurel. Tell him you changed your mind."

She pretended to pout. "You're the one who convinced him to hire me."

"That's bull!" Joe Harrington winced visibly. "Hand me that ice pack, will you? Thanks. Anyway, that's bull and you know it. All I did was tell him what a wild woman you are in the courtroom. Who knew he'd take it the wrong way?"

"Meaning what?"

"Meaning, he's gonna be all over you the minute he gets you alone in that suite." The prosecutor's bloodshot eyes narrowed. "We both saw that movie, Laurel. You said yourself that desktop stuff looked painful. And speaking of pain . . ." His tone softened to a whimper. "Do you still carry aspirin in your purse?"

"Once we broke up, I didn't need to anymore."

"Man, you're mean today."

She grinned and pulled out her pill case. "Here, you big baby. Try to learn a lesson from this. You can't take hard liquor."

"I know, I know. You should have gone with me, Laurel, to protect me from my dark side. It's all your fault."

"You didn't take a date?"

"Nah. I kept thinking you'd change your mind. And"— he eyed her dourly—"you definitely should have come. You hurt the old guy's feelings by staying away." When she jutted her chin forward in defiance, he scolded her. "You know how Judge Seaton feels about you. *He's* the one who got Grainger's motor running, I'll bet. He probably told him about that hot little body of yours." Joe's grin had widened predictably. "After all those tall, stacked models that throw themselves at celebrities like him, Grainger probably found someone like you refreshingly different."

"Meaning what?"

"Meaning you're little. Tiny. Petite. Like a scale model of a woman. Everything's there, and the proportions are dynamite, but—" He chuckled wickedly. "Where's the rest of you?"

"Five-foot-four is not short, dear. It's average. The only short, petite, scaled-down organ in this room—"

"Time out!" He shook his aching head. "What's up with you today? Can't you take a joke?"

"Apparently not."

"You know how I feel about your body," he insisted. "It's my all-time favorite. I was just harassing you out of jealousy."

"That's silly. We broke up six months ago. Get over it."

"Never."

"Well, there's nothing to worry about anyway. I'm a great judge of character, and I could tell Grainger was a complete professional. But just to be safe, I inserted the standard no-sex clause in our contract."

"Huh?" Joe's scowl faded. "You really did that?"

"Yep."

"Man, that brings back memories. I remember how torturous it was for *me*, working side by side with you when you were clerking at our office every summer during law school and wouldn't even let me look at you. And you'd wear those damned spike heels, just to cause me pain." He leaned back against the sofa cushion and rubbed his eyes. "I almost feel sorry for Grainger now."

"That's the spirit."

"However . . ." He opened one eye and tried to glare. "I'm coming by that suite, every single day, at varying hours, unannounced. Make sure you tell him that."

"Yes, dear."

"Am I still your date for the wedding?"

"Of course. My nieces would disown me if I showed up without their Uncle Joe."

He nodded smugly. "It's hard to believe, isn't it? Little Elaine, getting married."

"Little Elaine is only three years younger than me," Laurel reminded him. "Even Jessie will be twenty-one next month. Our girls are growing up."

"I guess you're right. Man . . ." He rubbed his eyes again.

"It's tough being a surrogate uncle, you know. Especially when it's all nieces and no nephews."

"Poor Joe."

"Yeah." He struggled to his feet and reached for the ice pack. "I hate to be a bad host, but I'm going back to bed. Feel free to join me," he added over his shoulder as he lumbered down the hall.

Laurel watched in wistful silence as the lanky, golden-haired giant peeled off his rumpled bathrobe just before disappearing into the bedroom. She'd been down that hall more than once, and remembered all too well how warm and cozy things could get in Joe Harrington's king-sized bed. In addition to his other lovable attributes, the man was a born cuddler—in fact, given his hangover, cuddling was probably all he could manage for the next few hours—and she could use some of that right now. Of course, it would be a mistake in the long run, but for the moment . . .

If only Joe could have been "the one." It would have made life so simple. They'd be married by now if she had just allowed him to take the lead. Instead, she had had the bittersweet insight to recognize their romance for what it was—an amazing friendship in disguise—and had set him free despite his fervent protests. Still, until one of them found someone else, the danger of backsliding was ever-present, especially now, with a living legend lurking in the shadows, threatening to challenge both her self-image and her self-confidence. Without a doubt, Joe Harrington could make her feel like a success again, at least temporarily.

Don't let Derek Grainger psych you out! she ordered herself sternly. *He's just a lawyer with a little more experience and a lot better press than you. And appellate work? Big deal. Once you've found out more about the case—about the verdict, and the client— you'll do great. So,* she took one last, longing look toward Joe's bedroom, *get out of here before you do something really, really stupid.*

Two

Derek Grainger studied his newly arranged temporary office with quiet satisfaction. It had everything he and Laurel Banyon would need—three phone lines, a fax, two powerful notebook computers, and two large desks with handsome leather armchairs. He smiled, remembering his fleeting urge to order glass-topped desks, just to amuse his new associate. Working with her was definitely going to be interesting. On the other hand, working with her could be distracting, and he couldn't allow that. He needed to concentrate. He needed to win this case, for his little daughter's sake.

And Laurel's never lost a case, he reminded himself. There had been something in those wild violet eyes of hers—sly challenge, backed by solid confidence. She was competitive. He liked that. He needed it, and needed to channel it for the appeal. Hopefully, some of the electricity that had been generated by the startling clash of those fabulous eyes with the burnished hair would lend energy to their association and, ultimately, to their appellate brief.

A knock at the door pleased him. Was she here, one day early, eager to get to work? They needed every precious moment, and he was grateful she understood that.

When he pulled open the door, his hopeful smile turned into a rueful grin at the sight of his friend and mentor, Matthew Seaton. "You're the last person I expected to see today, sir," he confessed, extending his hand in welcome. "Come on in."

"You thought I'd be sunning myself on a beach somewhere?" Seaton shook his bald head emphatically. "I intend to continue keeping an eye on things around this town. When I heard you were still here, I wanted to say goodbye, and to thank you again for making the trip."

"I wouldn't have missed your retirement dinner."

The judge eyed him with practiced suspicion. "Not only are you still in town, but you've traded your room for this suite. When the desk clerk told me that, I assumed you'd met a woman here in town and were staying over for some sort of liaison tonight, but all this"—he swept his arm broadly—"doesn't look very romantic."

"Actually . . ." Derek paused to clear his throat. "I'm setting up a combination office and hideout here for a few weeks. I'm knee-deep in a complex appeal and need to really focus."

"In Sacramento? Why not use your beach house in Monterey? Or rent a cabin in the mountains? Why here? What's going on?"

The tenacious questioning didn't surprise Derek. Seaton was the prototypical litigator—perceptive, blunt, and tenacious. He had been a fine professor, and undoubtedly an excellent judge, but just the same, had been born to cross-examine, not to instruct or mediate.

And he was waiting impatiently for Derek's answer.

"I've hired a young Sacramento attorney to help me with this appeal, sir. So, it made sense to set up here."

The judge lowered himself into the nearest chair. "What's so tough about this particular appeal?"

"Everything. I'm highly motivated to win. But—" Derek paused to shrug. "I've spent weeks going over the damned record and I can't find reversible error."

"If *you* can't find it, it's not there. You're the best."

"Thanks. Can I get you a drink? Coffee?"

The judge waved away the offer impatiently. "Sounds like you've got a loser on your hands. Just turn it over to your assistant and forget it." His eyes narrowed slightly. "A young Sacramento attorney, you say? Did you meet one at the dinner? The only person I saw you spend any time with was Joe Harrington, and he's not exactly looking for defense work." Then his eyes widened in feigned horror. "Tell me it's not the redhead."

Derek chuckled. "Her hair isn't really red."

"Not this week," Seaton agreed. "But with her, you never know what's coming next." He leaned toward his protégé and demanded, "Are you profoundly insane? Laurel Banyon? She's a renegade, Derek."

"I *need* a renegade. I need a flash of inspiration. Creative lawyering."

Seaton was shaking his head frantically. "You said yourself there's no reversible error. Not even Laurel Banyon can find something that isn't there."

"She thinks she can. She says there's always a way to win,

and when you look into those eyes of hers and see that energy—that pure inspiration—you know it's true."

The judge seemed to consider this, then rose to his feet, his expression grim. "I'm going to give you a piece of advice now, Derek, and it's going to offend you, but bear with me, because you need to hear this." He waited for Derek to nod, then continued. "Order up a bottle of champagne and a dozen roses. Then bring Laurel Banyon here and get it over with. That's all you're going to get out of this mess anyway, and you'll save yourself a whopping hotel bill and a truck-load of frustration."

Derek's entire body had tensed, with anger and with disappointment. Still, he respected this man—a little less now, and that was a shame, but respected nonetheless—and so he hoped only the disappointment showed in his eyes. "Let's drop it, shall we?"

"I'm all for equal rights, son. You know that. Women lawyers make a fine, substantial contribution to the profession. But when a man tells me he's looked into a woman's eyes and seen 'pure inspiration,' I repeat, get the champagne and roses and get it over with, or your client'll be the one who suffers."

"Apparently, I gave you the wrong impression," Derek assured him through gritted teeth. "It isn't like that between Laurel and me. She's attractive, but the relationship is strictly business."

"What color are her eyes this week?"

"I didn't even notice her eyes," he lied. "It was her brain that impressed me."

"What is it they say today?" Seaton glared. "The brain is the real erogenous zone?" When Derek returned the glare, the judge nodded. "Forget I said anything. If I'm right, it'll happen—slowly and painfully but it'll happen. So? Who's the defendant in this little drama? What'd he do?"

For the first time in his life, Derek wished he had never met Matthew Seaton. This was definitely going to set him off again, and Derek didn't need any more incendiary advice. Still, his respect for the man prompted a civil reply. "I'm representing George Perry, sir."

Seaton's face was ash gray as he again settled himself into the chair. "You've really done it."

"I have a tiger by the tail," Derek admitted quietly.

"Two tigers," Seaton corrected. "Why touch the Perry appeal? You didn't try the case."

"He contacted me. I went to see him, and . . ." Derek hesitated, wary of further lying to a veteran bluff detector like Seaton. "I don't think he got a fair shake."

"A fair shake? Did his little girl get a fair shake when she roasted to death in that mountain cabin? He had good lawyers, Derek. From what I hear, he deserved what he got. What's more, I'm told he didn't cooperate in his defense, which means he's dead on appeal. And so are you."

"Maybe so."

"It's a loser case. That's why you're bringing that wild woman into it, and you know it." He chuckled reluctantly. "She's creative, yes. No doubt about that. But she can't work miracles. If anything, she'll make this worse. The federal judiciary isn't ready for Laurel, son. If you're not careful, the next movie they make about you will be a screwball comedy."

"I think you're underestimating her, sir," Derek replied stiffly.

"Me? I'm her biggest fan. She's lively and shapely, she can light up a room with that angel face of hers, and yes, she's bright and inventive. But she doesn't know her place."

Derek's fists clenched in complete disgust. "Her place?"

"I'm not talking civil rights here, I'm talking about Laurel Banyon. She doesn't play by the rules. She makes them up as she goes along. If it were just ambition, I could live with it. But it's more than that. I can't put my finger on it . . ."

"It's ambition, Your Honor," Derek insisted, relieved at the semi-retraction. "It just looks and feels different with Laurel. I noticed it too. It's her style—competitive and gutsy. I liked it. I think she's just a lawyer with a twist."

"Or a twisted lawyer?" Seaton grumbled. "Fine. Here's my last piece of advice. Turn this Perry mess over to her completely. Maybe you're right. Maybe she can pull it out of the fire. Just get yourself out of the picture, so *you* don't get burned." He nodded, mumbling almost to himself, "Maybe she can do it, after all. She'll either save it or make it worse."

"Thanks for the advice," Derek interrupted. "Are you sure I can't offer you something to eat or drink?"

"If you end up staying in town, you can buy me dinner some night." Seaton grinned, easing himself out of the chair and moving toward the door. "Bring the gutsy redhead."

"We'll be buried in transcripts and precedents for the next few weeks, but after that, you and I'll have to get together."

Seaton flushed. "If I offended you, Derek, I'm genuinely sorry. On the other hand"—his pale blue eyes grew steely—"you haven't worked with her yet. She's different, and that's not male chauvinism or sour grapes."

"'Different' is just what this case needs," Derek said with a shrug. "Let's wait and see what happens, shall we? In the meantime"—his stern tone faded—"take care of yourself. Enjoy your retirement, and don't worry about me. I've won tougher cases than this, remember?"

"You're the best." The older man gripped his protégé's hand and added, pensively, "That's why I'm so worried."

◗ ● ◖

The Sutter Plaza had been in existence for only four years, yet had managed to become a focal point in Sacramento for both travelers and locals, due to its central downtown location and lavish accoutrements. From its plush maroon carpets and solid brass fixtures to the profusion of rich oak molding that framed and accented every architectural angle, there was an opulent warmth that made even the driest business seem enjoyable. One tended to linger in the brightly lit lobby or the dark-paneled bar, adapting easily to the unhurried pace that was the essence of the Plaza's charm and sophistication.

It was Laurel's favorite building in all of downtown, yet

when she approached the desk clerk for a key to "Mr. Grainger's suite" she was mentally kicking herself for having agreed to make this their headquarters. How could she have agreed to spend ten hours a day in a stranger's hotel room when her own, perfectly good office was only three blocks away! It had been a power play on Grainger's part, and she had fallen for it, just as she'd allowed him to keep the identity of their client a secret. For some reason, he was intent on controlling her, which didn't bother her half as much as the fact that she had let him get away with it. Twice!

All of that was about to change, she assured herself as she reached the fifteenth floor and strode toward the Eureka Suite. She intended to greet him as one professional to another, then grill him without mercy until she was truly his co-counsel and equal on this case. In a perfect world she would have begun by executing a dramatic entrance into the suite, but this wasn't a perfect world, it was his hotel, and it was early in the morning, and the last thing she needed was to catch sight of him half naked, so she decided to knock, this time at least, rather than to use her key card.

The door flew open almost immediately. "Finally! I was beginning to think you'd changed your mind."

"It's seven-thirty in the morning, Derek," Laurel retorted. "What's the problem?"

"No problem." He grinned sheepishly. "You're absolutely right. This is the first day and we should ease into it. Welcome aboard."

"That's better." She returned his smile, then quickly scanned the room, noting and appreciating the no-nonsense arrangement of the sitting room before looking back to her new boss. He was dressed in jeans and a loose-fitting plaid flannel shirt. Perfect. Not too formal, not too anything. She herself had chosen to wear smartly tailored black pants and a matching jacket, more out of deference to the Plaza than to Derek, and was now glad she'd stuffed jeans and a UCLA sweatshirt into her briefcase.

"You can have your choice of desks, Laurel. Take a look around while I pour you some coffee."

"Thanks." She eyed the furniture warily. If she chose the desk by the door, she'd seem like a receptionist. Of course, if she didn't, and Joe and the nieces actually had the nerve to show up, Derek would have a right to be annoyed, so . . . "I'll take this one." She plopped her briefcase onto the closer of the two desktops and settled into a luxurious black leather chair. "This is great."

"The master bedroom is basically for my personal stuff, but there's a smaller one, through that door, for you. And there are two bathrooms, so you can have the little one to yourself. I doubt we'll be having any guests."

"You're expecting me to sleep here? My condo's only ten minutes away, Derek, and my office is right down the street."

He shrugged. "It's there if you want it. And as you can see, we've got all the comforts of home, including a microwave. I'll have the refrigerator stocked with whatever you like, and if you can think of anything else I've missed, just speak up. You'll be spending long hours here, without any significant interruptions, so make yourself comfortable."

"Okay." She accepted a steaming cup of black coffee and sipped appreciatively. "Delicious. Now, before I die of curiosity, tell me about our client."

"Patience," he counseled. "Finish your coffee first. Fill me in on your schedule for this week."

"I'm all yours, except for a couple of hours Wednesday morning and all day Saturday. So? What did our guy do?"

"Wednesday? What's that about?"

"Derek?" Her gaze locked with his. "Are you stalling?"

"Pardon?"

"I get the feeling there's something about this I'm not going to like." Straightening in her chair, she murmured, "I'm beginning to think you've gotten me involved with a rapist or a child molester after all."

"He's no child molester," Derek said, his voice close to a growl. "And I *don't* want to hear that kind of talk around here." When Laurel stared in complete dismay, he winced and forced a smile. "You were kidding, right? Sorry. I'm a bear in the morning."

"Tell me what's wrong. Right now, or I'm out of here."

"He was convicted of kidnapping."

"Kidnapping?" She allowed herself to relax, but only slightly. "That's not so bad. Do you think he's innocent?"

"I want him to go free."

"That doesn't exactly answer my question, Derek. Is he a friend of yours or something?"

"That's irrelevant. You wanted to hear about the case, and so here it is, in a nutshell." His navy blue eyes cooled visibly. "Our client is George Perry."

Laurel counted to ten—a useless tactic under the circumstances—then snarled. "Do you think that was *clever*? This is *exactly* the kind of case I detest! It makes my skin crawl and I can't be objective."

"I told you—"

"Be quiet! You told me he's no child molester and that's cold comfort, Derek Grainger! He kidnapped his own daughter—that sweet little baby!—and now she's dead."

"You haven't read the transcript—"

"I don't have to. He was innocent until proven guilty, and that's just what happened. He got a fair trial and was convicted, and now I hope he rots."

"You're being unreasonable."

"I'm being creative. That's why you hired me, remember? To see the emotional errors in the transcript? But instead, I see the emotional error in this whole business, and I don't want any part of it."

"Laurel . . ."

"Be quiet! You called this my ticket into the big leagues and I guess I'm just destined to stay in the minors, Mr. Grainger, because I *don't* want to spend ten hours a day, seven days a week, trying to get a creep like George Perry out of prison."

"Are you finished?"

"Yes."

"Can I say something now?"

"There's nothing you can say that'll make me want to slave over this case, Derek. Save your breath."

"Even if the girl's mother was a perverted psychopath who would have made any child's life a living hell?"

Laurel counted to ten again. Again, it didn't help. "You have thirty seconds to substantiate that."

"George Perry claimed all along that he'd done the whole thing out of necessity. He honestly believed the girl's safety and sanity were at stake if she stayed in her mother's custody." When Laurel reached for her briefcase, he added sharply, "I met the mother once, years ago, and I totally agree with Perry's assessment. The woman's dangerous and unbalanced."

"Good grief." Laurel closed her eyes, fighting a vicious rush of pain through her temples. It was a warning—from instinct, or conscience, or both—telling her she was on the brink of disaster.

"Laurel? Talk to me."

"I followed the story in the newspaper," she murmured finally. "Not closely, but close enough to know that *both* those parents had problems. The real lawsuit is against society, for allowing the child to stay with either of them."

"We're in agreement on that."

"Okay." She reached for her coffee and took a fortifying gulp. "Maybe I overreacted. Fill me in."

"You said you followed the story. Why don't you tell me what you already know."

"Okay. George Perry and his wife—I don't remember her name . . ."

44

"Veronica."

"Right. Veronica. They divorced and had an unusually savage custody battle over the little girl. Allegations of alcohol and drug abuse, *and* sexual molestation." She paused, daring him to take offense, then continued. "The mother won. George had a fit, right there in the courtroom, which resulted in some contempt proceedings, right? But after that, he managed to get some very restricted visitation rights. On one of those visits, he drugged the mom and took the little girl—Amy, right?"

"Right."

"By the time the mom woke up, George and Amy were in the Sierras. He hid her in a remote cabin, left her alone with some sort of defective propane stove, and the place burned down. He was charged with kidnapping and felony-murder. Didn't testify, right? And defended, like you said, on the grounds of necessity. He lost, big-time, and got twenty years."

"You call her 'the mom,'" Derek muttered. "Like she's June Cleaver or something."

"She may not be June Cleaver, but she's been through hell. To lose her only child—" She stopped herself, alarmed by a flash of disgust in his eyes. "What?"

"Veronica Keyes Perry is a heartless, twisted, psychotic woman. Our client did what he did out of love for his daughter. If I'd been in his shoes—"

"You would never be stupid enough to endanger a child like that."

"True. George Perry was stupid. Phenomenally stupid. Is that suddenly punishable by twenty years in prison?"

"You bet. When someone's stupidity takes an innocent life—when a man disobeys court orders, drugs women, violates federal law . . . Even if Amy hadn't burned to death, she was *five years old*." Laurel's fist pounded the desk in anguished frustration. "He left her all alone in the middle of the big, bad forest with nobody to hear her crying. Her mother may have been a shallow, self-centered bitch—and I'm *real* sorry she broke your heart, Derek—but she was better than nothing."

He stared for a full moment before demanding, "What did you say?"

"You heard me."

"I heard it," he agreed dryly. "I just don't believe you had the nerve to say it."

"Am I fired?"

"Actually, I'm considering giving you a raise." He grinned when her mouth fell open. "I didn't fall in love with Veronica Keyes, but yes, I had a memorable affair with her. And you picked up on that right away. This is just the kind of mental gymnastics I was hoping for."

"I'm not afraid to make a fool of myself," she quoted. "Isn't that what you said last Saturday? Why do I get the feeling this case is going to make fools of us both?"

"It won't. I guarantee it."

"Have you met George Perry?"

"Yes."

"And . . . ?"

Derek shrugged. "He's a wreck. His life is a shambles. He's broke, his daughter is lost to him forever, his ex-wife is vengeful and ruthless—"

"Hold it."

"Huh?"

"He's *broke*?"

Derek laughed ruefully. "Did I say that?"

"I need an explanation. Fast."

"Don't worry about your thousand a day," he said soothingly. "The entire cost of the defense is being borne by the little girl's great-grandmother. A lover of justice."

"It's all so sordid," Laurel whispered. "Tell me why you're so hot to help him."

"Because I'm the only lawyer in the country who can win this. That's an awesome responsibility."

"Coupled with awesome conceit."

"Do you think so?" Derek's blue eyes challenged her confidently. "No one else came forward to defend the guy. His trial attorneys don't want anything to do with him, and vice versa. If nothing else, he clearly needs psychological help that he's not getting. Maybe there are other lawyers who could theoretically win this, but they don't have the combination of resources, talent, and gut reaction that I have. For better or for worse, I'm in the spotlight, thanks to the book and the movie."

"That's what brought you to the great-grandmother's attention?"

"Let's just say, I made a definite impression on her," Derek agreed. "And *you've* made a definite impression on *me.* Help me with this, Laurel, and I'll send your career into orbit."

She glanced at the stack of transcripts on a nearby coffee table. "It's in there, you know," she cautioned him quietly. "I'm not positive we can get him off, but I'm positive we can get him a new trial. *That's* the awesome responsibility here. Our responsibility to society, not to help free a kidnapper."

"There are worse people in the world than kidnappers, Laurel. Grow up and help me with this case. Do you want to be a defense attorney or not?"

"I don't know."

"Well, maybe it's time you found out."

◑ ● ◐

"Call me old-fashioned, but I think eight-thirty in the morning is a strange time to meet anyone, including your sister, in a dimly lit bar."

Laurel turned gratefully toward her big sister's teasing voice. "Thanks for coming, May. I need advice, quick." She patted the bar stool to her right. "One of the busboys slipped me two mugs and a carafe of French roast. He can probably get you a Danish if you haven't eaten yet."

"I'll pass." May Banyon-Connor shook her head as she settled into her seat. "I was just opening the door to my office when you called."

"It's convenient having my own analyst right around the corner."

"Yesterday, you were lecturing all of us about staying away from this place for the next few weeks so that you and your famous boss could work without interruption. What changed?"

Laurel took a deep breath. "Remember how I told you Derek wouldn't give me the details of the case on Saturday?"

May nodded. "You said he was trying to establish control right from the start."

"Well, I think it's worse than that." Laurel sifted her fingers through her hair, then shook the whole mane defiantly. "He knew there was a chance I'd turn his offer down if I knew who the client was. Remember that guy who took his little girl up to the mountains and left her alone in a cabin and she burned to death?"

"George Perry? Good grief, Laurie."

Laurel nodded. "That's what *I* said. Derek wasn't just controlling the situation, May, he was manipulating me— letting me invest some time and planning, so I'd start to count on the experience and the money—so there'd be less chance I'd back out. Plus, Derek's personal motives are all screwed up, because . . ." She paused dramatically, then finished with, "He once had an affair with George Perry's wife, so he's out for some weird kind of revenge."

"Incredible."

"Exactly. He's using me, manipulating me, and who knows what else."

"Or, he's manipulating himself," May mused.

"What?"

49

The older sister grinned. "I read that book of his last night. I figured if my baby sister was going to be alone in a hotel room with him day and night, I should check him out a little."

"And?"

"He usually works alone. In his office in San Francisco. He's very independent, but for *this* case, he's renting rooms and furniture and computers, and hiring *you*—a complete stranger. Why?"

"Because I'm creative," Laurel supplied, although the explanation now sounded somewhat thin.

"That's true. You're extremely imaginative. But you're also objective in a way *he* can't be if he's emotionally involved. He may seem to be controlling you, Laurel, but the truth is, he may be hoping you'll keep *him* in line, professionally speaking. You don't know him, and you don't know the Perrys, so you can be objective in a way he could never be."

She paused to brush a lock of hair from Laurel's cheek, then continued. "He holds himself to very high standards. Ethically, professionally, intellectually. He knows that objectivity is the key to all those areas. If he hates George Perry's ex-wife, he can't be objective."

Laurel was staring in complete adoration. "I love it when you do this. It's like being at the optometrist's office, and he clicks the thingamabob, and presto, all the blurriness goes away."

May laughed. "Thanks. Of course, this is just a theory. He may actually be a domineering jerk, out for revenge, with no respect for truth or justice, so don't let your guard down."

"Don't worry. I don't trust him."

"Neither do I." May arched an eyebrow and demanded, "Can you be objective about this case? I know you don't like it when little children are involved."

"It shook me for a minute, but now I'm sure I can handle it. It's a challenge. A real stretch for me."

"Because you're not going to trial?" May smiled sympathetically. "You really do love to perform, don't you?"

Laurel nodded. "It's my favorite part of the job. But I'll also miss a defense attorney's most lethal weapon—the presumption of innocence. My clients and I have always had that in our favor. But at the appellate level, George Perry is no longer presumed innocent. He's been proven guilty, and if Derek and I don't find the right kind of error in the trial below, we're sunk."

"In a big trial like Perry's, there must have been lots of mistakes," May said reassuringly.

"True. But ninety percent of the errors in the trial court are useless on appeal. If the mistake couldn't possibly have affected the outcome, it's called 'harmless error,' and it's not good enough to get him a new trial."

"So, you're looking for harm*ful* errors?"

"They're called reversible error. Prejudicial to the defendant. Of course, if the attorneys below made an inordinate number of harmless errors, we could try to prove that they were ineffective, overall. That *could* work. But these guys weren't beginners. I'm sure they did a fairly competent job."

"So, reversible errors are big ones? Like evidence coming in that should have been excluded?"

"It's even more complicated than that." Laurel sighed. "If the trial attorneys didn't object to the inadmissible evidence, we're still sunk because the appellate court will say it was part of their trial strategy to let the evidence in."

"Strategy?" May frowned. "That sounds like pure incompetence. Why would a lawyer ever knowingly let harmful evidence in if he could keep it out?"

Laurel smiled, amused by the psychologist's dogged interest. "Remember in the movie they made about Derek's case? Remember when that sweet old woman was babbling about all the ugly rumors she'd heard about the defendant, and your heartthrob Trevor Harris didn't object? And *you* insisted it was hearsay?"

"Well, wasn't it?"

Laurel nodded. "Joe and I agreed with you, remember? But Joe explained that Trevor Harris didn't object because he didn't want the jury to think he was being mean to a sweet old lady."

"Trial strategy?"

"Exactly. So, even if Derek and I find some really juicy issues, they may not be enough. It's tough to win on appeal, May, but I'm determined, and Derek's even worse."

"Tell me more about him."

"There's nothing else to tell, yet. Anyway—"she slid off her barstool—"I should get back upstairs. He thinks I came down here to think about quitting."

"Quitting?" May shook her head in genuine amusement.

"He doesn't know you very well yet, does he?" She stood to heartily embrace Laurel. "If it helps, honey, I feel sorry for George Perry. I think it was unfair to call him a murderer. After all, that fire was accidental, and so was the girl's death. Accidents aren't murder."

"It's called the felony-murder rule," Laurel explained. "Any time there's loss of life during the commission of a dangerous felony, the felon is held accountable. Like, if a robber holds up a store with an unloaded pistol, and the store clerk is so scared he has a heart attack and dies, that robber is guilty of felony-murder. He didn't intend to kill anyone—he used an unloaded gun, right? But we still call it murder."

"And since George Perry committed a kidnapping . . . ?"

"Right. Felony-murder of his own kid, even though he was arguably trying to make her life better, not end it. It's such a mess. I can't *believe* I've gotten myself involved in it."

May patted her sister's shoulder. "You may not want to hear this, Laurel, but in some ways, this sounds like just your kind of case."

◖ ● ◗

This time, she used her key card to enter the room, keeping her face carefully expressionless as she greeted a wary Derek.

"So?" he demanded, his brusque tone softened by the hopefulness in his eyes.

"I'm going to change into my work clothes, then we can

finish our case conference. And, Derek? No more games, okay?"

He nodded solemnly. "I'll tell you everything you need to know. You have my word on that."

"Fine." Grabbing her briefcase, she headed for "her" bedroom, where she quickly traded her pantsuit for the jeans and sweatshirt, then pulled her curls back into a practical ponytail held in place by a band of elasticized black velvet. The image that stared back at her from the mirrored wardrobe door was exactly right—confident, unpretentious, and just unpredictable enough to keep him in line. After all, if May's theory was correct, that was precisely what she'd been hired to do.

THREE

"Okay, I think I'm up to speed on the basic facts and procedure, so . . ." Laurel slipped her hair free of its ponytail and pulled her legs up under herself, snuggling into her chair. "Tell me more about George."

Derek groaned. "We've been at this for three hours straight. I thought *I* was a workaholic, but you're worse. Let's order up some food at least. I'm not trying to stall again," he added with a playful glare. "I'm just plain hungry."

"Order food then. I'll have whatever you're having and some club soda." She was rifling through a folder filled with photographs. "Our guy has the saddest face."

"In person it's worse," Derek confirmed without looking up from the room service menu. "When he sent for me, I figured I'd do him the courtesy of listening to his story, then bow out, but he doesn't have a friend in the world. Twenty-eight years old and his life is over."

"What about his parents? Are they supportive?"

"In their own way, maybe, but I got the impression they don't visit him."

"Does anyone?"

"Apparently not." He closed the menu and reached for

the phone. "Is swordfish okay? I had it yesterday, and it was excellent."

"Whatever," Laurel mused. "I wouldn't mind going to visit him, Derek. Alone, or you could come too."

"I'll ask him the next time I talk to him. But I got the impression he doesn't really want company. What he wants is to be free. To start over."

"As a makeup artist in his parents' mortuary?" Laurel shuddered. "He's not thinking of going back to *that* life, is he? All that death, combined with the poor man's memories and guilt. It's too much."

"I don't think he'd go back there. On the other hand, there aren't many ways for an artist to earn a living, and apparently he was pretty good at it. That's what initially attracted Veronica to him, you know. She went to a funeral, decided the deceased woman looked better dead than she'd looked alive, and adopted George as her personal makeup artist in residence."

"Veronica Perry is obsessed with her looks," Laurel agreed. "You can tell that from these photos. She's practically a caricature of a beautiful woman. Curves and angles, but zero warmth. Of course, she managed to impress you and George, so maybe I'm just being overly critical."

Derek seemed about to retort, but room service had come on the line and he turned his attention to placing their order while Laurel once again studied a handful of shots of Veronica Keyes Perry. Statuesque was one word that came to mind. Bitch was another. Everything about her appearance was an exaggeration of womanhood, from her enormous chest to her ridiculously tiny waist, always cinched with a bright sash or silver conch belt. Her thick platinum hair—waist length and artfully crimped into thousands of tiny waves—had such an artificial tone to it that Laurel wondered how any man could find it alluring.

Sour grapes, she chided herself finally. *Admit it. If you'd been born with these looks, you could have been a superstar actress. And if Derek Grainger measures other women against her, no wonder he hasn't given you a second look.*

And he definitely hadn't. While she had requested and wanted professional behavior on his part, she also wouldn't have minded an occasional appreciative or admiring glance. After all, *she* was managing to be strictly business, yet to still be aware of his denim blue eyes, well-toned body, and devastating smile. She could appreciate his sexy voice, square jaw, and rumbling chuckle without losing sight of the fact that they were two experts conferring on sobering topics with no danger of romantic overtones or distractions.

"They said it'll be less than half an hour," Derek informed her, standing and stretching as he spoke. "Did you still want to know about George, or . . ." The blue eyes teased her. "Did you want to hear more about Veronica?" When Laurel flushed, his smile softened. "I appreciate the fact you haven't asked about my relationship with her, but I promised to give you any information you needed, so . . ."

"I'm dying of curiosity," Laurel admitted, gathering her hair back into its ponytail and anchoring it securely. "What happened?"

Derek began to pace. "I met her when I was twenty-six. Just one year out of law school. She was twenty-seven, I think, but infinitely more experienced than me, although you never could have convinced me of that at the time. I considered myself a man of the world, but I wasn't ready for Veronica." He grimaced, as though still pained by the memory. "She came to my office and asked me to prepare her will. It wasn't my area of expertise, so I reluctantly referred her to a colleague. But"—he flushed slightly—"she insisted that she had to have me."

"Literally."

"It gets better." Derek grinned. "She seduced me, right there in my office, then invited me to spend the weekend at her place in Sausalito."

"You weren't seeing anyone else at the time?"

"It wouldn't have mattered," he admitted sheepishly. "She knocked me out, not just because of the way she looked, but because she was so obsessed with sex. It was an irresistible combination."

"So you went to her place? And?"

"She wanted me to review some papers she'd drafted for herself. She claimed there wasn't any attorney in the world she trusted beside me, and I made the obvious disclaimers—that it wasn't my specialty and I might make mistakes—but she insisted."

"And . . . ?"

"That's when I got my first hint of how unstable she was. Her will had only one provision—a single sentence forbidding any autopsy in the event of her death. She didn't want to be 'disfigured,' as she called it, in any way, after she was gone."

"Good grief."

Derek nodded. "I tried to explain that there are certain situations that demand an autopsy, and she got upset. Then she sprang an even weirder document on me. A durable power of attorney, providing that, in the event she was ever unconscious and in need of medical treatment, she absolutely did not authorize any medical or surgical procedure that would cause any scarring or disfigurement."

Laurel bit her lip. "That's actually kind of sad, don't you think? What did you say to her?"

"I told her she needed to see a therapist. To find out that there was more to her than her looks."

"That was right." Laurel smiled fondly. "But after that, you stayed?"

"For the rest of the weekend, and believe me, it was unforgettable. By the time I realized how perversely unstable she really was, I felt like an idiot for having become so intimate so quickly."

"Did you continue to see her after that?"

"No. Once I came to my senses, I hit the ground running and never looked back."

"Until the trial."

"Right. I kept imagining Veronica as a mother, and it was very disquieting. And I felt sorry for George. He was fresh out of college when he met her, so he was even more vulnerable to her 'charms' than I'd been. She was twenty-nine years old by then, and he was still a kid."

"And a year later, he was a father." Laurel shook her head. "It's odd, isn't it? She was paranoid about scars, et cetera, but was willing to go through childbirth where the risks of quote-unquote disfigurement run from stretch marks to C-sections."

"According to George, she starved herself during the entire pregnancy, to the point where outsiders couldn't even tell until almost the final month. She was determined to retain her shape and avoid any stretch marks. And she was also determined not to consent to a C-section, even if the baby's life were at stake. She actually made George promise not to consent on her behalf either, if it came down to that."

Laurel shook her head again. "Why bother having a baby at all if that's the way she felt?"

"George says Veronica had a child in an attempt to immortalize herself—or more specifically, her beauty—then couldn't handle it when little Amy's beauty wasn't a carbon copy of her own."

"That's sad."

"Sad? Try 'chilling,'" Derek drawled. "If half of what George says is true, Veronica obsessed about things like the shape of Amy's eyes, and the fact that her teeth were a little crooked. She argued with the dentist about putting braces on the baby teeth—fortunately, he was too professional to do so, even in the face of Veronica's brand of persuasion. But you can imagine how nervous George got when she started having an affair with a plastic surgeon after their marriage broke up."

Laurel stared in dismay. "He actually believed she might have cosmetic surgery done on a little girl's *eyes?* That's pretty far-fetched, Derek." When he just arched an eyebrow in response, she felt a chill run down her spine. "Go on."

"It gets pretty rough," he warned. "You already know George's visitation rights were extremely limited, so it was tough for him to keep tabs on Amy. But a few of their old friends were sympathetic, and one day, one of them called George to tell him Amy had been hurt playing catch. Supposedly, a ball hit her in the face. She came to school all bandaged up. When George heard that, he freaked."

"Because he thought it was just a cover story, and she'd had some surgery done? But that can't be true. It would have come out at the trial."

Derek nodded. "But get this. It was Veronica who threw the ball that hit Amy in the face."

"No!"

Derek's blue eyes were alive with disgust. "Veronica took her to the emergency room, crying and upset over the so-called accident, and insisted that they send for the plastic surgeon. Fortunately, the guy had principles, and didn't exploit the opportunity to do what Veronica wanted." Derek took a deep breath, as though the telling of the story was beginning to wear on him. "Needless to say, that was the end of Veronica's affair with the doctor."

"If she threw a ball at that adorable face on purpose, she really *is* a monster."

Derek nodded. "By the way, this is all privileged information."

"Are you saying he didn't use any of this during the custody hearings? Or the trial? It's dynamite!"

"It's all just conjecture on George's part, right? And he didn't testify. The plastic surgeon was a married man, so he wasn't about to take the stand and say Veronica offered him sex in exchange for mutilating a child. Without any corroboration, all they were left with was the fact that Veronica had hurt her, and everyone believed that was an accident. She played the frantic, loving mother to the hilt at the emergency room, couching her demand for plastic surgery in terms of getting the best medical treatment to make sure there was no lasting damage to Amy's breathing or vision." Derek moistened his lips before adding, "There's another factor at play here, Laurel. George wasn't exactly the boy next door, in terms of some of his idiosyncrasies. He might not have been a danger to Amy, but he was a strange guy. I got the feeling that during the early months of the custody battle he and Veronica agreed, either overtly or otherwise, not to make their respective dirt public."

"Dirt?" Laurel yanked the band from her ponytail and tossed her hair angrily. "We need all the dirt we can get. And the last thing George should be worrying about is his image! It can't get any worse." She eyed Derek coolly for a moment before adding, "He trusted you to keep his secrets and take his defense. Why? Do you think Veronica told him about the affair?"

Derek nodded. "She probably mentioned it when the movie came out. It stuck in his mind, and when his first team blew the defense, he took a chance I'd remember

Veronica's sex games and be sympathetic to his plight."

"Sex games?" Visions of whips and handcuffs were slithering through Laurel's imagination. "That must have been a strange attorney–client interview."

"You have no idea."

"How was George holding up?"

"Not well. By the end of the meeting, he was practically a basket case."

"And why not? Good grief, Derek, the man lost his liberty and his baby girl in one tragic, unendurable moment. Poor George."

He chuckled. "Listen to yourself. Four hours ago you were ready to lock him up and throw away the key. Now he's 'poor George'?"

"Four hours ago, he was a stranger," Laurel reminded him quietly. "Now he's my client."

"Right." A loud knock drew his attention. "That was quick."

"I'll get it." Laurel sprinted for the door, half expecting to see Joe Harrington's disapproving face, but it was room service and so, as she ushered the bellboy and his cart into the room, she made a mental note to call her overzealous ex-fiancé and compliment him on his restraint. Maybe she'd even reward him with a quick lunch the next day, if things with Derek were still going smoothly.

"This looks delicious, Derek. Thanks."

"You deserve a break. We have to pace ourselves through this thing or we'll get burnt out."

"I agree. In fact . . ." She smiled tentatively. "I was thinking I'd meet Joe downstairs for a forty-five minute lunch tomorrow, if that's not a problem. You're invited, of course."

"I'll pass. But go ahead, and take a full hour if you want."

Laurel laughed. "You're a total control freak, do you know that? I'm taking forty-five minutes. If I wanted an hour, I'd take it."

"Fine."

"You should join us."

"Now who's trying to control whom?"

"Good point. Come anyway."

Derek shook his head. "I'm sure Harrington wants you all to himself. I got the distinct impression he still considers you his girlfriend."

"His *best* friend," Laurel corrected. "The rest is just a memory."

"Like when you clerked for him in high heels? I heard all about it at Seaton's dinner."

She liked the soft chuckle he hadn't even tried to suppress. "From now on, Mr. Grainger, every time you tease me about that dinner, I'm going to dredge up an embarrassing moment from your film career."

"Thanks for the warning." His smile warmed. "Harrington told me the D.A. offered you a job, but you had your heart set on defense work. Did you consider the public defender's office?"

"It wasn't my style. Of course, it would have been more sensible. As it stands, I end up taking civil cases to pay the bills, and they distract me from the criminal stuff."

"That's a problem." Derek gave her a sympathetic smile. "If you want to do criminal defense work, you have to be available—like a hired gun, in a way—sharp and ready for action at a moment's notice. And like a hired gun, you have to be ready for the prosecutor who's heard you're good and wants to take a crack at you.

"That's the stage you're at now, Laurel. All of that laughing at Seaton's retirement dinner didn't fool me. Those guys are nervous—or maybe 'threatened' is a better word—and they're going to come gunning for you. You can't be going cross-eyed over some cross-complaint when they do. You have to be watching your back. Or get someone to do it for you."

Laurel leaned back in her chair and savored the image of Derek as a gunslinger—sharp and straight, his eyes fixed on his prey—ready to take on any challenge. A hired gun. She had never really thought about herself as one before, but it was exactly right. And exactly what she wanted.

"You're at a crossroads," he was warning. "You've got to go for it now, while your reputation's hot."

She sighed, banishing the fantasy of six-guns and showdowns in favor of a dose of reality. Her "hot" reputation wasn't going to pay her bills, and this kind of daydreaming wasn't going to help her new client. "Is there any chance we can get George out on bail pending appeal? It's dangerous in prison for guys like him, you know. Because he's perceived as a child-murderer."

"I spoke with the warden about that. He said there was a buzz about George during the trial, so they kept him out of the general population at first, but it all seems to have died down."

"Still, if we can get him out, we should."

"That's not a possibility. Even if it were, he feels safer where he is for the time being. Did I mention that Veronica swore to hire a hit man to follow him and kill him if he dared step foot outside prison before his sentence was served?"

"Like we care what *she* says?" Laurel tossed her hair contemptuously. "Tell him not to worry. If we get him out, he can come and stay with me."

Derek frowned. "I hope you're kidding about getting involved on that level—with George Perry or any other client. It's a bad idea, Laurel. Not only is it unprofessional, it's dangerous."

"*You're* lecturing *me* on getting personally involved in a case?"

Derek chuckled. "I didn't realize I was lecturing. Go ahead and eat your lunch in peace."

She had expected him to take offense. Maybe she had even been trying to goad him, although she couldn't imagine why. She was no longer angry over his earlier deceptions. If anything, he'd been disarmingly candid and frank since their initial disagreement. He had been steadily earning her trust, which was probably the reason she now felt the need to put a little emotional distance between them. It was too soon to let down her guard. The stakes were too high, both in terms of George Perry's future and Laurel Banyon's career.

"Laurel?"

She flushed and pulled herself back to her immediate circumstances. "Are you finished eating already? You didn't take three bites!"

He had returned to his desk, and now reached into a drawer for a miniature tape recorder, which he brought over to Laurel. "This is for you. It's how I communicate with my staff. When you need to tell me something, just make a note of it here, and I'll listen to it when I'm taking a break."

"Excuse me?"

"I know it's bizarre, but I like to concentrate while I work. I'd rather not be interrupted, or interrupt you, with non-urgent matters. So record anything you need to tell me, and I'll do the same." He crossed to his desk and pulled a second recorder into view. "I'll leave this out for you, and you can listen to my messages at your leisure."

"You're kidding, right? Aren't we going to be working ten feet from one another? Can't you just say, 'Hey, Laurel, do you have a minute?'"

"If it's important, I will. If it can wait, I'll record it. Or if you're not here—"

"What about that? If your office calls, am I supposed to take messages for you or something?"

He tapped a nearby machine with an impatient finger. "This is hooked up, so we don't need to answer the phone at all if we're both absorbed in what we're doing."

She could imagine the messages she might get—bluster from Joe, melodrama from Jessie—and insisted quickly, "I

67

don't get as easily absorbed as you, so I'll just answer the phone if you don't mind."

"Fine. Whatever. Now——" He exhaled sharply, as though frustrated by her lack of cooperation. "I'm going to look over some of the pretrial publicity. When you're finished eating, I can answer more questions, or you can look through some of the documents. I'd like you to start with the custody hearing. It gets rough, but it's necessary background for the trial, believe me."

She watched, intrigued, as he turned his attention to a thick looseleaf binder. He had called himself "detail-oriented," with a tendency toward becoming completely engrossed in his work. She herself was almost the complete opposite—restless, easily distracted, depending more on intuition and brainstorming than actual concentration. Would they be able to function together in the same room? She'd be afraid of disturbing him with her occasional jumping jacks and humming, and he might just bore her to death with his plodding, deskbound focus.

Except he was too handsome to bore her. In fact, she could easily imagine spending hours pretending to study the transcripts while secretly studying his anatomy as she waited for inspiration to strike. She liked the way he had rolled his sleeves up to expose the taut muscles of his forearms, and she loved the way he raked his fingers through his dark hair as he read. Most of all, she liked watching him concentrate, finding it amazingly attractive for reasons completely unrelated to law.

When the phone rang and he still didn't move a muscle,

she was tempted to see if he could really work straight through a message, then thought better of it and dove for the receiver, demanding breathlessly, "Can I help you? This is Laurel Banyon speaking."

"Good afternoon," a soft, cultured voice responded. "Have I reached Derek Grainger's room?"

"Yes. Could I take a message for him?"

"This is Ellen Grainger—Derek's mother. If he's not too terribly busy, I'd like to speak with him."

"Oh, hold on, Mrs. Grainger. He's right here. Derek? It's your mom."

A scowl had crossed his handsome features. "Tell her I'm working and I'll call her later."

Laurel shook her head, pressed her palm to the mouthpiece, and drawled, "You're not paying me enough to be rude to your mother."

"Fine. I'll tell her myself." Reaching for the phone, he boomed, "Mother? Is anything wrong? We're busy here." Then he grimaced as he listened, responding finally, "Yes, she's as lovely as her voice. She's also extremely busy assisting me on an important case, so if there's nothing urgent, let me get back to you . . . Fine . . . Right . . . Have a nice afternoon . . . Yeah, goodbye."

He hung up the phone and seemed about to return to his reading, but Laurel's annoyed expression had apparently caught his attention. "Did you want something?"

"No."

"Are you finished with lunch?"

"Yes."

"Fine." He closed the binder and smiled. "Where were we?"

"We were being rude to your mom."

"Drop it."

"I would except, I couldn't help overhearing. Did she really ask if I was as lovely as my voice?"

Derek was chuckling reluctantly. "Yes. She called long distance just to compliment your voice. Any other questions?"

"If I have anything else to ask, I'll use my recorder," Laurel retorted, reaching past him to sort through a pile of documents until she'd located the custody materials. "Don't let me distract you."

"Too late." He gripped her shoulder and turned her to face him. "If you've got something to say, just say it."

She flushed, wondering how he could touch her so nonchalantly, when she'd been fantasizing about bold physical contact and the provocative effect it could have on their relationship. Apparently, his superior concentration skills had kept him from forming any such hang-ups. He was glaring down at her with those gorgeous blue eyes without any hint of awareness of the proximity of his elbow to her left nipple, and so she forced herself to ignore it as well. "I apologize, Derek. I didn't know you were touchy about your mother."

"I'm not. But apparently you are."

"She sounded sweet. And lonely."

"Her?" He moved even closer, his breath now warm on her cheek. "If she's lonely, it's the ultimate irony, believe me."

As Laurel backed against the edge of his desk, a scene

from the film *False Pretenses* flashed through her mind. Trevor Harris as Derek Grainger, angry and impassioned, bullying a voluptuous female witness who, in a magnificent burst of illogic, found his manner arousing and pulled him onto herself, precipitating a full-blown, extremely memorable desktop love scene.

Grateful that Derek hadn't seen the movie, Laurel forced herself to glare back at him as she wriggled out of his grasp. "What's with you? First you bully your mother and now me?"

"I thought *you* were bullying *me*." He grinned, his anger gone as quickly as it had come. "Don't worry about her, Laurel. She can take care of herself, believe me."

"Okay, fine. The subject's closed."

"Good." He piled two bound transcripts into her arms. "These should keep you busy for the rest of the day. And if you have any questions"—he flashed his most devastating smile—"please feel free to interrupt."

◐ ● ◑

Ordinarily, concentration came easily to Derek, but this case was profoundly different from all the others. He could scarcely read a paragraph without encountering his daughter's name. And the photographs! George hadn't been exaggerating when he'd called Amy an angel. There was such innocent delight and purity to her expression that love seemed to radiate from it, straight into the heart of the father she'd never met.

71

Distraction, worry, anticipation—all these and more were beginning to take their toll on the frustrated attorney. He needed to know where she was. Needed to know she was safe, and happy, and cherished, until he himself could gift each of those basic necessities to her.

Despite George Perry's stern warnings against any attempts to try to locate Amy, Derek had already tried and failed. He'd hired an investigator, warned him to be discreet, and had him thoroughly check the backgrounds and current living arrangements of each of George's known friends and relatives. The detective had done an admirable job—at least, in terms of the purported assignment, which was simply to gather information for George's defense. In terms of the true but undisclosed objective—identifying the person to whom George had entrusted guardianship of little Amy—the investigation had been an unmitigated failure.

And so Derek had temporarily abandoned his search for the child, searching instead for the elusive reversible error that would lead to a retrial. George Perry had given his word that he would tell Derek everything once such a retrial had been obtained, and Derek had no reason to think his client was lying. It wasn't George's principles that were less than noble, it was his methods. Unfortunately, the error had proved as elusive as the girl herself.

Unaccustomed to failure, Derek had doggedly persevered. He hadn't found Amy, and he hadn't found a surefire error, but he had found Laurel Banyon. Could she be the key to success?

He glanced toward her just in time to see her pull the stretchy band of black velvet from her gorgeous auburn mane, which would now cascade about her shoulders. Did she have any idea, Derek wondered, how many times per hour she did that, or how provocative it was? The second half of the ritual—the scooping up and imprisoning of the curls, thereby unveiling her long, slender, kissable neck— would soon follow, and would be equally distracting. Not that he had any plans to kiss her, of course; still, there was no denying that it was a neck made to be nibbled.

And her eyes! They were widening now, outraged apparently by the words she was reading, but that expression would change easily, like her moods. She could be pensive one moment, indignant the next, amused moments later. And woven throughout was her playfulness, the quality Derek found the most appealing and most thoroughly confounding.

What mood would those violet eyes betray should Laurel learn the truth about this appeal? He almost wanted to tell her, just to see her reaction. She'd be livid, he knew, over having been further deceived and manipulated, but that would fade fast, into a euphoric energy—a celebration of Amy's continued existence. After that, what? What would a woman like Laurel do?

One thing was certain: she wouldn't feel bound by George Perry's rules. She'd do something unpredictable and wild, and while Derek was dying to know just what that would be, he didn't dare chance it. There was too much at stake. And he didn't dare jeopardize Laurel's career by asking her to knowingly present false information to an appellate court. Derek's own license to practice law was at risk, but for him, the risk was well worthwhile. He loved his profession, but Amy . . .

She was his child, despite the fact that he had resigned himself, years earlier, to a childless existence. Having known he wouldn't have time to devote to parenting, given the intense mix of ambition and pride he had inherited from his own parents, he had been unable to imagine how or where to find a woman unselfish and unambitious enough to balance out those faults and to fully meet their child's needs. It had seemed the height of arrogance to bring a life into the world without being certain one could provide the necessary attention and nurturing, and so he had reluctantly denied himself the right to fatherhood.

Sliding open the upper right-hand desk drawer, he stared down at a miracle: a three-by-five school portrait— *of his daughter.* It humbled him, and he might have slipped into a full-blown reverie, but at that moment his attention was grabbed by his associate's absentminded corralling of her hair into a ponytail, and it was all he could do to keep from chuckling aloud. Between Amy's angelic face and Laurel's alluring neck, he apparently wasn't going to get much done for the rest of the day.

FOUR

Hours later, Laurel's eyes were burning as intensely as the setting sun that was visible through the window of the suite, so she pushed the hearing transcripts aside and used her imagination instead, groping for an understanding of the rancor and animosity that had dominated the custody battle over little Amy Perry. The pages had indeed been rough reading, as Derek had predicted. They were also profoundly sad—a record of a child's future being decided on the basis of which parent was the least hazardous to her mental and physical health.

"Are you burned out?" Derek sympathized. "I could use a break myself."

"Great." Laurel beamed at her associate. "I have a million questions."

"I can imagine. Custody fights are always murder, but this one took the cake."

"It was rough, I agree." She gathered her legs under herself and loosened her ponytail. "But it's the trial itself that I'm curious about. When you read the transcript, could you tell anything about the atmosphere there, in the courtroom? Was it hostile, or mournful, or what?"

Derek scratched at the stubble that had begun to shadow

his chin and jaw. "Actually, it was surprisingly civilized, given the nature of the charges. Things only got emotional twice: first, when Veronica took the stand—she really made a scene; and second, when two of Amy's preschool class-mates testified."

"In other words, all the drama went to the prosecution's advantage?"

Derek nodded. "Unfortunately, yes. It might have been different if George had testified, but like I told you earlier, he categorically refused."

"If I'd been his lawyer, he would have taken that stand."

"Actually, that isn't true. Wild horses couldn't have dragged him up there, believe me."

Laurel smiled coolly. "Are you saying *you* wouldn't have made him testify?"

"You can't force a client to take the stand."

"Sure you can. If you really need his testimony, then you've got to find a way to convince him. That's part of a defense counsel's job, right?"

Derek hesitated before responding. "Believe me, George Perry was adamant about it. And he won't testify during the retrial either. He and I went over all that last week."

"That's nuts." Laurel scowled in disgust. "What's the point of getting this mess reversed if you're just going to make the same mistakes again? He *has* to testify. The jury has to see how grief-stricken he is. In fact," she added, springing to her feet and staring Derek down, "it shouldn't even *be* a trial next time. It should be a wake! A primitive ritual. Not 'civilized' at all." She tossed her hair, suddenly and completely indignant. "Jurors take their responsibilities so seriously anyway, but when a dead child is crying out from the grave for vengeance and justice, they must really go nuts with dedication. They'd be obsessed with doing the right thing, for little Amy's sake. The power in that court-room—the drama—would be so intense, all you'd have to do is tap into it and *boom*! Don't you see that?"

His unreadable expression galled her. Didn't he under-stand how basic this was? How on earth had he ever won a case, much less carved out a successful career? She stepped closer and warned, "This is crucial, so pay attention. Jurors want justice. Justice for Amy and, if you're not careful, jus-tice for Veronica, the bereaved mother. You have to make them understand that George needs justice too. It's all he *ever* wanted—justice for Amy, because he adored her more than freedom itself."

Righteous indignation, the most valuable tool a defense counsel could employ, coursed through her at that moment, making her crave a judge and jury before whom she could rage and wheedle. But there was only Derek Grainger—cool, detached, and probably inwardly scoffing. It was absolutely infuriating! "You have to paint George as the victim!" she chastised sharply. "The heartbroken father, shattered beyond recognition, consigned to a lifetime of guilt and grief. And George has to do *his* part, by testifying. He just *has* to."

"Go on."

"What?"

"You were mesmerizing me," he insisted. "Is that how

you do it? It's really terrific, Laurel. Go on with it."

Forcing herself to take a deep breath, she returned sheepishly to her chair. "All I'm saying is, you *have* to put George on the stand. The jurors will want to hate him, but only because they think he stole life from a child. If you can show them her life was already in jeopardy, and George was willing to sacrifice anything, even his own freedom, to save her, you might just be able to turn things around. At the very least, the sentence won't be so harsh. He *has* to testify, Derek. If you can't convince him of that, I will."

"How?"

She shrugged her shoulders. "Beg, plead, bully, threaten . . . I'll think of something. I'll probably end up guilt-tripping him, but until I meet him, I can't really be sure. Anyway . . ." She squeezed her eyes shut again, belatedly drained by her outburst. "It's not just the problem with him testifying. All the stipulations his attorneys made at the beginning of the trial really messed things up too."

Derek's blue eyes narrowed. "What are you talking about?" Before Laurel could respond, he was chiding, "Those stipulations were absolutely essential. You'll never convince me otherwise. By conceding from the start that the cabin belonged to George, that the stove was defective, and that Amy's death was the direct result of the fire, George's defense counsel kept out a whole flood of prejudicial evidence." He paused to scratch again at the stubble on his chin. "If they hadn't stipulated, the prosecutor could have brought in graphic pictures of the crime scene, along with hours of expert testimony about the cause of death. It would have been gruesome, and the jury would have despised George for sure."

"They despised him anyway," Laurel muttered. "Sometimes you need to wallow in the gruesome details and force yourself to work through them. Otherwise, the jury thinks you're hiding something."

"That's ridiculous."

"Is it?" Laurel arched an eyebrow in sharp disagreement. "The newspapers kept saying Amy *burned* to death, when I'm sure she must have died of smoke inhalation, right? But everyone, including the jury, imagines her little body engulfed in flames. *That's* gruesome, and that image really hurt George."

"The prosecution stipulated to the fact that death was by smoke inhalation, Laurel. It helped George's case."

"Apparently not enough," she said with a disdainful sniff. "Anyway, one little stipulation can't compete with live testimony, from a doctor, saying that Amy was bless-edly unconscious before the flames reached her, or whatever. All I'm saying is, sometimes the crime scene stuff helps the defense as well as the prosecution. It goes hand in hand with what I was saying before. The trial is a cathartic, cleansing experience for the jury. You have to take them through things, step by step. Give them a chance to be horrified, confused, compassionate, exhausted. Lead them by the hand, right to the place you want them. By agreeing to make dry, unemotional stipu-lations instead, the defense lost the chance to guide that jury through the pathos and into the light of forgiveness.

Show me a civilized trial," she added in disgust, "and I'll show you unfinished business."

"I disagree."

"Really?" She folded her arms across her chest. "Would you like a little demonstration?"

"Pardon?"

Reaching for the clipboard on his desk, she summoned her most litigious tone. "We're all impressed with your credentials, *Doctor* Grainger. In your capacity as head of the Burn Victims Research Institute, I'd like you to consider a hypothetical. You heard the prosecutor tell us that Amy Perry's burned remains were found on and around a brass bed in the corner of the one-room cabin. Assuming, for the sake of this hypothetical, that the child became bored, alone in the cabin, crawled into that bed and fell asleep—" She leaned closer and demanded, "Wouldn't you say she never awoke from that nap? Wouldn't you say that the smoke invaded her lungs as she slept, causing her to lose consciousness without ever awakening?"

Laurel's words became sharp, staccato accusations. "Isn't it a fact, Doctor, that sixty-two percent of all smoke inhalation victims die in their sleep without *ever* becoming aware of the presence of the fire or the danger? And that *ninety-eight* percent of all smoke inhalation victims are dead before the flames ever reach them?" She glanced across the room toward an imagined judge and purred, "Your Honor, would you please instruct this witness to answer the question?"

Derek moistened his lips, tugged at a nonexistent necktie as though thoroughly unsettled, then cleared his throat and responded, "The truth is, Ms. Banyon, we at the Institute have conducted exhaustive research on this subject and our results, as detailed in *The New England Journal of Medicine,* indicate that in eighty-five percent of smoke inhalation cases in which the victims are sleeping when the fire begins, the intense fits of coughing caused by the smoke are enough to rouse them, even from a sound sleep, at which time they experience intense panic and pain for up to five full minutes before lapsing into coma."

"Wow." She stared admiringly into his twinkling eyes. "You're pretty good. Usually . . . well, never mind."

"Remember this," he drawled as he stood to tower over her. "You're good too, Banyon, but you're in the big leagues now. No one's going to roll over and play dead just because you can talk a good game and toss around some phony statistics."

"So I noticed." She could feel a flush spreading across her face but didn't care. He deserved to see that he had completely shaken and impressed her. That was part of the fun of winning these impromptu mock trials, which until now had been her personal stomping grounds. Her nieces and sisters always succumbed to her interrogations, and even Joe could usually be reduced to a babbling idiot when suddenly plunged into the role of air traffic controller or accident reconstruction expert.

Derek Grainger was something new in her life—a challenge. Maybe even a mentor. She could learn from him—from his deceptive cool and his quick, measured responses. If she paid attention to him, over the next few weeks, she might walk away from this with more than just rent money and appellate experience.

"Are you suddenly speechless?"

"Never," she assured him with a smile. "Just recalibrating my weapons."

Derek chuckled and backed a respectful distance away. "While you do that, I'm going to clean up for dinner. Take a look at the room service menu if you'd like, or"—his smile broadened—"are you just going to copy me again?"

"You're my new hero," she admitted sheepishly. "Why don't you let *me* buy *you* dinner? There's a little teriyaki place around the corner that's really scrumptious."

"Jot down what you want to order, while I shave, then I'll call the desk and have them send someone over there. *My* treat."

It seemed like a waste of money to pay for delivery when the restaurant was so close and a walk would do them both good, but she wasn't quite ready to tangle with Derek again, so she reached for a pad and pen, scribbling while he moved toward his bedroom to make good on his threat to remove the sexy five o'clock shadow. If she asked him not to shave, he'd be momentarily speechless himself, she was sure, but she didn't dare raise the stakes in that particular direction—tempting as it might be—so she forced herself to think about less volatile but equally mouth-watering temptations like crispy tempura and spicy sesame chicken.

"It's almost eight o'clock, Laurel. Shall we call it a night?"

"I'm exhausted," she admitted, leaning back in her chair as she spoke. "I'm also completely discouraged."

"I know." Derek stood and stretched. "Every mistake we've discussed so far has been trial strategy—completely useless to us. And to the extent George refused to cooperate with his trial counsel—and by the way, I'm sure they begged, pleaded, *and* bullied, trying to get him to take the stand— our hands are tied on appeal. The court isn't going to let George profit now from his refusal to participate below."

"So, we're back where we started," Laurel agreed. "Trying to find an inspired error in a completely uninspired trial."

"Tomorrow you can start going over the transcript," he reminded her soothingly. "I have a feeling it won't seem so uninspired to you. I think you could find drama in a dead fish."

"Is that a compliment?"

"Absolutely. You would have made a great actress."

She waited, assuming he would now tease her about her aborted acting career, then prodded, "Didn't Joe tell you I was a drama major in college?"

"Seriously?" He nodded his approval. "I'll bet you were terrific. What happened?"

Laurel shrugged. "I wasn't really very good. I mean, I didn't stink, but I wasn't a major talent."

"And so you switched to law?"

"During my senior year at UCLA, a friend of mine wrote a play for one of our classes, and he gave me the part of a witness in a murder trial. We decided to check out a few real trials, to get the flavor of the scene, and it literally changed the course of my life. I sat in that courtroom," she added dreamily, "and all I could see was this incredibly accessible stage, complete with a captive audience, where the lawyers could perform in the spotlight every day of their lives. There was drama, suspense, passion—but the most amazing thing of all was that none of the attorneys I watched seemed to appreciate what they had. They didn't project their voices, didn't learn their lines, didn't emote for the jury . . ." She smiled sheepishly. "I figured I'd have a part for life if I went into law, and it's been everything I expected, plus more."

Derek nodded. "Courtroom drama—the perfect setting for a performer with a talent for arguing."

"I love trial work," she agreed. "I guess I'm just enough of an attention junkie to really thrive on it. Which means, of course," she added more soberly as she slung the strap of her briefcase over her shoulder and prepared to depart, "I'm probably not suited to appellate work. It's like asking an actor to become a drama critic."

"The appellate justices are the drama critics," Derek corrected. "You're more like a detective. Finding the clues in the transcript."

Laurel nodded. "That's true. I always wanted to play a detective. Maybe—"

"There's no maybe about it. You were born for this role. And the rehearsals are going to be grueling, so go home and get plenty of rest."

She stared into his deep blue eyes and murmured without thinking, "You know what I like about you?"

He cocked his head to one side. "What?"

She had been about to compliment him on his skill at improvising—he seemed to instantly catch on to her games, and he played along so effortlessly!—but their gazes had made a more personal kind of contact—the kind that made her pulse race and her throat tighten with anticipation. It was definitely time to go home. "I like it that you're so smart," she salvaged lamely as she backed toward the doorway. "I think I'm going to learn a lot from you."

"We'll learn a lot from each other," he agreed. "Last week, I was completely discouraged over this case. Now, I'm seeing it through your eyes, and it's a whole new ballgame. That's what *I* like about *you*."

"Well, then . . ." She continued backing away from him until she was flush against the door. "See you tomorrow, bright and early."

"I'll walk you to your car."

"No." She coughed to get rid of the tell-tale huskiness in her voice, then insisted brightly, "The valet will bring it around for me. Just get some rest, and don't worry about the case. And," she gave him one final, weak smile, "don't forget to call your mom."

◑ ● ◐

Derek stared at the door for a full minute after his new co-counsel had disappeared. There had been such energy in the

85

suite when she'd been there—excitement, challenge, intuition—all of which had departed with her, leaving him virtually exhausted. And wary. Of her.

Matthew Seaton, a wise and experienced jurist, had called her a renegade—a woman who didn't play by the rules. Joe Harrington, an extremely bright and capable giant of a man, had characterized her as an uncontrollable, irresistible brat. As much as Derek had discounted such images as exaggerations, he was now beginning to understand them. Laurel had been a whirlwind the entire day, commanding his attention and mesmerizing him with her double-talk and brilliance, while simultaneously intimidating him with unspoken consequences should he dare cross or deceive her.

And yet he had had no choice but to continue the deceptions. In a perverse way, he had even enjoyed the sense of danger those lies had evoked. Her bursts of displeasure were almost as attractive as the adoration she had directed at him more than once, most notably during their good-byes.

He was more convinced than ever that she was going to blow this case wide open. She'd find reversible error, or she'd create it out of thin air, like the preposterous statistics she had invented for her impromptu cross-examination. But would she stop there? If she could see error where there was no error, wouldn't she see the lies as well? Could he risk that? Did he have a choice?

He needed her, but he also needed to find a way to control and channel her curiosity—to keep her focused on the transcript rather than on the drama that lurked behind it. She was independent by nature, but she was also his assistant, hired to do what *he* told her to do, and he had to learn to assert that authority firmly and consistently.

With a grin of relief he recalled how she'd looked in her oversized sweatshirt and ponytail—a kid, really. A novice who had made it clear she wanted to learn from the legendary Derek Grainger. That was the key.

He headed for his bedroom to change into workout clothes, pleased that he had resolved the dilemma so easily. All he needed to do was to dominate Laurel, benevolently but also unwaveringly. Under any other circumstances he would have found the concept somewhat distasteful, but this was for Amy. He'd do anything for her.

He had age, experience, size, and mystique on his side. All Laurel Banyon had was energy, instinct, and a slight case of hero worship. And of course, an incredibly sexy neck. Grateful to her for having so wisely anticipated and forbidden *that* particular complication, he forced himself to forget about Laurel Banyon, and to concentrate instead on the missing child that needed him in a way no one had ever, ever needed him before.

◐ ● ◑

"I can learn a lot from him, May. He's *so* calm, and he *exudes* confidence, not to mention self-control."

"And control of you too?"

Laurel grinned and shook her head. "He'd be crazy to

try anything like that. Anyway, he brought me in on the case for a second perspective, so controlling me would be counterproductive, right? But I'll bet he controls a courtroom with an iron hand, and that's something I'd like to learn."

"You always win your cases, Laurel. Doesn't that mean *you* control the courtroom too?"

"I disrupt it, which works well for small cases. But for something complex, where you're going to spend days with a jury, I'm sure Derek's method—earning their trust instead of just entertaining them—would be better."

May smiled. "A controller and a disrupter, working together for twelve hours a day. It sounds explosive. And exhausting. Why are you here instead of home in bed?"

"For one thing, there's no food at my place," Laurel admitted, taking a bite from the enormous sandwich she'd made for herself the moment she'd crossed May's threshold. "And for another, I'm too pumped up to go to sleep. Too stimulated."

"Professionally? And . . . romantically?"

"This relationship is strictly business." Laurel jumped to her feet and began to pace. "Joe called *that* one right. Derek's so used to supermodels and femmes fatales, I don't even register on his Richter scale."

"You're not exactly a wallflower, Laurel. He's probably just respecting the parameters *you* set—quite wisely, I might add. So?" Her stern expression flickered with sisterly curiosity. "Does *Grainger* register on *your* scale?"

Laurel pretended to ponder the question. "He's a little too civilized for me—that's his favorite word, by the way.

Civilized. And every time he uses it, he looks at me like I'm a striking example of just the opposite. But right around dinnertime, he started developing this very sexy, very *un*civilized five o'clock shadow, and I had a weak moment. Aside from that, and a couple of fleeting urges to sit in his lap, there was no chemistry at all."

May was laughing helplessly. "You're nuts, you know."

"Is that your professional opinion?" Laurel grinned, then plopped into an overstuffed chair and admitted, "He thinks too much. All intellect and no emotion. And he might have a good heart, but it's not open for business. Plus, he has a crummy relationship with his mom."

"That's a bad sign."

"I know."

"My girls will be disappointed, especially Jessie. They think you're having a passionate affair at the Plaza."

"I should be so lucky." Laurel studied her sister intently. "The timing of all this is lousy. I wanted to spend this week fussing over Elaine and the wedding. I'll probably miss the rehearsal dinner, and maybe even the bachelorette party."

"She understands," May assured her firmly. "This is a great opportunity for you, Laurel, and we're all behind you. So don't blow it," she added teasingly.

"I won't." Laurel snuggled back into the cushions. "My adrenaline's fading . . ."

"Do you want to crash here for the night?"

"I wish I could, but I need to get a couple of dressy outfits from my place, to keep at the suite. Other than that, I've decided to live in jeans for the next couple of weeks, and just use the elevator directly from the parking lot to the suite instead of going through the lobby."

"Maybe you should start sleeping there, like he suggested. It would save you time, and you wouldn't have to drive late at night—"

"Very funny." Laurel grinned and struggled to her feet. "I can't wait for all the half-baked innuendoes you guys'll be flinging around at the wedding."

"Bring him with you," May suggested slyly. "Then we'll have to behave."

"He already turned me down this afternoon, which is probably for the best, since I'm sure we'll be sick of the sight of each other by then."

"Assuming you can stay out of his lap?" May patted her sister's arm fondly. "Go get some sleep, Laurel. I have a feeling you're going to need it."

FIVE

Bursting with renewed enthusiasm, Laurel arrived at the Eureka Suite at seven the next morning with an armload of clothes and a cheery hello for her co-counsel. Having expected to ease into the workday with some casual conversation, she was annoyed when a cordial yet detached Derek offered her coffee, croissants, and a microcassette tape filled with observations and instructions to "consider at her own pace." He was back at work, ignoring her completely, before she could think of an appropriate response, and so she escaped into her bedroom and glared at her reflection in the mirrored wardrobe doors.

"Are you going to let him boss you around?" She eyed her faded jeans and white silk tee with disgust. "You really are a flunky, you know." But it was too late to make a more dignified entrance, so she resisted an urge to put on the black suit she'd brought in case she needed to dash off to court unexpectedly. Why should she? She needed to be comfortable if she was going to work long days under *these* conditions.

Still, she had to do something, and so she rummaged in her makeup case until she'd found her green contact lenses, which she immediately popped into place. At the very least, they made her look less naive. In fact, she'd been told more than once they gave her a more sophisticated air. Maybe the effect would catch him off guard, and prompt him to treat her with more respect. If only she'd thought to bring her blond wig! She'd like to see him try to ignore her in that!

Returning to the work area, she settled down at her desk and sipped at her coffee while listening to the tape. Ten feet away, Derek seemed oblivious to the sound, which might have amused her if she weren't so annoyed. How could he sit there *listening to himself* and not see the absurdity of this system? Fortunately for him, none of his instructions was particularly offensive. In fact, he was basically telling her she was on her own, which was exactly the way she wanted it, and so she eventually decided to just bury herself in her work and make the shunning mutual.

She was soon genuinely engrossed in her client's disastrous life as portrayed in the custody transcripts, investigators' reports, and pretrial newspaper accounts. George Perry—a quiet, creative, harmless man—had lived a slightly morbid but solidly middle-class life until he fell into Veronica Keyes's clutches. And Amy—what a doll! While her predicament had been heartrending and her ending tragic, the girl herself had apparently been a sheer delight—polite, sweet, intelligent, and adorable. Teachers, baby-sitters, psychologists, neighbors—all painted a picture of a child who had been relatively happy and healthy, at least until the custody battle began, at which point everyone had attributed her weight loss and withdrawal to the strife between her parents. Given the things George had told Derek, Laurel knew it was much more than that.

One thing was clear: George had been a terrific enough father to balance out a very *un*balanced mother. For that reason alone, Laurel *had* to successfully represent him. In time, if he were free, he might put together a new life for himself. Perhaps he would even have another child, to love and nurture as completely as he had Amy. The world needed parents like George Perry.

She grinned at the thought, remembering Derek's words: "*. . . you were ready to lock him up and throw away the key. Now he's 'poor George'?*" And she remembered her reply: that he was no longer a stranger who'd kidnapped a little girl and left her alone in a cabin to die a horrific death. He was Laurel Banyon's client.

And he was Derek Grainger's client too, and so, for George's sake, she decided to give her co-counsel a second chance to behave like a human being. Picking up her recorder, she dictated softly, "Listen, Derek, these notes your investigator made during this background check are pretty strange. I hope you didn't pay him too much. When you have a minute, would you please explain why he never asked any of these people what they thought of George's character, but he made copious notes about how many people lived in each house and the ages of each child? It's like he was more interested in finding out about *their* lifestyles than about George's! And when you have a chance, could you let me know why—"

"Laurel?"

She looked up innocently from her recorder. "Did you say something?"

"Go ahead and ask your question."

"Did I distract you? Sorry."

"You're not sorry." He grinned, standing and stretching, then crossing the room to stand beside her desk. "What's the problem with the background check?"

She took a long moment to admire him in his tan slacks and navy polo shirt before explaining. "The first investigator—the one the trial attorneys hired—was pretty good. Uninspired but good. But yours! He spent most of his time on irrelevant stuff. Look at this: a detailed description of each kid in George's second cousin's household—including two who aren't even related to George! But does he bother to ask whether George was a good father? No. What's that about?"

"I told you how I am." Derek grimaced. "Just ignore the detail if it bothers you. It's my way of being thorough."

"What about this?" Laurel challenged firmly. "Asking each relative if they had any artistic ability! What does that have to do with anything?" Her eyes narrowed as she demanded, "Do you think George may have been adopted?"

He seemed about to deny it, then shrugged. "It crossed my mind. He doesn't look like either of his parents. But it turns out he's definitely their biological offspring."

"He doesn't look like Amy either," Laurel noted. "I guess she's all Veronica. So? What if he *had* been adopted? What difference would that have made?"

Derek's jaw visibly tensed. "None. I just like to know as much as possible. Is that a crime?"

"You don't fool me, Derek. I know exactly where you were going with all this, so level with me. You think he had an accomplice, right?"

He looked stunned, then almost angry. "That doesn't make any sense. An accomplice for what?"

"Someone to hide Amy with, right?" She noted his startled reaction warily. "I thought you told me you weren't going to keep anything from me. What's going on?"

Derek moistened his lips, then sat on the corner of her desk. "Someone to hide Amy with? Explain that."

Laurel uncrossed her legs and shrugged to her feet. "Simple. Suppose Amy hadn't died. What was George's plan? He couldn't have hoped to hide her from the authorities for long, right? He left a trail any amateur could follow, and he didn't try to keep his identity hidden from Veronica, so . . ."

Derek's smile was guarded. "You think he made arrangements to hide her with someone else? But of course, the plan never got to that stage because Amy died in the fire."

"Either that, or someone was going to help him get out of the country." Laurel nodded. "Don't pretend to be surprised, Derek. I'm sure you thought of this weeks ago."

"You're giving George too much credit, Laurel," Derek insisted. "He's no master planner, believe me. He was just acting spontaneously—"

"Spontaneously?" She began to pace as she logically refuted that notion. "He had to arrange for the cabin and stock it with food. He had to procure the drugs he used to knock Veronica out with. Why go to all that trouble when he couldn't possibly get past the next step?" She paused in front of Derek and caught his gaze in her own. "I need to talk to him. Can we arrange that? Thursday or Friday would be good for me."

"You don't need to see him, Laurel. I can answer all your questions. For example—" Derek took a deep breath and flashed his first real smile of the day. "I'm sure he thought that, if he kidnapped Amy, the authorities would finally realize how desperate the situation was and would reconsider the custody decision. That was probably nine-tenths of his plan."

"Is he that naive?"

"Absolutely. Did I tell you what he said about not cooperating in his defense?" When Laurel shook her head, he revealed, "He was sure the judge and jury would see that he acted out of fatherly love and concern, and so they'd either find him not guilty, or decide that he'd suffered enough and set his punishment at time served. He gambled on their pity."

Laurel felt a new wave of sympathy for her hapless client. "Poor George."

"He didn't have an accomplice," Derek added firmly. "I asked him about that, and he said there's no one in the world he trusted that much."

"That's even sadder." Laurel sighed, then reached for her briefcase, locating an elasticized hairband through which she proceeded to pull her hair into an efficient ponytail. "Maybe there was no accomplice, then. But something about this just doesn't add up. I don't think we should be concentrating exclusively on finding error here, Derek. I think there's something else—something bigger. Some huge, gelescent fact that will bring all this into a new focus for us, if only I can put my finger on it."

"'Gelescent'? Is that really a word?"

"Sure. It means, when everything comes together and gels."

"I don't think so." He flipped open one of the notebook computers and, to her annoyance, began searching through the dictionary program. "Gelatinous . . . gelled . . . but no gelescent."

"Are you for real?" Laurel glared. "Forget the vocabulary lesson and pay attention to what I'm telling you! There's some huge fact missing from all this—I feel it in my bones!"

"There's no gelescent fact here, Laurel," he assured her with a patronizing smile. "This isn't a movie of the week, you know. You're looking for a staggering plot twist, and I'll admit that would be nice. But the truth is, we have a lot of unglamorous, hard work to do, and the sooner we get started, the better."

"But, Derek—"

"Your drama training may work well in the courtroom, but here, it's just disruptive. We have to sift through all this information, as boring and trivial as it may seem to someone like you. All the theatrics in the world aren't going to change that."

The look in his eyes was all too readable—the look of a man who was beginning to think he'd made a huge mistake. He was wishing he'd never hired her, and as unfair as that was, Laurel knew she had to reassure him. "Just hear me out, Derek. Please? Remember why you hired me? Not to sift detail—that's your job. You wanted inspiration. Creativity. Right?"

His eyes were still cool. "I want you to creatively manipulate the information in the transcript."

"My instincts tell me we can't get the whole picture from transcripts and reports. I really, really need to talk to George."

"That's not going to happen, so forget it."

She stared for a long, stunned moment before murmuring, "I beg your pardon?"

"I already interviewed George. Very thoroughly. And now he wants to be left alone. If something crucial comes up, I'll go see him again, alone. Otherwise, just work with the materials I've provided."

"I'm his attorney—"

"No, *I'm* his attorney. You're my assistant."

"I see." She turned away, not yet daring to respond—not because she was speechless, but because the retorts on the tip of her tongue were temporarily laden with expletives. She had to compose herself, before she said or did something she'd live to regret, his arrogant provocation notwithstanding.

Derek stared at Laurel's back, knowing he probably had less than a minute to decide what to do before she got control of her temper and turned to face him and quit. Because he knew that that was exactly what she would do. He had left her no choice. But did he really want her to leave? Did *he* have a choice?

The potential for disaster was too enormous to ignore, and his plans to control her had proven laughably ineffective. He had asked for creativity and inspiration, but hadn't dreamed that, in less than twenty-four hours, she'd be narrowing in on "George's accomplice," and honing in on "a place to hide Amy." It was all too close to the truth. What if she took it that one, crucial step further?

And what if she did? he challenged himself desperately. *If she's this intuitive about George's thought process, maybe she could actually find the hiding place! That's what you really want, right?*

But what if he took a chance and confided in her, and then she failed to uncover Amy's whereabouts? What if she decided to tell the authorities, or to go and badger George, who would undoubtedly consider all this a gross violation of their deal? He'd lose his chance to find Amy forever. Worse still, Laurel might decide that "the mom" had a right to know her child was still alive. *That* was the most chillingly unacceptable possibility of all!

And even if Laurel agreed to play along in order to help him free George and find Amy, she'd be jeopardizing her entire career. He couldn't in good conscience ask that of her. She was destined to be one of the great criminal defense attorneys, and he couldn't ask her to put all that on the line for him or for anyone else. She was an officer of the court and couldn't afford to participate in this fraud, even for the most laudable of causes.

He knew he should just let her quit—let her storm away from this incendiary situation, for both their sakes. Who knew what she'd do next? She wanted to see George—*that* would be a catastrophe. And even if he could talk her out of that, what would be next? Would she want to visit the crime scene? It was all cleaned up, of course, but to Laurel's eye—the eye of a former drama major—it would still all seem too neat. The setting, the photos, the sheriff's testimony—she'd guess the truth. That brilliant, dangerous curiosity was as unquenchable as the fire that George had so carefully staged.

His gaze traveled, from her long, sexy neck, over her slender shoulders, and down to her nicely filled jeans. Any second now, she was going to loosen her hair and turn to face him. To give him the tongue-lashing he knew he deserved, and then, to walk out of his life, taking her energy, brilliance, and innocence—all of which he so desperately needed.

He remembered how he'd felt, when he'd reached a dead end in his own quest to find Amy, or the reversible error that would lead to Amy. Exhaustion and disillusionment, bordering on despair, had threatened to sabotage his only hope for finding his daughter. Then he'd heard about Laurel Banyon. Met Laurel Banyon. Watched Laurel Banyon in action . . .

"We can work this out, Laurel. I'm sure of it."

She turned, pulling the band from her hair, allowing soft waves to fall freely around her shoulders. "Can we? I don't think so. Unfortunately," she added sharply, as though anticipating an argument, "I can't just abandon George, so if you have a suggestion, please make it."

"You're worried about *George?*" he murmured in disbelief.

"Who else?" Her tone dripped with mockery. "Me? Don't kid yourself, Derek. If I walked away right now I'd be just fine. I don't *need* this case, or you and your money. But George Perry would be up a creek without me, and I don't do that to my clients."

She wasn't quitting, and he should have been grateful, but instead he felt insulted by her insinuations. "You don't think I'm competent to represent George on my own?"

Laurel shrugged. "As far as I can see, you're representing yourself. This is all some sort of weird scheme of revenge—*don't* deny it! You want to win the case for personal reasons, which makes *me* the only professional on this so-called team."

He took a deep breath and tried to smile. "You're oversimplifying things, but I see your point. I do have a personal stake in the outcome of all this. But George knows that, and he still wants me as his attorney. His *only* attorney. After that debacle in the trial court, he doesn't trust any other lawyer in the world."

"Including me? Did you even tell him about me?"

"No. He'd never agree to my sharing confidential information with anyone else. I know that for sure. But I also know I need an objective, creative counterpart, so I didn't ask his permission to hire you. I just did it." He stepped closer and insisted, "He'd never agree to talk to you, Laurel. He'd probably want you to withdraw from the case. And you're right—losing you would be a disaster for him. And for me."

"I don't care about *you*."

"That's understandable."

She moistened her lips, then turned away again, this time crossing the room to pour herself a second cup of coffee. As she moved, she unconsciously gathered her hair back into its ponytail, and Derek found himself relaxing and enjoying the show, certain for the first time that she was really staying.

She turned to eye him critically. "I *knew* you were keeping something from me, Derek. You're a good liar, but I've been studying performers all my life. I know an act when I see one."

"I apologize. For deceiving you, and for the way I treated you this morning."

"Oh?"

He grinned at the haughty tone. "I wanted to establish my control—my dominance—right from the start. And I wanted to keep you—"

"In my place?"

"No!" The grin turned sheepish. "Not exactly. I wanted to keep you in the dark, I suppose. For fear you'd see the extent of my personal involvement in all this. But you're so sharp, Laurel. You saw it right away. Except . . ."

"Yes?"

He waited until she'd settled back into her desk chair. "Revenge against Veronica isn't my motive here. You'll have to take my word for that. I haven't been carrying a grudge or anything. In fact, I rarely thought of her these last seven years, except as a bizarre but harmless side trip on an otherwise straight and narrow path."

Laurel stared up at him coolly. "Don't bother telling me your motive is to get justice for George, because I'm not buying it."

"Not justice for George. Justice for Amy." He watched her eyes widen and, despite the interference from the green lenses, could see he had won her over at long last. It wasn't really a surprise—he was persuasive by nature, and accustomed to eventually getting his way. What surprised him was how he was feeling—not just relieved or grateful, but also profoundly stimulated. Energized. Aroused. And he knew that her most brilliant move so far had been to keep them at arm's length from one another at moments like this.

"You said it yesterday," Laurel was murmuring softly. "That if you'd been as young and naive as George when you met Veronica, you might have been the one to marry her and have a child with her. *You* might have been the one confronted with the need to save a helpless little girl from an unbalanced mother. But, Derek . . ." She stood and took his hands in her own. "*You* would never have screwed it up the way poor George did. If you were Amy's father, she'd be alive and safe today."

"Don't sell George short," he whispered hoarsely. "He did one helluva job, considering what he was up against."

"Okay, okay." Her tone was now soothing. "Come over here now and sit with me on the couch. We're going to have a long talk."

"About Amy?" He winced, annoyed with himself for having pointed her in a disastrous direction. "That's not necessary, Laurel."

"Sit." She settled onto the sofa and patted the cushion beside her. "We're not going to talk about Amy. We're going to talk about you."

"Me? That's *really* not necessary." He chuckled nervously.

"I can't work with a stranger, Derek. At this point, I feel like I know George a little, but I don't know you at all, except what I learned from the movie, and let's face it," she finished teasingly. "No one's *that* perfect."

"I think I've proven that today." He sat next to her and tried not to think about kissing her neck. "What do you want to know?"

"Hmm . . ." She pursed her lips thoughtfully. "Let's start with your mom. Did you call her last night?"

He scowled and started to stand. "Let's get back to work."

She grabbed for his hand, restraining and coaxing in one gentle motion. "In other words, you didn't call her? Fine. That tells me all I needed to know on *that* subject, so let's move on to—"

"Wait!" He shook his head, smiling despite himself. "Your turn. Tell me something personal about you. About you and Harrington."

"Joe? I thought you knew all that. We worked together, became friends and lovers, then backed off and concentrated on the friendship."

"You were the one who broke the engagement."

"And you want to know why?" Laurel flashed a mischievous smile. "It seems crazy, doesn't it? I mean, he's Prince Charming. Every girl's fantasy, right?"

"I wouldn't know."

She grinned. "He's handsome and sweet and smart and big-hearted. Right from the start, we had a perfect relationship."

"I see. That must have been a nightmare for you."

"Very funny." Laurel laughed lightly. "What I'm saying is, it was too comfortable, right from the first moment. I like drama, remember? I want trial by fire—for myself, and for Joe. I love him so much," she added sincerely, "that I can't wait to see him fall hopelessly into love. I want him to lose sleep, and babble, and rage with jealousy, and—"

"Suffer?"

"Exactly! I'm glad you understand."

Derek studied her closely. "What you're describing is a hot love affair. But is it the basis for a good marriage? Maybe what you and he had would have been best for your kids—"

"Good grief, Derek, I don't want *endless* conflict. Just an exciting courtship. After that, I'm sure my husband and I, and Joe and his wife, will settle down and be blissful. I just don't want to start out with bliss and end up with boredom. See?"

"You plan to have kids, though?"

"Of course. Eventually." She seemed to be enjoying their new relationship as confidants. "But right now, I can barely spare the time and energy for dating, which means I'm definitely not ready to be a wife *and* a mother. So I've put all that on hold, temporarily."

"Have you ever considered the modern woman's solution?" He eyed her cautiously. "Having a baby without having a relationship with the biological father?"

Laurel laughed with musical delight. "*My* baby's going to *need* his or her biological father. With me as the mother, the kid'll need a whole team of auxiliary caretakers, including a dedicated father, slavishly devoted aunts and uncles, and a full-time nanny." She noticed his frown and added quickly, "That's just me, of course. I know plenty of women who could handle single parenthood and a career without losing their minds. I'm just not one of them. Did I say something to offend you?"

"Hardly. Just the opposite, actually. I've been asked, more than once, to— Never mind." He coughed nervously. "How did we get on this subject?"

"You brought it up," Laurel reminded him, patting his hand in amused reassurance. "So? You've been asked to contribute sperm to some liberated would-be mom? You should take that as a compliment. You're intelligent and good-looking and healthy—the perfect donor, or whatever they call it."

"I'm just grateful they asked, and didn't just help themselves to the donation," he admitted wearily. "It was that damn movie that made things crazy, you know. Like you said, they portrayed me as some sort of perfect specimen. Little did they know, right?"

"Good grief. I think that's the most paranoid thing I've ever heard!"

"Pardon?"

"You're glad they didn't just help themselves?" She was

grinning impishly. "How exactly would they do *that*? Are you a really sound sleeper or something?"

"Laurel . . ."

"You use condoms, don't you? No one can steal your sperm unless you let them, Derek. I mean, theoretically, if you went to some sort of sperm bank, I suppose, and then *they* released it without your permission—"

"Laurel!"

"Huh?"

"I shouldn't have said anything," he grumbled. "I forgot about your warped imagination. No one's paranoid about stolen sperm. Plus, we were supposed to be talking about you."

"But you're so much more interesting," she said teasingly. "Movies, and stolen sperm, and—hey!" She grabbed again for his hand as he shrugged to his feet. "Don't go. I won't tease you anymore, I promise." When he'd relaxed back down beside her, she coaxed, "I told you I want to have children some day. The *normal* way. Do you?"

He studied her for a long moment, then admitted, "I decided a long time ago that perfectionism and parenthood don't mix. I'm more realistic than you are, Laurel. I don't see having a kid and then consigning it to a string of baby-sitters for eighteen years and expecting anything but heartache. Ambition like mine—and I suspect like yours—doesn't leave room for much else." He noted her silence with fond amusement. "Now who's being moody? Can't you take the truth?"

"I want it all," she repeated stubbornly, "and I'll have it.

It's just going to take a little of my infamous creativity."

"What's the point? Are you afraid of being alone when you're old, because I'll tell you a secret." He stretched his arm across the back of the sofa and leaned toward her coolly. "If you neglect your kids when they're young, they'll return the favor when you're old. That's only fair."

Laurel glared. "You're the most depressing guy I've ever known, Derek Grainger. Just because *your* mother neglected *you* doesn't mean *I* can't juggle motherhood and a career, does it?"

"As long as you *keep* juggling, and don't just drop the ball, which in this case would be a human being," he retorted. "Work forty hours a week if you want, but don't go for sixty. Travel occasionally, but try to be home at least one weekend a month, and when you *are* home, spend at least five minutes a day off the phone. Then maybe you can call it juggling instead of neglect."

Laurel's eyes had widened with dismay. "I'm sorry, Derek. It doesn't sound like very much fun."

"It wasn't."

She touched his tight jaw apologetically. "I'll bet you were such an adorable kid too. I can't believe she managed to resist you. Where was your father?"

"He died when I was five. So my mother had to work hard. Long hours. I understand that. But . . ." He shrugged and tried to smile. "Can we drop it?"

"She sounded like a nice person on the phone. You don't hate her or anything, do you?"

"No. I just don't have any particular need to spend hours

on the phone with her. She's retired, and finally has some time on her hands, but if she's lonely, she can remarry. She's nice-looking and well-to-do, so don't worry about her."

"Did she beat you when you were little?"

"Of course not."

"Well, she should have." Laurel grinned. "You're an ingrate."

Derek pretended to glare. "Do we have to have these personal talks very often?"

"Twice a day," she assured him. "In the meantime, I guess we'd better get back to work. But first . . ."

He liked the hesitation in her voice. And he liked the fact that she was nervous, just a bit. He could tell *that* by the way she fidgeted with the hairband she had slipped onto her wrist for safekeeping. "Is something bothering you?"

"No, not really. I just wanted to say . . . to admit, I guess, that you were right about one thing, earlier."

"Oh?"

"That crack about my looking for a 'movie of the week'-type plot twist in our case. It's a bad habit of mine. When I'm faced with a pile of hard work, I start looking for an easy out—a secret passageway, right through the middle. But sometimes"—she sighed—"it's just a lot of hard work, with no shortcuts. If that's what we're facing here, I'm ready. I promise."

"Well, since we're leveling with one another," he said with a smile, "I should tell you you were absolutely right about those background checks I had my investigator do. I *was* looking for George's accomplice. He denies having had once, and I didn't find anyone who'd be just right, but I agree with you: he must have had a plan for what to do with Amy eventually."

"Thanks, Derek." She cocked her head to the side. "So? The reason you had the investigator find out the number of kids in the households, and their ages and descriptions, was because you thought George would hide Amy with a family that had built-in playmates for her? Right?"

The last thing he wanted to do was to tell another lie to this remarkable woman—now or ever. But he couldn't very well tell her he'd requested ages and descriptions in hopes of finding little Amy herself. So, for the sake of his child's happiness, he nodded and lied. "That's right."

"Was that so hard?" She paused to flash a teasing smile. "From now on, just tell me the truth, Grainger. Don't make me grill you."

"You think you're pretty smart, don't you?" He chuckled, standing and then reaching for her hand, assisting her gallantly to her feet. For the tenth time that day, he wondered what she'd do if he pulled her into his arms. Most likely, she'd question his ethics and his commitment to George Perry's defense again. And she'd be absolutely right, so he released her hand quickly, gave her a sincere but detached smile, and headed back to his desk.

Six

The rest of the morning was everything Laurel had hoped it would be. She and Derek conferred—sometimes soberly, sometimes militantly, but always productively, and the insights and advice he offered never ceased to amaze her. She had wanted so badly to learn from this talented man, and thanks to their no-holds-barred fight, they had reached a point where that was both possible and enjoyable. They were now equals, bowing to one another's strengths. Questioning, but never doubting, one another's styles. Appreciating the company, yet working basically alone, as they approached George Perry's quandary from completely different angles. There was no doubt that, if this kept up, they'd blow this case wide open before the end of the week, and that thought excited Laurel as much as it clearly did Derek.

She almost hated to break for lunch, but Joe Harrington wouldn't take a last minute brush-off well, and maybe Derek needed a little break from her hyperactive style, so she reluctantly tidied up the pile of clippings and transcripts on her desk as noon approached. "I'd better get dressed. I'm meeting Joe in a few minutes. Are you sure you don't want to come along?"

"He'd love that, I'm sure." Derek grinned. "But I'll pass.

Did you find anything special in all that pretrial publicity?"

She shook her hair free of its band. "It's just like you said: their decision not to try for a change of venue was just trial strategy, pure and simple. Still, we'll make the argument that it was ineffective assistance of counsel, right?"

"It's a losing proposition, but yes, we'll use it. We'll use anything we can get, and hope we can convince the court that all these little miscalculations added up to one crummy defense. But . . ."

"I know, I know." She sighed as she edged toward her bedroom. "We need to find one real eye-opener. And I'm still sure it's in there, Derek. We've only just started, right? We'll find it." She had reached the doorway, then turned to add, "If you're keeping track of these mini-errors, be sure to include all that evidence of George's drinking habits. None of that should ever have come in."

He nodded. "It's on the list. Anything else you've noticed so far?"

"Nothing that we haven't already discussed." She left the door open a crack as she began to shed her jeans in favor of a soft, flowing skirt that was feminine enough to please Joe without being sexy enough to provoke him. "I wish we knew someone who attended the trial," she called out mournfully. "I'd love to know more about the atmosphere. The witnesses' demeanors, the judge's tone of voice . . ."

"I can arrange for you to talk to Ted Payne, if you think it might help," Derek called back.

"The U.S. Attorney who prosecuted the case?"

"Right. I'm sure he'd be glad to answer any reasonable question."

"I don't get my information from the enemy," Laurel assured him haughtily.

"Ted's fair. He's a little like your Joe Harrington, in fact. You'd trust *him* to give you accurate information, wouldn't you?"

"If Joe were the prosecutor in a case I was defending? No way! I wouldn't trust him, and he wouldn't trust me. That's the way it works, Derek," she added as she stepped back into view.

"Thanks for the tip." He chuckled. "You look pretty, by the way."

"Don't try to change the subject." She was slipping her feet into a pair of low-heeled pumps as she scolded him. "If we're going to work together, we'd— Oh!" She brightened instantly at the sound of loud knocking. "That must be Joe now." Ignoring Derek's grimace, she pulled open the door and was startled to see not an ex-boyfriend but an ex-judge. "Your Honor! What a great surprise." Giving Matthew Seaton a warm hug, she added sincerely, "I'm sorry I missed your party. Congratulations on your retirement."

"You should have come. Everyone missed you."

"I didn't want to steal the spotlight," she told him teasingly. "And I've heard that beauty salon story once too often."

Seaton laughed and stepped into the room. "You'll be happy to hear I've turned over a new leaf in that department. No more Laurel Banyon stories." For the first time, he looked directly toward Derek. "How's the new partnership working out?"

"Nice to see you, sir." Derek crossed and offered his hand to his former professor. "Can I get you some coffee?"

"I'm here to take you both to lunch."

"Laurel already has plans."

Surprised by Derek's brusque tone, Laurel interceded quickly. "I'm meeting Joe Harrington downstairs, Your Honor. I'm sure he'd love to see you. Why don't you join us?" Turning to Derek, she added quickly, "And you should change your mind and join us too."

"Maybe I will."

"Really?" She smiled toward Seaton and explained, "He kept turning me down before, so you should take this as a compliment."

"Actually, I think it's a compliment to *you*." The old man's eyes twinkled. "He's coming along to protect you from my prejudices."

"Oh?" She glanced toward Derek and was surprised to read confirmation in his expression. "Well, it hardly seems necessary, but if it gets Derek away from these transcripts for an hour . . ." She shrugged and glanced at her watch. "I told Joe to wait downstairs, so . . . Shall we go?"

When they'd reached the lobby, she sent her companions into the dining room and headed for the bar to find her date. Predictably, Joe Harrington's handsome face lit up when he saw her. "You look terrific, Laurel."

"Thanks."

"I thought you said there was nothing going on between you and Grainger?"

"Hmm?"

"Why are you wearing your sexiest outfit—"

"What?" She stood back from him and glared. "*This* skirt?"

"You were wearing it when we had our all-time best sex," he reminded her. "Don't you even remember?" When she shook her head, he added with a huff, "On the deck! Remember?"

"I was wearing this then?" She almost laughed at his illogical annoyance. "That may have been a memorable moment for you, but all I got out of it was splinters."

"Well, get used to it. I'm sure *my* deck is more comfortable than *his* desktop."

She patted his cheek. "You'd better get a life soon. Or get the Playboy Channel."

Joe grinned in defeat. "Well, at least, for the next hour, you're all mine."

"Actually, I'm not. Judge Seaton came by, looking lonely, so I invited him to join us. Is that okay?"

"I guess so," Joe grumbled. "He can't get the hang of retirement, huh? I could have predicted that."

"And Derek's coming too."

"What?"

She touched his scowling face pleadingly. "It was unavoidable, believe me. Plus, it'll be fun. You enjoyed talking to him at the retirement dinner, didn't you?"

"Yeah, because I didn't realize he was pumping me for

information about you. What's his problem, anyway? He can't spend one hour away from you?"

"Actually, he's being gallant. He thinks the judge will tease me or something, so he's coming along to protect me."

"Like I wouldn't be able to handle that alone?"

"You're a lover, not a fighter," Laurel said soothingly. "Anyway, they're waiting, so stop pouting and let's go."

They found the two men seated in a huge, circular leather booth and, to Laurel's amusement, Joe steered her so that she would be strategically placed between himself and Seaton, and away from Derek. Despite the fact that pleasant greetings were exchanged by all, the rampant testosterone level was unmistakable.

And of course, Joe Harrington threw the first verbal punch. "So, Grainger? Laurel tells me you've dragged her into George Perry's appeal. Don't you think that guy should quit while he's ahead? A lot of people think he got off easy."

"A lot of people in the D.A.'s office." Laurel eyed him sternly. "That's hardly an accurate reflection of public opinion, dear."

Seaton was chuckling at the open sniping. "High-profile cases certainly make entertaining topics for lunch conversation."

Joe, who was apparently bent on harassment, continued. "The most entertaining thing about the Perry case is his ex-wife. Have you seen her, Grainger? Is she as drop-dead gorgeous as the papers claimed?"

"We have a bunch of pictures of her up in the office,"

Laurel interrupted again. "You'd love her, Joe. She's the original blond bombshell."

"Bombshell?" The prosecutor's gray eyes twinkled wildly. "What does that make *you*? A grenade?"

Seaton and Joe chuckled boisterously, but Derek seemed completely annoyed, and for the first time Laurel began to see him as a prude. Then she remembered his relationship with Veronica Keyes Perry, and sighed. He was definitely not a prude. Just protecting his co-counsel again, for some unfathomable reason.

"Let's change the subject," she insisted. "Derek and I need a break from the Perry case. Tell us what you've been up to, Your Honor. Are you planning on traveling, now that you have some free time?"

He nodded. "Yes, eventually. But for now, to be honest, I want to dedicate myself to our profession. I'm thinking of writing a series of articles praising the fine attorneys I've worked with over the years, including, I might add, each of you seated with me here today. There's too much irresponsible criticism of attorneys these days, and I'm damned tired of it."

"You won't get any argument from us," Joe said with quiet enthusiasm. "It's easy for politicians to blame the problems in the criminal justice system, and the jury system as a whole, on attorneys, instead of dealing with the underlying social problems."

"Exactly!" Seaton pounded the table angrily. "Between the recriminations and the jokes, the lack of respect for our hard work and dedication is positively sickening. If I hear the word 'shark' one more time in connection with one of my colleagues . . ."

He paused to take a breath, and Laurel exchanged concerned glances with Derek. If Matthew Seaton didn't lighten up, he was going to have a heart attack right there at the table. And if he was this agitated now, how would he feel alone, in his big house, working on these emotionally laden articles?

Joe seemed to be on the same wavelength when he jokingly revealed, "Laurel takes it as a compliment when someone calls *her* a shark, sir. Maybe you should get that perspective on all this."

"Pardon?"

Laurel smiled sweetly, so that the old man wouldn't suspect she was kicking her ex under the table. "It's true, Your Honor. I taped a wonderful documentary on sharks off a nature channel, and believe me, they're amazing animals. And when they go in for the kill, well . . . let's just say, I'd like to be that effective some day."

Seaton stared for a long moment before bursting into laughter. "Do you see, Derek?" he insisted with delight. "She's not normal. I wasn't insulting her the other day. Just stating a fact." To Laurel he explained, "I told Derek you didn't know your place, and he took it as a sexist remark."

"You? Sexist?" Laurel drawled, and again the judge burst into laughter. And again, Joe Harrington joined him, while Derek Grainger scowled.

This is going to be a long, long lunch, Laurel mourned silently. *I should either go to the ladies' room and never return, or invite some females from the other tables to come over here and neutralize some of this.*

As though in answer to her prayer, a familiar figure appeared in the doorway of the restaurant, waving shyly in their direction. Melissa! Instantly proclaiming the lovely, twenty-one-year-old girl to be her favorite niece, Laurel motioned eagerly for her to join them. "Look, Joe. Derek? Your Honor? This is my niece Melissa."

"Hey, Melissa." Joe stood and guided the willowy blond newcomer into the booth by his side, again ensuring that no female would be seated next to Derek. The obvious gesture made Laurel kick him again as she made more formal introductions.

"I remember you from the beauty salon that day." Judge Seaton beamed. "All of the pretty nieces, lined up in a row, like a human chemical spill."

"You knew those customers were ringers?" Joe grinned. "Laurel thought she put that one over on you for sure."

"It's nice to meet you, Your Honor," Melissa insisted in a soft, sweet voice. "And you too, Mr. Grainger. I really liked your movie."

Derek grinned. "Thanks. Are you planning a career in drama too?"

"Me?" She flushed earnestly. "No, that's Jessie. I'm a history major."

"Melissa's going to be a teacher," Joe explained proudly. "Of all our nieces, she's the smartest."

"*Your* nieces?" Seaton chuckled.

"Joe got joint custody when we broke up," Laurel explained. "He's a terrific uncle, isn't he, Melissa?"

The girl blushed again. "He's wonderful."

Not wanting to overuse her niece, Laurel decided to rescue her. "Are you meeting someone here, Melissa? Or, were you looking for us?"

"I was looking for you, to tell you . . ." She hesitated, then explained, "I have a message for you. It's not personal, and I don't think it's confidential or anything . . ."

Laurel was about to urge her to speak freely when the waiter appeared to take their orders. "Stay and eat with us, Melissa. Please?"

"I can't. I have class in half an hour. But . . ." She waved her hand to indicate that they should proceed without her, and so Laurel quickly ordered a salad, then winced as the men each ordered a macho entrée. No swordfish for Derek today, apparently, nor was Joe having his usual turkey sandwich. It was a steak-eating sort of lunch, and Laurel could only hope she'd find a reason to leave with Melissa before things got any more pugnacious.

When the waiter had departed, Melissa murmured, "I was at your office, Laurel. Working on an assignment. And that bear guy came over, and he said he needs to talk to you right away."

"'Bear guy'?" Joe Harrington's eyes narrowed as he turned to Laurel and demanded, "Is she talking about Oso Morales? Is he still hanging around you?"

"Relax, Joe. It's under control." Laurel frowned. "He was polite to you, wasn't he, Melissa?"

"He behaved the way he always does. Really . . . complimentary."

"He *flirted* with you?" Joe roared. "Goddammit, Laurel, you let a guy like that bother the girls?"

"Shh! Good grief, Joe, lower your voice."

Ignoring her, he turned to Melissa and slipped his arm around her shoulder. "Did he scare you, honey?"

"No. Not at all." She cuddled against him gratefully. "I just never know what to say to him when he comes to the office."

"You were there using Laurel's computer?" Joe shook his head. "It's not safe there, apparently. And I have a better set-up at my place, sitting vacant all day, so why don't you and the other girls just start going over there? I'll get you a key."

"My office is safe," Laurel interrupted. "And Oso's not one bit dangerous. But I'll talk to him and tell him to stay away. So," she added coolly, "let's drop it."

"Oso Morales," Judge Seaton murmured, as though Laurel hadn't closed the conversation. "The name sounds familiar. Drugs?"

"Yeah," Joe confirmed with a low, ominous growl. "And who knows what else."

"I beg your pardon," Laurel interrupted again. "Oso doesn't have *any* convictions, drug-related or otherwise."

"Because he uses other people to do his dirty work. And he's trying to use you too, Laurel. We've discussed this—"

She glared pointedly at Joe. "That's right, we've discussed this. He's not my client and he never will be, but he's also not public enemy number one."

"You've told him you won't represent him and he's still coming around, so . . ." The prosecutor's gray eyes glinted wildly. "I think it's time some of the guys on the force had a little talk with him about leaving you alone."

"Don't you dare!" Laurel fumed. "It's not illegal to try to hire an attorney, Joseph Harrington. If you dare violate Oso's civil rights, I *will* become his attorney, and we'll sue you and your office."

Flustered, Joe turned to Derek. "Talk to her, Grainger. Maybe she'll listen to you."

To Laurel's absolute delight, her handsome co-counsel straightened and met Joe's gaze calmly. "I agree with Laurel. The guy has a right to legal representation. As long as he's not harassing her, the authorities should stay out of it."

"You haven't met him—"

"I don't have to meet him to know what he is and what he wants," Derek countered coolly. "If he's dealing drugs, I want him off the streets as much as anyone. But that's a separate issue."

"Oso Morales's constitutional rights," Joe muttered. "I doubt whether Thomas Jefferson and the gang had this guy in mind when they gave us the right to the pursuit of happiness."

"You're wrong, Joe," Laurel murmured. "Oso's exactly the guy they had in mind."

"I agree with Joe," Seaton interrupted brusquely. "This Morales character may have gotten away with his crimes so far, but it'll all come crashing down on him one day soon, and you *don't* want to be standing next to him when it does."

Laurel shook her head in defeat. Arguing with Joe Harrington was one thing, but Matthew Seaton was the most close-minded man she'd ever met, and she'd learned long ago not to waste her breath on him, so she turned a bland smile toward her niece and inquired, "Wouldn't you love to skip your class and stay for round two?"

Melissa flashed a grateful smile. "I'd love to, but I really have to go right away. It was nice meeting you, Judge Seaton. And you too, Mr. Grainger."

"I'll walk you out, honey," Joe offered, sliding out of the seat behind her. To Laurel he added teasingly, "Try to do one of those subject changes before I get back, okay?"

"You read my mind. Bye, Melissa."

"Bye."

"They make a charming couple," Seaton observed as Joe and Melissa headed for the lobby. Turning to Laurel, he goaded, "Does that bother you, counselor?"

"You're just *full* of it today, aren't you, Your Honor?" she accused between gritted teeth.

To her surprise, Derek belatedly joined in the teasing. "What a mouth! Does she always talk to judges that way?"

"Get used to it." Seaton beamed. "Never a dull moment with Laurel, especially when she's wearing those green contact lenses. That's a signal she's ready for a fight."

"You might want to write that down, Derek," Laurel admitted.

"I won't forget, believe me. After all of Harrington's experience with you, I'm surprised *he* still stands up to you the way he just did."

"Me too." She grinned. "I thought I had him trained better than that."

"Here he comes," Seaton warned. "And since I see our food is also arriving, why don't we all just declare a four-way truce?"

Laurel smiled in quiet gratitude. "Good idea."

Despite an occasional volley between Joe and Derek, the meal eventually settled into a pleasant, almost mellow experience, and by the time Laurel had taken her last sip of coffee and was searching for her purse, she felt refreshed and ready for another crack at the Perry case. But first she needed a few minutes alone with Joe, and so she smiled and hugged Seaton warmly while insisting that he and Derek "probably had a lot to talk about," after which she quickly shooed a willing Joe toward the doorway.

Derek watched in quiet envy as Joe Harrington draped his arm around the auburn-haired beauty's slender shoulders. They were friends, yet much more. One day, if he was lucky, he might have that with her too. But he couldn't afford to think about that just yet. He needed to concentrate on the relationship he wanted so desperately to have with his missing daughter . . .

"She's an amazing female, isn't she?"

Startled and sheepish, Derek turned to Judge Seaton and nodded. "Working with her is great."

"You two obviously make a good team. And you were right to back her up on that Morales business. I would probably have been disappointed in you if you hadn't, but—"

"I'll talk to her about it, sir. Don't worry. For now, she's too involved with the Perry appeal to take on any new clients, and after that . . ." He took a deep breath and revealed, to himself as well as to his mentor, "I think my professional association with her might just continue indefinitely."

"That's fine, as long as you direct your combined talents toward defendants who are worthy of you. George Perry and this Morales character belong locked up or executed." When Derek scowled, the judge just shrugged. "To paraphrase our young prosecutor friend, I doubt whether Tom Jefferson rolled over in his grave when the verdict against George Perry came in."

"And to paraphrase my new partner," Derek retorted, "my client is exactly the guy our legal system was set up to protect."

"Do a competent job, then drop it. Don't let it drain you, personally or professionally. *Or* financially."

"I know what I'm doing."

Seaton patted Derek's shoulder. "I see it in your eyes, son, and it worries me. This case has its hooks in you on a personal level. We've all been there, myself included. Our passion for justice is part of what makes us the best, but in this case, your passion is misplaced. Wasted. Undeserved. Let it go."

Derek tried to smile. "Déjà vu, right? First Laurel and Morales, now me and Perry. I guess you and Harrington just can't see it from a defense attorney's point of view."

"We see it clearly—not just the waste of talent, but the potential for disaster." A confident smile flickered over the judge's weathered face. "You told me earlier you'd discuss the Morales situation with Laurel. All I'm asking is, when you talk to her about him, pay attention to your own advice. Fair enough?"

◐ ● ◑

"I'm thirty and she's twenty-one. That's hardly cradle robbing."

"It's still sick and incestuous," Laurel said, arching her eyebrow to further tease her prey.

Joe flushed but persisted. "Is she seeing anyone? Do you know if she's bringing a date to the wedding?"

"You're *my* date, Joseph Harrington. Are you trying to ditch me?"

"I'll be your date for the wedding. But when the reception starts, I'm asking Melissa to dance," he declared, adding in a more guarded tone, "okay?"

Laurel grinned and kissed his cheek. "I can hardly wait. You two are adorable together. I just never thought of you with one of the nieces, but it's perfect! I'll bet they've all had secret crushes on you at one time or another."

"Thanks, Laurel." He eyed her quizzically. "Is Grainger invited?"

"Of course. But he declined. He'll probably go to San Francisco to take care of some business. Or maybe he has a date. Either way, he says he won't come."

"Has he hit on you yet?"

"He's strictly professional, all the way. Just like I knew he'd be."

"Well, watch him. And watch out for Morales too." Joe hesitated, then pulled her into his arms and murmured, "Are you sure you're okay with this Melissa thing? You keep saying it's over between us . . ."

"The affair is over," she confirmed with a wistful sigh. "But we'll never be through with each other. I need your friendship. If dating Melissa won't change that, then I'm fine with it."

"I felt like a real pervert today when I put my arm around her to hug her, like a concerned uncle, and—"

"Spare me the pornographic details." Laurel grinned, then added gently, "She seemed different to me. I thought it was because she was shy about meeting Derek, but now I think all the blushing was about you."

"Yeah?" He cleared his throat, then admitted, "I'm going to miss being in love with you, but . . . maybe you were right about that lightning bolt business. I mean, that's how it seems, even though of course I've known her for years. But not the way it seemed like I could know her today . . . Do you see what I'm saying?"

"You're babbling," Laurel murmured as she fondly stroked his face. "It couldn't happen to a nicer guy. Or a more wonderful girl. Just don't get your heart broken or anything. I didn't give you up for that, you know."

"Yeah, I know. I'll be careful. And I'll be a perfect gentleman with her, of course. You can count on that. I mean—" He paused for a long, husky breath. "Just to spend time with her would be enough for a long, long time. And she's so sweet. And fragile and delicate. I'll need to be extra careful, so to start with, I'll just call her, I guess. Right? I mean, I don't want to scare her or anything, but—"

"Good grief, Joe, just pull yourself together and go back to work. Don't you have to be in court this afternoon?"

"Huh? Oh, yeah. Court." He chuckled sheepishly. "I'll go to work and then, when I get home, I'll call her. Right? I mean, is that too fast, do you think?"

"I think she'll be disappointed if you don't."

"Really?" He beamed at the thought, then leaned down to kiss his friend's cheek gently. "Thanks, Laurel. You're the best."

She smiled in quiet envy. "So are you. Now wipe that silly grin off your face and *get back to work*."

$$\text{◑ ● ◐}$$

It didn't surprise Laurel to find Derek hard at work when she returned to the suite, but when he stood and motioned for her to sit on the sofa with him, she was completely amazed. "Is everything okay?"

He nodded. "I just wanted to thank you."

"Oh? For what?"

"For not telling Harrington about my relationship with Veronica. I appreciate that, Laurel. I know he's your best friend—"

"Anything you tell me about the case, or about your personal life, is confidential," she assured him, adding sheepishly, "except I usually end up telling my sister May everything. But that's okay, because she's a shrink, so there's a sort of umbrella of confidentiality that basically protects you as well as me."

"That's fine." He studied her carefully. "Did you and Harrington have an argument after you left the table?"

"You mean, because of that Oso Morales thing?"

"Actually, I meant, over him and your niece."

"You picked up on that too? I completely missed it! But it's true, and I couldn't be happier. Plus, it explains why he was so militant about Oso. He wanted to impress Melissa with his connections on the force and his ability to protect her. Isn't that sweet?"

"Well, he *is* Prince Charming after all," Derek drawled. "So, tell me about your drug dealer friend."

"His name's Justin Morales, but they call him Oso, because he looks like a bear—stocky, dark, handsome, and shaggy. To *me*, he looks like a rock star, and if I had any real influence over him, he'd be in drama school instead of on the streets. He's only twenty years old, but very smooth and charming. He was born in Spain—at least that's what he tells me—and his mother was apparently French. She moved here with him when he was in high school, and either he fell in with a bad crowd, or was already corrupt. Anyway—" She paused for a new breath. "He wants me, but it's not going to happen."

"Wants you?"

She glared playfully. "As his attorney. You Hollywood types really have warped imaginations, don't you? I told you, he's only twenty years old."

Derek chuckled. "So? How'd you meet him?"

"Jonathan—the guy my niece is marrying on Saturday—was driving to Los Angeles last January when his car broke down. He needed to get going quickly, so he decided to hitchhike the rest of the way. Oso picked him up, and they got stopped by some cops, who found a load of marijuana in the trunk of the car. Elaine called me in tears, and I went down there and got both of them released. Ever since then, Oso has seen me as some kind of super-lawyer, but the truth is . . ." She smiled slyly. "Any first-year law student could have handled it."

"Let me guess: Fourth Amendment?"

Laurel nodded. "The first person I talked to was the arresting officer. I asked him what made him stop Oso's car, and he said, 'When you see a Mexican and a clean-cut college kid like that together, it's gotta be drugs.'"

"In other words, he handed you the case on a silver platter?" Derek chuckled, then added more soberly, "It's always disheartening to hear how much ignorance and prejudice is still out there, isn't it?"

Laurel nodded again. "That's why I don't want to hear that garbage about our Founding Fathers not including Oso in their Bill of Rights."

"On the other hand," Derek murmured, "he had a trunk-load of marijuana. It's just a matter of time for him, Laurel."

"I know, I know. *Please* don't lecture me about it. Especially considering the fact that *you* feel comfortable representing rapists and child molesters—"

"Let's not argue," Derek suggested. "It sounds like you're handling this Oso guy intelligently, so there's no problem. I was more curious than anything else. I'd even like to meet him sometime."

Laurel shook her head, frustrated that her supposed equal was protecting her again! And she suspected Matthew Seaton had played a part in fostering that reaction. Men! "Forget about Oso Morales. We're supposed to be worrying about George, right?"

Her offhand comment subdued Derek easily, and she found the reaction disquieting. Was he *that* wrapped up in their client's fate? *But it's not George he's thinking about,* she reminded herself soberly. *He said he's looking for justice for Amy. Almost as though, if we free George, Amy will be alive again . . .*

Of course, Derek Grainger wasn't *that* irrational. Still, he was letting this thing tear him up inside, and she simply wasn't going to allow it, any more than he was going to allow her to get torn up over drug dealers. Like it or not, they were becoming true partners, at least temporarily, and so she had every right to interfere. "Listen, Derek, I meant to say this to you earlier. About Amy . . ."

His eyes clouded ominously. "There's really nothing to say about her. She was sweet and innocent, and she should have had a wonderful childhood, but she didn't. End of story. You were right the first time—we should just get back to work."

Laurel shrugged. "Maybe her childhood wasn't as awful as you think. I mean—" She paused dramatically. "Do you want to hear this or not?"

He scowled but nodded. "Make it fast."

"Charming, as always," she muttered under her breath, then smiled blandly. "I've been over and over the custody transcripts, and the depositions of her teachers and neighbors, and the psychologists. And one thing stands out, almost glaringly. That kid was absolutely precious. And well adjusted. And happy. Her life was cut short, and that's an awful tragedy, but while she was alive, I don't think she was horridly mistreated or psychologically tormented. I think George showered her with love, and people generally responded to her with warmth and affection, and I think she was thriving. She probably had no idea that Veronica was plotting reconstructive surgery behind her back, right? It scared George on Amy's behalf, but I'll bet Amy herself was oblivious to most of that, thank God. I'll bet she never suspected that her mother threw that ball at her face on purpose, either. The bottom line is, I think she believed she was loved, and that's the most important thing a child can feel. Right?"

Derek was staring as though thunderstruck. "You saw all this? Where? I mean . . ." He stood and began to pace. "I got that feeling too, I think—that she was pretty well adjusted—but I thought it was just wishful thinking. She looks genuinely happy, in those school pictures and all, but I worried it was just a mask. I mean, with Veronica Keyes as a mother—"

"That's another thing," Laurel interrupted. "I agree, Veronica was a monster, but it appears that she cherished Amy in her own warped way, at least at the start. Maybe it's like you said: maybe, as Amy grew up and went out to school, and people started making a fuss over her—as someone other than just Veronica Perry's daughter—it started bothering her. But that was probably gradual, Derek. At the beginning, when Veronica saw Amy as an extension of herself, she would have enjoyed the child's beauty, right? It was only later that it possibly turned overtly harmful."

For a few moments, he seemed so lost in thought, she wondered if he was going to respond at all. Then he crossed to Laurel, took her hands, and requested hoarsely, "Could you do something for me?"

"Anything."

"Could you find those sections—of the transcripts, and depositions, and anything else—and photocopy them, and put them in a file for me? I'd like to take a look at them tonight, after we're finished working."

"When we're finished working, you should rest. Looking at that stuff is still work, Derek. But—" She touched his shoulder and smiled. "I'd be glad to do that for you. Anything else?"

"Yes. One more thing. Don't wear contact lenses to work anymore, please."

"Pardon?"

A teasing grin had finally replaced the look of heartache on his handsome face. "The best part of working with you is watching those eyes of yours dance and sparkle. I can't see half the show through those lenses."

It was as close to flirting as he'd come, and probably as close as he'd *ever* come—at least, until the case was wrapped up—and so she nodded and dared to ask a favor in return. "I won't wear lenses, and you won't shave more than once a day. Deal?"

"Huh?"

"You shaved at dinnertime yesterday. I *like* five o'clock shadows. They're very dramatic. So?"

The grin turned slightly wicked, as though he too liked the idea of tweaking their no-flirtation clause. "Anything else?"

"Actually," she admitted quietly, "there is."

Derek seemed to sense that this next request wasn't going to be quite so frivolous, and so he stepped back and sat on the edge of her desk, then motioned for her to continue.

She wanted to kick herself for ruining the moment, but their conversation about Amy's childhood had reminded her that she needed to ask the most difficult question of all if she was going to truly understand George's motivation, and so she tucked her legs up under herself, nestled into the sofa cushions, and began. "Like I said, the psychologists didn't seem to feel Amy was in any real danger from Veronica. In particular, the psychologist appointed by the federal court—"

"The *male* psychologist," Derek interrupted coolly.

"Don't be silly." She fought a wave of jealousy, lost, and murmured, "Is Veronica really that attractive?"

"Yes."

"You're actually suggesting that the court-appointed expert slept with the subject?"

"I have no idea. All I'm suggesting is, he couldn't possibly have been objective."

"That's why George's team brought in a female shrink?"

"Probably. Not that it mattered." Derek shrugged. "Women can't be objective about Veronica either. For different reasons, of course, but—"

"So? If I met her . . . ?"

"You'd hate her."

"I already do."

"Good."

Laurel grabbed for her purse, located a lacy hairband, and bundled her hair up in one quick, frustrated move. This was going to be rough, apparently, and so she needed to focus, which she couldn't do when *anything* was touching her neck. Composing herself quickly, she locked eyes with Derek and continued. "I hate her, but I'm not convinced she's a complete psycho. More like a spoiled bitch, with the face and body to back it all up. If there's more to it than that, I think I need to hear it."

Derek flushed but nodded. "I'll try. Just stop me if it starts getting too perverse." He paused for Laurel's gesture of consent, then stood and began to pace again. "She and I were as different as night and day. But at the same time, there were certain fantasies I apparently had—not the same ones *she* had, thank God, but still—"

"Just spit it out, Derek. You liked big breasts, and she liked . . . what?"

He grinned darkly. "Let me ask *you* a question. How do you feel about death?"

"I'm against it."

"So am I. Veronica's obsessed with it."

"That's not exactly perverse, Derek. It's sad, like you said yesterday."

"Okay, question number two. When you die, what do you want done to your body?"

"You mean, do I want it buried or cremated?"

"I mean, what do you want done to it, sexually."

"Yuck." She ignored his sympathetic chuckle and tried to rally. "I already know all this. She married George because he could make her appearance beautiful after she died. That's not sexual. It's just . . . aesthetics, right?"

"Veronica has a game. In fact, she calls it *The* Game. And I was such a walking hormone at age twenty-six that it took me an entire weekend to decide it wasn't worth it."

"The Game?"

"One of us—usually me—would lie in a dark room, with only candlelight for illumination. My instructions were to try not to react, no matter what she did to me. No talking, no moving, no visible breathing. It was like a test of my self-control, or so I told myself. She'd go to work on me . . ." He shook his head, as though still amazed at his youthful indiscretion.

"You enjoyed it?"

"Sure. I would have preferred something a little more active and a lot more tender, but it worked. And I wasn't that good at staying still, believe me. But Veronica was a different story. When it was her turn to lie still . . ." He shook his head again. "I was such an idiot."

"You enjoyed the challenge," Laurel guessed. "You wanted to make her react."

"But she never did. She stayed completely limp and motionless. She was aroused—the usual signs were there— but her limbs, her breathing . . ." He shuddered, then glared. "Aren't you going to stop me soon?"

Laurel grinned. "I played a corpse once, but I wasn't limp. I had rigor mortis. Not the kind *you* had, of course, but the all-over kind." She paused while he laughed, then insisted, "Limp would be tougher, especially if someone were touching me."

"But she stayed that way, right up to the moment of orgasm. And even then . . ."

"Yuck. You're the only guy I know who can make orgasm sound unappealing."

"I do my best," he said with perfect deadpan delivery. "Anyway, I went along with it for a while, but eventually, believe it or not, it just got boring. And when I tried to convince her to try something a little more interactive, she rattled off so many morbid variations on her game that I just split."

"But George stayed."

"He met her two years later. When he was still just a kid. And it's possible she'd learned to be more subtle by then. Or maybe . . ."

"Maybe George liked The Game?"

"That's my guess. He didn't want to discuss it specifically, but he didn't deny that they shared a definite taste for kinky stuff. Which of course is why he couldn't use any of it against her during the custody battles. He was as vulnerable as she."

"Kinky views toward death, and creepy plans to re-do her own child's face. Who could blame George for trying to get Veronica out of that sweet kid's life? I won't say she's better off dead, but he certainly had to do something drastic." Unfolding her legs, Laurel stood and moved to stand in front of Derek. "I know it was embarrassing for you to have to give me the details of Veronica's games, but I needed to hear them. Thanks."

"Thank *you* for listening without judging me." He took her hand, raised it to his lips, and kissed it gently. "Now, go take out those lenses and let's get back to work. I'm not paying you to stand around looking beautiful."

"It's better than lying around looking dead," she quipped, then turned and hurried to the bedroom to find her lens case *and* her equilibrium.

SEVEN

Over the next three days, Derek's spirits soared as he worked side by side with the dynamic woman who was going to help him find his lost child. Life was filled not only with hope but with danger and suspense of the most provocative sorts. What would she wear? What would she say? Would he be able to keep his hands off her? Would those amazing violet eyes, which insisted on studying crime scene photos despite his futile protests, widen at any moment with understanding, accusation, and joy? And what of her stubborn search for George's accomplice? Would she find the "gelescent" fact that would lead them to Amy's caretaker? And if she did, would he ever, *ever* be able to thank her?

Fortunately, she didn't *know* she was looking for Amy. Instead, she was planning the retrial, as though supremely confident that there would be one. And so, at least twice a day, she would erupt into her favorite diatribe—the failure of the original defense team to put George on the stand and "the absolute vital necessity" that Derek convince him to testify in the new proceedings.

He was dying to tell her the truth—that George hadn't dared take the stand. Not because he feared perjuring himself—he'd do that in a heartbeat for Amy—but because Veronica had been sitting in that courtroom, and she knew him *so* well. She would have sensed that he was lying—about the fire *and* the loss of their daughter—and then the nightmare would have assumed even more horrific proportions.

On the bright side, watching Laurel emote was one of the most fascinating side benefits of their association and so, whenever she sprang to her feet and began to rail, he would simply lean back in his chair with his fingers laced behind his head and pretend to nod in agreement while secretly enjoying the show put on by her petite, provocative body.

Derek Grainger now had *two* incredible prospects in his future—rescuing Amy Grainger and seducing Laurel Banyon. He'd ply the latter with flowers and compliments and kisses and entreaties and, because she loved to wring every drop of drama and anticipation from every scene, she'd pretend to resist before surrendering into his arms. He could almost taste that moment, and when such thoughts began to make his pulse race too wildly, he reminded himself he had to be practical, for Amy's sake.

Amy was the ultimate priority and, while he intended to one day enjoy both fatherhood *and* Laurel, he'd willingly abandon all thoughts of the latter if it were the only way to be certain of the former. As much as he wanted to enjoy Laurel as a woman, it was the attorney in her that made her so priceless, and he couldn't afford to distract the attorney by making love to the woman.

He wasn't even certain Laurel would allow it until a

winning brief had been designed and completed. But he suspected, from the mischievous smile that so often played on her lips when they were arguing, that she might. And so *he* had to be strong for both of them.

◐ ● ◑

Each day, after lunch, Laurel strolled over to her office, to sort through her mail, listen to her messages, and remind her body that fresh air and sunshine still existed in the outside world. Only once, on the fourth day of their association, did Derek deign to come with her, and they ended up discussing the case the entire time, hardly noticing the gorgeous spring day until a school bus filled with boisterous children rattled past them and Derek stared as though he'd never seen kids before. And Laurel knew he was thinking about Amy Perry again, or about the children he had so stubbornly decided never to have, or about his own lonely childhood. And she wanted to take him into her arms and comfort him but instead distracted him by mentioning a visit to the crime scene—a ploy that always provoked an exasperated lecture from him.

On Friday, she made the trip by herself, but found herself missing him almost immediately, and so she was back within a half an hour. To her surprise, Derek wasn't at his desk. His bedroom door was closed, and she hoped he'd finally taken her advice and tried to grab a nap. It had been a grueling week of twelve- to fourteen-hour days for her, but she knew that, for Derek, it had been even worse. He continued to work at night, when she staggered home to collapse into bed, and he was already poring over notes or documents each day when she arrived. The man definitely needed a break.

It had become second nature for her to reach for her recorder and so, as she slipped off her shoes, she pressed the play button, smiling at the gentle teasing behind his tone as he reported:

"Your niece Elaine called. She said you told her not to use this number unless it was an emergency, and she was sure this qualified, because she wants to change the song you're supposed to sing tomorrow at the wedding. I wrote it down— 'Till There Was You'— so apparently the crisis has been averted. She was sweet. Told me she loved my movie and was looking forward to the sequel. What's that about, anyway? And of course she graciously invited me to the wedding, but I told her I was going down to my office in the Bay Area. She sends her love.

"And your sister Amber called. Her emergency is that she found a headboard that matches your armoire and she wanted your permission to put a deposit on it before it got away. I told her to go ahead and buy it—I'd take the responsibility. She sends her love. She loved my movie too, by the way.

"If I'm asleep when you get back, wake me up. We've got a lot of ground to cover if you're really going to abandon George for a whole day tomorrow."

"Laurel? You're back already?"

"Oh!" She spun and grinned into his sleepy eyes. "You look awful. Go back to bed."

"I'm fine. I just needed to close my eyes for a minute."

She smiled apologetically. "Sorry about all the messages. Elaine's changed the song fifty times already. She's a walking panic attack. But that headboard really *was* an emergency. We've been looking for it for two years, so thanks for handling it for me."

"No problem. They were a pleasure to talk to, especially compared to Matthew Seaton, who called right after them."

Laurel waited while he ambled over to the coffeepot and poured himself some fortification, then she prodded. "Did the judge want to bother you about George and Oso again?"

"More or less." He slumped into his desk chair and rubbed his eyes. "Do you remember that tangent he went off on during lunch? About the public's disrespect for the legal profession?"

Laurel nodded. "It's been an obsession with him these past few months. I thought retirement would help, but I guess not."

"I actually considered inviting him to join us on this appeal, thinking maybe he just has too much time on his hands. What would you think of that?"

She crossed to stand directly in front of him and glared ominously. "*Please*, tell me you're kidding."

Derek scowled in return. "Why? He has a brilliant legal mind, Laurel. We could benefit from his experience and insights. Plus, he cares about both of us. Plus," he added more weakly, "he keeps calling me 'son' these days, and I'm worried about him. He doesn't have anyone, you know."

"Don't you dare let him psych you out," Laurel warned.

143

"He's *not* your father. He's a controlling old man with delusions of omnipotence, and we have too much work to do to baby-sit him—"

"What?" Derek was on his feet, towering over her in outraged disbelief. "You're a lousy judge of character, do you know that? He's probably the finest man you'll ever meet!" When she simply shrugged, he added sharply, "Just because he ruled against you a few times—"

"I never lost a case, remember? Seaton always found a way to rule *for* me. Now, sit down," she instructed coolly, "and I'll tell you a few things you don't know about your hero."

"He's not my hero," Derek muttered. "But I have a lot of respect for him, and so should you."

"He may have been an incredible attorney, long ago, and I'm sure he was a wonderful professor, but he was a lousy judge. He's so opinionated and domineering, it makes him absolutely incapable of being neutral or impartial. And these days, I don't even think he's capable of being rational."

"He's really fond of you," Derek chided softly.

"It's mutual, but it doesn't blind me to the facts." She sighed as she loosened her hair and perched on the edge of Derek's desk. "I think he retired because he knew, deep inside, that he was getting a little squirrelly. I'm sorry if that hurts you, Derek. If you want to spend time with him, I think that's great. Like you said, he's all alone and it's sad. But don't let him manipulate you into inviting him into your practice."

"Into *our* practice," he corrected with a rueful smile. "Right?"

Laurel flushed, hoping he couldn't guess how thrilled she was with that offhand invitation. "We'll see."

He grinned, grabbed her by the waist and pulled her to her feet. "We haven't had a good fight like that in days. It's nice to see I can still irritate you."

"It was good for me too," she quipped, exhilarated by the feel of his hands on her. And the reference to *their* practice! And the sexy twinkle in his dark blue eyes . . . "Come to the wedding with me tomorrow," she dared to plead. "We're both starved for a little fun and relaxation. I know you like to put your social life on hold during tough cases, but—"

"But that doesn't mean *you* should," he agreed, dropping his hands to his sides. "Elaine told me you're skipping the rehearsal dinner, and you already missed some wild bridal party and a week's worth of dance classes. Just because *I'm* obsessed with this case. I'm sorry about that, Laurel."

Disappointed that the flirtation had mutated so easily, she sighed. "I'm as obsessed as you are these days. And contrary to popular belief, I'm not a party girl. When I'm working on a case, I'm as single-minded as you are, believe it or not."

"I believe it. That's why you insisted up front that we keep our relationship on a strictly professional level. Of all your brilliant strategies," he assured her sincerely, "that one may have been your best."

"Pardon?"

145

He seemed to miss the hurt in her voice as he insisted, "You were able to trust me more quickly, knowing I wasn't going to hit on you. Knowing that my interest in you was as an attorney, not a woman. I think it's been crucial to our success—"

"Success?" she interrupted softly. "A list of harmless errors is hardly success, Derek. We have a lot of work ahead of us, and tomorrow is completely shot, so . . ." She turned away, still hurting, but knowing it would be unfair to allow him to see it. Everything he'd just said had been meant as a compliment. A tribute, in fact. And he was right—the whole hands-off policy had been *her* bright idea, and if that was going to change, it would have to come from her too.

But if she suggested something more intimate, and he turned her down, she wouldn't just have hurt feelings to deal with, she'd have an awkward situation that neither of them could afford. Derek would be uncomfortable with having rejected her, and she'd be mortified beyond belief. And George Perry would be the real loser.

So just wait one more week, she counseled herself as she returned to her desk and flipped open her computer. *Unless you can somehow lure him to the wedding and weaken him with champagne and dancing, you just can't take the risk. Your only other hope is to find a big, beautiful reversible error this afternoon, spring it on him, then attack him mercilessly—so . . . stop looking at that rugged jaw and those sexy blue eyes and start looking at those transcripts!*

Ordinarily, Laurel loved weddings more than any other social event, but that was before she met Derek Grainger. Not only had he exhausted her by keeping her at the suite the night before until after one A.M., but he had made himself so pivotal in her life that she couldn't seem to be happy for more than a few hours away from him at a time. Her only hope, as she suffered through the boisterous wedding reception, was that he would change his mind about going to San Francisco and would appear in the doorway of the rented hall to rescue her. With his broad shoulders and lean, tapered body, he'd look sensational in a suit. And in a tuxedo . . .

She had dressed for him, just in case, in a skimpy, royal blue lace halter dress that was backless, braless, and borderline shameless. On a more voluptuous woman it would have been completely inappropriate for the occasion, but on Laurel's trim curves it was simply playful and provocative. She'd received dozens of compliments—on the dress, and on her soft, throaty rendition of "Till There Was You"—but she honestly didn't care what all these insufferably cheerful partygoers thought. She only wanted Derek's praise . . . Derek's appreciative glances . . . Derek's body dancing close to hers . . .

Instead, she was stuck with Joe Harrington, who was too busy mooning over Melissa to notice that his dance partner was not exactly having the time of her life. "I don't want to embarrass her, Laurel. I mean, don't you think everyone will be shocked if they see me dancing with her, after seeing me so many times with you?"

"No one will be shocked," Laurel assured him petulantly. "Everyone *knows*, Joe. Rumors spread quickly in my family, especially when one of us has been having phone sex for a whole week with a D.A."

"Phone sex?" He was visibly panicking. "I've been calling her, yeah, but it's been clean, Laurel, I swear it. We've just been talking—"

"I was kidding." Laurel glared. "Good grief, Joe, what's happening to you? Just go ask her to dance and get it over with. Word on the street is that she's had the hots for you for months, so it's about time, don't you think?"

His face lit up at the news. "Really? Did Melissa tell you that?"

"Apparently all the nieces knew, but they were afraid I'd misunderstand. The bottom line is, you're bothering me. Go bother *her*, please?"

Oblivious to Laurel's mood, he kissed her cheek gratefully and insisted, "Of all the great things you've ever done for me, getting me together with Melissa is the best. I'll never forget it, Laurel. If you ever need anything—"

"Go!"

She watched in rueful amusement—a thirty-year-old man doing a perfect impression of an insecure, inexperienced high school boy at his first dance. And Melissa was almost as bad, blushing so deeply that it could be seen from anywhere in the huge hall. And indeed, all eyes were on the pair, so much so that, when Joe finally took the girl into his arms for the first time, a raucous cheer went up that made Laurel laugh for the first time that day.

"They're so cute, aren't they?" Jessie squealed from behind her. "Honest, Laurel, don't you feel like you're witnessing the beginning of something really, *really* red-hot sexy?"

"Always a witness, never a bride," Laurel agreed sourly. "And speaking of red-hot, I was watching you with Clay. Shouldn't you try to leave something for the honeymoon?"

"Huh?" Jessie studied her anxiously. "What's with you? Oh, no!" She clasped her hand to her mouth. "You're jealous of Melissa? *You want Joe back?* Oh, no!"

"Shh! Stop shrieking," Laurel warned with a rueful laugh. "Honestly, Jessie! Derek thinks *I* overdramatize everything, but you're ten times worse. I'm not jealous, I'm just tired. And envious, which is something completely different."

"Derek?" Jessie's eyes began to twinkle. "Oh, I get it. You're missing him? That's *so* romantic! Mom's been telling everyone nothing's going on between you two at the Plaza. But I knew it!"

"Jessie?"

"Yes?"

"Go stick your tongue down Clay's throat and leave me alone."

The pretty blond giggled, then pulled her aunt away from the dance floor and insisted, "Tell me the details. Cry on my shoulder. Don't keep me in suspense! Have you made love with him yet? He's so handsome, Laurel. I'll bet he drives you wild with desire!"

Before Laurel could protest, her niece continued imp ishly. "Don't try to deny it. I don't know why we didn't see it sooner. We all thought you were just tired, but when you sang that love song so beautifully, we should have known—"

"Go away."

"Here comes Mom," Jessie warned. "Don't even bother trying to hide it from *her*. You know how *she* is."

Laurel groaned and nodded. She had, in fact, been avoiding May all day, knowing that her older sister would see in an instant what Jessie and the others had almost missed. "Go have fun with Clay. And *don't* spread any rumors about me. Your grandfather already interrogated me for twenty minutes outside the church."

"I know. He's says you'll be the death of him yet." Jessie grinned as she turned her over to May. "Be careful with her, Mom. She hasn't been getting much sleep, if you know what I mean."

"Jessie!"

When her niece simply flashed another impish smile and escaped back to the dance floor, Laurel turned toward her big sister and smiled wanly. "Nice wedding. Elaine looked radiant."

May was eyeing her knowingly. "That's an interesting dress. Too bad he didn't show."

"I'm really, really not in the mood, May. I'm tired and cranky, so be careful what you say."

"I'm surprised you're not a total zombie, with the hours you've been keeping," the older sister said. "Any progress with finding the harmful error?"

"Nothing," Laurel admitted sadly. "But remember how I told you that, if we find enough little stuff, we might be able to get it reversed anyway? Well, Derek thinks we're almost there."

"What do *you* think?"

"I think he hired me to be creative, and I've been a total flop."

"I thought he hired you to keep his personal involvement from interfering with his professionalism."

Laurel grinned darkly. "On that front, I've been an amazing success. There's no personal involvement whatsoever."

"I was talking about his revenge problem, not your urges to sit in his lap." May's eyes twinkled. "I've never seen you like this, Laurel. Have you told him how you feel about him?"

"He keeps thanking me for ruling out any possible romantic complications," she explained with a sigh. "It makes it kind of hard to jump his bones. Plus," she added pensively, "his personal involvement is more serious than just revenge. It's almost as though, by identifying with George as Veronica's lover, he's also imagining himself as Amy's father, and mourning her that way. Do you see what I mean?"

May nodded warily. "Are you sure it's just his imagination? I mean, you said he slept with her years before Amy was born, but is it possible—"

"No, definitely not. Once he broke off his affair with Veronica, he says he never looked back. She's twisted, sexually—don't ask for the details, they're creepy. Anyway, combine *that* with Derek's natural paranoia about fatherhood—"

"I beg your pardon?"

"He's sure he wouldn't be a good father because he's such a workaholic. Just like his mom was. Plus, he's afraid some woman will just have his kid, without telling him. He actually thinks someone could be loony enough to . . ." Her voice trailed into stunned silence as Derek's words resurfaced in her mind. *I'm just grateful they didn't help themselves . . .*

"Laurel?"

"Shh . . . Let me think."

The entire conversation was now echoing through her head. *How could someone steal your sperm, Derek? Didn't you use a condom . . . ?*

"Laurel?"

"Veronica Perry is so twisted, May. She wanted to have a beautiful baby—one worthy of inheriting her own looks. And George Perry was a terrific makeup artist, but not particularly handsome or intelligent." Her voice was trembling slightly as she asked, "How long do you suppose sperm lives, after . . . ?"

May bit her lip thoughtfully. "Not too long, I suppose, unless you take special steps to preserve it. And not just in the kitchen freezer. You'd have to have a special set-up . . ." She locked eyes with Laurel and murmured, "Exactly how twisted is this Veronica?"

Laurel was battling a wave of nausea and disbelief. "I've got to go. Please explain to Elaine for me."

"Stay and talk, Laurel—"

"No! I have to go help Derek. I can't just let him be alone with this. Not for one more minute." Her eyes were stinging with tears. "Why didn't he *tell* me?"

"Maybe he didn't want to make you cry," May suggested gently. "He's in San Francisco, Laurel. Stay and talk—"

"I want to find reversible error for him. When he walks into that suite tomorrow morning, I want to take him in my arms and tell him we've done everything we could for his little girl." The tears were now streaming down her cheeks. "He must see her every time he closes his eyes, May. Burning to death . . . helpless . . . calling for her daddy . . ."

"I know, I know," May mourned, pulling Laurel into a hearty embrace. "Go and help him, then. Help him past this awful tragedy. Show him that the future can still be good. And the future with you could be great."

"There's no future until he deals with this awful past." Laurel was sobbing softly. "No future for Derek, and maybe not for me, either. Or for poor George. I *have* to find something in those stupid transcripts to help them."

"Listen to me, Laurel Banyon," May interrupted firmly. "Find that error for them, and get the conviction reversed, if you think it'll give them closure. But remember something: all the brilliance and creativity in the world isn't going to bring that little girl back. I have a feeling those fathers haven't come to terms with that yet, so be prepared—"

"I will. I promise." She dabbed at her damp face with a

hankie and tried to summon a smile for the sake of the guests. "I really have to go now. Will you make my excuses? Please?"

"Go on. And call me, Laurel. Day or night. Let me help."

"You already have, as usual. And maybe, someday soon, Derek'll agree to talk to you too. Professionally. Eventually. But for now"—she squared her shoulders—"at least he's not alone anymore."

"Laurel, wait a minute." May's eyes were bright with concern. "You'd better brace yourself before you go back to that suite. He may not have gone to San Francisco after all, and for the moment, you're as vulnerable as he is."

"At this moment," Laurel agreed, "I need him as much as he needs me. I hope he *is* there, May, so I can do whatever it takes to help us both get through the night."

Eight

By the time she reached the Eureka Suite, all traces of exhaustion had vanished, and Laurel was bursting with energy and purpose. She would find an error that no appellate court could ignore. But first, she would pull out that file they'd been keeping on Amy—the one with the heartbreaking pictures of a little girl with her daddy's big blue eyes. Interspersed with the photos were anecdotes, culled from depositions and testimony, detailing the child's sunny nature and precocious intellect. Amy had inherited the latter from Derek too, Laurel knew. She also knew that that file must have been torture for Derek, despite its avowed purpose of proving that Amy had had a decent, happy childhood.

And no wonder he'd balked every time Laurel had tried to examine the crime scene photos! Photos of the place where his precious child had burned to death. If only she had known. She would have done so many things differently. But she knew now, and she was going to reorganize each and every file—the entire office, if necessary—so that Derek's pain could be lessened while they worked through his grief. And if May was right, and he hadn't gone to San Francisco at all . . .

She took a deep breath, then slid her key card into the slot and cautiously pushed open the door. The office area was dark and deserted, but from Derek's bedroom came a spattering of sound and a flicker of light from a television screen. Instantly, Laurel's heart began to pound, as she wondered if she dared go to him and comfort him the way she so ached to do. Not that she had a choice—she was bursting with love and compassion, all of which she needed to lavish on Derek Grainger—and so she murmured softly, "You'd better not have a woman in there, partner," and tiptoed to the bedroom doorway.

An orchestra was playing waltzes—a PBS tribute to Strauss—but it was clear Derek had been simply using the show to help him fall asleep. The sound was low and the picture not quite within his field of vision, and the would-be viewer was snoring softly. Propped up against two pillows, dressed only in black silk pajama bottoms, he was so arrestingly handsome that Laurel almost sighed aloud.

She'd expected him to be in good shape, physically, but saw now that his chest was a virtual wall of hard, toned muscle, covered by a mat of wiry black hair as wavy and enticing as the tousled lock that had fallen across his forehead. Laurel's nipples strained through her skimpy lace bodice in a futile attempt to connect with that erotic display as her breath grew shallower and her willpower disintegrated into need. Thoughts of comforting him disappeared as well, subsumed by the desire to seduce him. To possess him. To devour him, and to be devoured . . .

Almost without thinking, she loosened the single button

that held her dress's halter in place and, with one slow, sensuous wriggle, sent the fabric into a lacy pile at her feet. All that remained was a black garter belt and stockings, black satin panties, and the stiletto heels that had so often made Joe Harrington drool. Derek wouldn't get the chance to appreciate *them* tonight, she knew, but they fit with her mood—the temptress, smoothly approaching her sleeping victim, ready to awaken him with an erotic invitation that even the most virtuous of men could not hope to resist.

She was only inches from him now, and so intense was her anticipation that she wouldn't have believed anything could divert it. Then her hungry gaze, sweeping over his rock-hard form, saw the tiny picture of Amy in his hand, and she winced with disappointment and self-recrimination. This man—this heartbroken father—didn't want or need her half-naked body in his bedroom. He needed her creative brain in the outer office, combing through the record, searching for the elusive justice for his daughter that would allow him to begin to grieve and heal.

Ignoring her own aching need, she turned and moved away, stooping as she moved to pick up the discarded dress so that she could begin to put herself back together. But before she could do so, his hands were on her waist, and he was murmuring her name, and she turned instinctively, needing to feel the brush of his wiry chest hairs against her swollen breasts, even if nothing more would come of this bittersweet fantasy.

She gasped then, with exquisite pleasure, as he pulled

her gently against himself and began to sway to the music, while he murmured into her hair. "I went crazy today without you. I thought you'd never get here."

She groaned, wrapping her arms hungrily around his neck. "Me too."

"I kept imagining you dancing with other men."

"There are no other men," she assured him with a sigh.

"Thank God." He was moving, in a slow rhythmic grind that let her know how fully aroused he had become, and her pelvis tilted greedily to enjoy him. He was dancing her toward the bathroom, and she didn't care, as long as he kept growling her name and kissing her neck while the heat between them rocketed toward its boiling point. Then he was rummaging in his shaving kit, retrieving a strip of condoms, and she thought briefly of Veronica's heinous invasion of his privacy, but her brain couldn't stay there for long. She didn't care about any of that. All she cared about was this. Here and now. Hot and hard. So dangerously close to perfection that she could hear herself moaning Derek's name even before he waltzed her back to the bed and tumbled her gently beneath him.

"Kiss me," she pleaded softly.

He hovered over her for a moment, his blue eyes dark with desire, and then his head dipped down, so that his lips could brush hers for the very first time, coaxing sexy sparks that made her tremble with anticipation. He tasted her again and again, gently, as though they had nothing but time. Then his hand slipped inside the stretchy fabric of her panties, and one finger began to tease at her, duplicating the soft strokes of his lips. In less than an instant, she was throbbing with need.

"Derek—"

"Shh." His tongue began to probe her mouth, and again his finger followed suit. Laurel groaned with delight, then laced her fingers behind his head and pulled his mouth down harder against hers, knowing that both his tongue and his finger would now plunge hungrily into her. Gasping with excitement, she greedily returned his kiss while pulsating against his hand. Then she moaned his name again, and this time, he groaned in return, then stripped her panties away and plunged himself into her with hedonistic insistence.

She couldn't get enough of him, nor he of her, as they writhed and teased and hurtled toward ecstasy. She had expected the expertise and the heat, but the outpouring of love—the absolute adoration they lavished on one another—utterly stunned her. And when at last they were still—drenched, exhausted, and silent in one another's arms—she wondered if either of them would ever be the same again. Never had she dreamed of such a night, and she had to believe that Derek Grainger, for all his worldliness and experience, had never known anything quite like this himself.

But she needed to hear him acknowledge it, and so, in a voice so husky it was almost raw, she whispered, "Derek? Was it my imagination, or was that incredible?"

"Sixty hours of foreplay," he murmured back, sounding as dazed as she herself felt. "We're lucky we're still alive."

"Sixty hours of foreplay," she agreed, seduced by the assessment as she cuddled against him. "I guess that explains it. That, and the fact that you're such a good dancer."

"And you do a mean striptease," he countered teasingly. "I think you missed your true calling."

"Mmm, so did you," she assured him. "But if we weren't both lawyers, we never would have met, so . . ." She slipped her hand behind his neck and kissed his mouth lovingly.

It wasn't the right time to talk about Amy, but somehow, some way, she was going to find the perfect time, and the perfect words, to help him through his loss. To make him as deliriously happy as he'd made her. There was nothing she wouldn't do for him now. And as her contented body drifted toward much-needed slumber, she assured herself that the love she felt for him—the love she'd always dreamed of finding—would guide her in her quest to fill his life with hope and happiness. And the love he felt for her would be the only reward she would ever, ever need or want in return.

◐ ● ◑

When she awoke the next morning, bright hot sunlight was already streaming into the room, and Derek Grainger was nowhere to be seen. "The ultimate workaholic," she reminded herself as she stretched her nude, rested body. "He's already out there at his desk, and it's going to take more than a striptease to get him back in here, but . . ." She grinned devilishly. She needed him, and it was still morning and her contract didn't call for her to report to work until noon on Sundays, and so she'd find a way to lure him if it took every ounce of "creative lawyering" at her disposal.

Then she noticed the tape recorder on the far side of his pillow, and she grimaced with fond disgust. The man was hopeless in his habits, but she would forgive him because he had talents that had essentially enslaved her forever. And there was always the possibility that this was a love message—an erotic proposition, or a tender thank-you for making him deliriously happy—and so she eagerly reached for the machine and pushed the play button as she snuggled back into her pillow, readying herself for his smooth, sexy voice.

"I have no idea how you're feeling right now, Laurel, and I don't have a clue how to make up for last night, but I'm willing to do or say anything to get us back on track. Let me start by apologizing for my predatory conduct. I know it sounds shallow, after the way I acted, but I've never respected a woman the way I've come to respect you. And my respect for you as an attorney is even stronger. Our professional association is so valuable to me—indispensable, actually—that I'd never knowingly do anything to jeopardize it. You made it clear, from day one, that you wanted me to keep my hands off you, and all I can say is that you're incredibly attractive. And my loneliness, combined with arrogance, made me forget my priorities. That's not an excuse, of course. Just an explanation.

"At this point, it's strictly your call, Laurel. If you want to yell at me, or talk this out, we'll talk. If you want to pretend it never happened, it never happened. All I ask is that you not let it affect

your dedication to the Perry appeal. That has to be our priority right now. We're too good together out of bed to let last night sabotage our efforts. My focus—my only focus—is winning this appeal. I can't afford to care about anything or anyone else, or to get hung up on you as a woman, when you're so indispensable to me as an attorney. And I think you're the kind of professional who feels exactly that way too.

"But like I said, it's your call. You can have the place to your-self until noon—to get yourself together in private, and to decide how you want to proceed. When I get back, we'll play strictly by your rules from here on out. You have my word on that. And again, I apologize. Especially for that crack about sixty hours of foreplay. The last thing I ever intended to do was trivialize the hours of dedicated professionalism you've given to this cause. So, again: I'm sorry. More than you'll ever know. All I can hope is that I'll see you at your desk at noon."

Numb with hurt and disbelief, she rewound the tape and forced herself to listen to the second half of the message again. *I can't afford to care about anything or anyone else, or to get hung up on you as a woman . . .*

She could have forgiven him the rest, knowing that he had a right to be confused and wary over breaking her no-sex rule. They'd never even kissed before, and so the intensity of their lovemaking must have been as staggering to him as it had been to her. And since he had apparently not experienced the rest—the *falling* in love—it must have been doubly confusing for him. As much as that hurt, she could have forgiven it. After all, a person didn't choose to fall in love, and if it didn't happen for him, well . . .

Yes, she could have forgiven him for being unromantic and confused. Given the way he had made her feel for one magical, unforgettable night, she could have forgiven him almost anything. But . . . *I can't afford to care about anyone else.*

She could *never* forgive him *that.*

◐ ● ◑

The elevator ride up to the Eureka Suite was almost too fast for Derek as he prepared himself for seeing Laurel again. When he'd left her, she'd been sleeping so soundly—the most achingly beautiful sight he'd ever had the privilege to witness. And the feel and smell and taste of her had still been pulsating in his senses, and it had taken his every ounce of willpower to trade that warm, loving bed for the cold desk in the office on the other side of the wall, where he had dutifully recorded his apology.

Even now, his memory of their night together threatened to subvert all rational thought. They had been insatiable, each for the other, and yet there had been such tenderness. Such absolute splendor. And for the first time since he'd met George Perry, he'd spent an entire hour—a fabulous, sensation-charged hour—free from all thoughts of Amy's dilemma. As selfish as that still seemed, he'd been humbly grateful for it.

Then, as Laurel had dozed peacefully in his arms, exhausted not only by the assault but by the ungodly number of hours of work he had required of her, he had imagined the morning to come. The awkward transition back into work. The potential recriminations. The methodical disintegration of his only real plan for rescuing his lost daughter.

No sex. She couldn't possibly have made her condition of employment any plainer, but he'd waited, like a lonely, sex-starved stalker, for the moment when her defenses had fallen. When she'd just come from an evening at a wedding—an evening of singing love songs, sipping champagne, and watching her ex-fiancé dance with her niece. All of that had clearly been too much for her, and she'd escaped back to the suite, needing to be alone, with every intention of burying herself in work.

But instead, she'd found Derek, and had been tempted to surrender herself to the quick fix of a night of passion. But something inside her had warned her to pull back—to be professional until the end—and she'd changed her mind and tried for a graceful exit. But Derek hadn't allowed it. His own need had been so out of control that he'd swept her into his bed, into a fantasy of his own making that had promptly engulfed them both, driving from them all thought of their priorities.

Amy, Amy, Amy . . . He *had* to find her. He couldn't let his own needs and desires stand in the way of that, or in the way of Laurel Banyon's career. These two females were his whole world, with one important difference: Laurel could survive, even thrive, without him. Could he say the same for his precious, golden-haired little girl?

He and Laurel were a great team because they were so different. Because they approached problems, and life, from such completely different angles. If they merged, they would lose their respective edges, and Derek couldn't allow that, despite the exquisite perfection of that merger on an interpersonal level. And so, if she was angry when he opened this door—or disdainful, or confused—he would have to weather it. For Amy's sake.

But to his relief, when he finally got up the nerve to slide his card through the slot, Laurel was seated at her desk, in her standard jeans and white silk blouse, poring over the record as though nothing unusual had transpired. It was a good sign. Except, she didn't look up at him, even when he approached her desk, and that, he knew, was a very *bad* sign.

And if she was wearing green lenses when she finally did look up, he sheepishly warned himself, he had better head for the hills. "Laurel?" he tried finally. "Are we okay?"

She raised her violet eyes from her reading and studied him as though seeing him for the first time. Then she observed coolly, "You said on the tape that we'd play by my rules from now on."

"Absolutely. Whatever you say. I'm just glad you're here." He tried for a reassuring smile. "Where do we go from here?"

"We'll work ten hours a day. Diligently. We won't speak to one another unless it's absolutely necessary and one hundred percent job-related."

"Laurel," he protested uneasily. "Maybe we should talk it out—"

"If you can't play by those rules, we'll just divide up the

documents, and I'll work at my office. And once a day, we'll have a short, to-the-point case conference. Take your pick."

He tried to remind himself that she had once been a drama major, and so it was possible she wasn't nearly as detached and scornful as she now appeared. It could be an act—an attempt to buy herself time, while she sorted through her conflicted emotions and got herself back on to the professional track that meant every bit as much to her as to him. With that in mind, he smiled again and nodded. "Whatever you say. Thanks for being here, Laurel. It means a lot. To me, and to George."

"Whatever."

He had been dismissed—by the word, the tone, and the cool dropping of her gaze. And part of him knew he should grab her and kiss her right then and there, while some vestige of their night together still lingered in the air. But she *had* been a drama major, and he didn't have a clue what she was thinking or feeling. And he didn't dare compound his sins by forcing himself on her again, so he convinced himself to return to his own desk and bury himself in detail.

◐ ● ◑

Up until now, Laurel had spent almost every waking hour searching for George's accomplice. For the place he would have hidden the girl had she not burned to death in the cabin. Now, she needed to change her focus—to find the goddamned reversible error that would get her out of this suite, and out of Derek Grainger's life, forever. The retrial, should there ever be one, would be Derek's problem. He was more than capable of handling it. It would be *his* responsibility to find the accomplice, and to force George to take the stand, and to do the thousand and one things that would make the difference in the jury's eyes. That was Derek's strength. That was the reason George had hired him. Laurel's only job was to find grounds for reversal without falling apart before her co-counsel's eyes.

She was going to find error if it killed her, and she was going to find it within forty-eight hours. The real question was, Why hadn't she found it in the first sixty hours? And the answer was clear—she had been too busy falling in love with a heartless bastard. With that complication blessedly out of the way, she'd be able to concentrate at last.

Sixty hours of foreplay. Fine. Maybe that was true. Maybe she *had* been nursing naive fantasies about herself and Derek right from the start, along with the more insidious fantasy of single-handedly freeing George and allowing little Amy to rest in peace at last. Those myths had now exploded in her face and she was glad of it. Now she could be the professional Derek so blithely assumed her to be.

At dinnertime she stood and left without a word to him. When she returned from her lonely meal in the coffee shop, she saw questions in his eyes but ignored them in favor of the one question that mattered to her at this point. "Can I ask you something, Derek?"

"Sure. Anything," he responded eagerly. "What is it?"

"Once we find the infamous reversible error, can you

handle the rest of this by yourself? The brief, the argument, the retrial?"

He was quiet for a long moment before murmuring, "Don't do this, Laurel."

"Don't ask me not to," she countered quietly as she seated herself at her desk and proceeded to tune him out as she'd done all afternoon.

A full hour passed before he spoke again. "Laurel?"

"Hmm?"

"Do you still have the tape I left for you this morning?"

She raised disbelieving eyes to his. "I beg your pardon?"

"I'd like to listen to it," he insisted stubbornly. "Apparently, I said something monumentally offensive, which was not my intent—"

"You were very clear and very eloquent," she interrupted haughtily. "You said it was my call. If I wanted to talk, we'd talk. If I wanted to drop it, we'd drop it. So—" She glared pointedly. *"Drop it."*

He stood and crossed to her desk, a nervous smile on his lips. "What I said was, if you wanted to pretend it never happened, we would. Which meant we'd go back to our old relationship—"

"Relationship?" She almost hated him for daring to use that word. "You can't afford to have a relationship, remember?" Slamming her computer closed, she warned, "If you can't just drop this, I'm going home. I'm tired anyway. Tired of this stupid case, and tired of you."

"We're both tired and confused," he agreed quickly. "Go

home and get some sleep. But tomorrow . . ." His blue eyes flashed with unmistakable determination. "We're going to talk this through, once and for all. I was crazy to think we could handle it any other way." Stepping closer, he added desperately, "I care about you. You must know that, in your heart. And maybe I underestimated us. Maybe we *can* handle being partners and lovers—"

"Don't insult me like that!" she warned through gritted teeth. "I'd never consider having either of those relationships with you. You lied to me from the day you met me, and when I gave you a second chance, you still didn't level with me. All you've done is lie to me and manipulate me, and you're still doing it.

"This isn't about last night anymore, Derek Grainger. It's about sixty hours of deceit and disrespect, and a man so wrapped up in his need for revenge that he doesn't have room in his life for anything or anyone else. *That's* what you said on the tape, and it was the first honest thing you've ever said to me. Now I think we finally understand one another. And I think you're right. I'm tired, and I need to go home."

"And tomorrow—"

"Tomorrow I'm going to find grounds for reversal," she announced boldly. "Grounds so explosive and unassailable that no appellate court in the world could turn you down." She smiled coolly at the flicker of greed in his eyes at the thought. "You were right, don't you see? We can't afford to waste time on our social life right now. I'm giving you my word that, if you let me work, undisturbed, for ten hours tomorrow, I'll present you with reversible error by the end of the day."

He didn't say anything. In fact, she could see that he was speechless at the unexpected guarantee, and while a part of her ached to hear him say that *she* was more important to him than any retrial could ever be, she was grateful at least for this opportunity to make a quiet, dignified exit. Still, as she reached the elevator, she had to admit that she had underestimated her need for him to take her into his arms. To run after her, even now, and beg her to forgive him. She had to admit it, because there was no other possible explanation for the tears that were streaming down her cheeks.

◗ ● ◖

Still stunned by Laurel's confident prediction, Derek moved to his desk and retrieved his favorite glossy photograph of his daughter. Then he sank onto the couch and remembered the blaze of drive and determination in Laurel's gorgeous violet eyes. She could do it. There was simply no doubt in his mind anymore. Unassailable grounds for reversal within twenty-four hours. He could almost *touch* it, it was so close! And if she really pulled it off, he could go to George and demand to know Amy's location immediately, and maybe, just maybe, he'd be holding his daughter in his arms before another forty-eight hours had passed.

And then Laurel will understand, he promised himself shakily. *Once Amy's safely hidden away in a place of your choosing, not George's, you can take Laurel there, and those magnificent eyes of hers will blaze again.With understanding and with love. And you'll find a way to make her keep it all secret from Veronica, and the authorities, until you can figure out what to do next.*

For now, all that mattered was finding the girl, so that her new life as a safe, happy, well-loved child could finally begin. If twenty-four more hours of hostility from Laurel could accomplish that, then he'd weather it somehow, despite the nagging need to run after her, even now, and tell her what she so clearly ached to hear. It would all be over soon. There would be a happy ending. And Laurel would understand. Because if she didn't, then the happiness he'd bought for Amy would have been purchased at a price so high it would haunt him for the rest of his life.

Nine

When Derek emerged from his bedroom at six the next morning, rubbing his eyes and still exhausted from having labored over documents long into the night, he was shocked to see Laurel curled up on the couch, already hard at work. And this wasn't just any Laurel—it was the most amazing Laurel yet: the blue-eyed one. The aloof ingenue, complete with pink cashmere sweater, pink socks, and pouty pink lips. Brilliant blue sapphires sparkled from her ring finger and on a slender golden chain around her neck, and his first thought was that some man had given them to her, and the thought infuriated him.

She apparently wasn't going to let him forget how great the sex had been between them, or how little chance there was of ever having it again. "Eat your heart out" was the message, and his body was receiving it loud and clear, which was understandable, since he'd been lying in bed only moments earlier, imagining what it would be like to wake up with her in his arms.

She noticed him. Barely. And apparently the sight of him bored her, because she went back to her reading without reacting at all, other than to tuck her legs more securely under herself and to stifle a tiny, provocative yawn. She was distant. Untouchable. And he had to have her. It was as simple as that.

"You look beautiful."

"Hmmm?" Tearing her gaze away from the transcript, she frowned pointedly. "Didn't we have an agreement?"

He nodded. "You need ten uninterrupted hours to find unassailable error. Mind if I watch?"

"Whatever."

He poured himself a cup of coffee, remembered that he must be presenting an awful sight in rumpled hair, stubbled beard, and pajama bottoms, and headed quickly back into his bedroom.

Laurel waited until his door had firmly closed, then sighed and set aside her reading. This wasn't going to work after all. She had intended to show him that she had been only momentarily hurt by his rejection. That it had upset her, but with a good night's sleep and some distance, she had gotten over it quickly and without any permanent scarring. But if he was going to walk around looking like *that*, she was doomed.

Still, the long night's rest *had* done her a world of good. She could now remember the stress he was under—the nightmare of losing the daughter he'd never known. And while a better man might have reacted in a different way, Derek's reaction—an insatiable hunger for revenge against Veronica—was understandable. And if he wanted to use Laurel to get that revenge, that was understandable too. Despicable but understandable.

Once her wounded pride truly healed, she would have

only pity for Derek Grainger, because he would learn a painful lesson during his lonely life—all the vengeance in the world wasn't going to bring back his little girl. He would never hold her in his arms, and that was a tragedy, but even more tragic was the fact that he'd never hold *anyone* in his arms with the kind of love and tenderness that made life worth living. It was such a waste of an intelligent, attractive man, but there was nothing to be gained from trying to help him, and everything to lose, so she'd just help him get his revenge, then banish him from her life before his shallow, unloving loneliness resurfaced and he turned again to her for something more.

Focusing her attention back on the transcript, she reminded herself of her plan. She would concentrate on the testimony of the prosecution witnesses. That was always the most fertile source of error in a criminal trial, and ordinarily she would have started with it the first day. But Derek had supposedly belabored those pages of the transcripts almost to death, and she had believed him to be so technically talented that he would have naturally caught any error in admission or exclusion of evidence. Now she knew her assessment had been wrong. He was good, yes, but so twisted in his relationship with this case that he couldn't possibly be professional.

There was a second reason she'd left this area of review for last. She would undoubtedly be caught up in all the melodramatic factors that made a good prosecutor's case so spellbinding and a good defense attorney's cross-examination so potentially explosive. Timing. Innuendo.

Orchestration of emotion, sensation, suspense . . . She *loved* this part, and had intended to wallow in it. But now there would be none of that. She had ten hours to get it done.

There were five main prosecution witnesses in this case, but two of them were children, and that didn't seem to be a promising area to explore. Wide latitude was traditionally given during direct examination of children—leading questions were officially permitted, obvious coaching was implicitly allowed, and unresponsive answers were simply tolerated as unavoidable unless egregiously prejudicial. After all, they were only children.

So for the time being she was ignoring "the little tattle-tales," as she called them, and concentrating first on the principal investigator. Then she would move on to the most damaging of the psychologists, saving the most notorious of witnesses—Veronica Keyes Perry—for last.

The phone rang and she considered letting the machine take over, but the odds of it being some member of her family bursting with embarrassing questions that Derek might overhear were too great, and so she dove for it on the final ring and breathed, "Derek Grainger's office. This is Laurel Banyon. Can I help you?"

"Oh, Laurel, forgive me. I hope I didn't . . ." Ellen Grainger cleared her throat and amended weakly, "I didn't imagine you and Derek would be working already so early. I just intended to leave a message . . ."

"I've been hard at work for almost an hour," Laurel assured her briskly, anxious to dispel the apparent impression that she and Derek were having an affair. "I'd be happy to take a message for you." She didn't want to add that Derek was in the shower for fear she would make matters worse, and so she explained, "Derek just stepped out, but I can have him call you—"

"Just tell him I called. Actually . . ." Ellen Grainger sighed loudly. "I was a little concerned. He always calls on Sunday mornings—I can usually set my clock by it, in fact—and so, when I didn't hear from him yesterday . . . But I suppose this case you're working on is absorbing every waking hour?"

"It really is. We're both totally absorbed by it. Derek probably didn't even realize it *was* Sunday."

"Goodness! Is this another murder case? I remember how that business with Carson Barrow drained Derek. Although"—she chuckled softly—"from the movie, one would think it was all car chases and seductions."

"Reality is much less exciting," Laurel agreed. "Just lots of detail and hard work."

"Derek *does* love detail, doesn't he?"

"Yes, he does. I'll tell him to call you—"

"No, dear. That's not necessary. Just give him my love and tell him not to work so hard. That goes for you too. There's a lot more to life than hard work, Laurel. Believe me, I know."

The wistful voice almost broke Laurel's heart as she reflected on Derek's dilemma. He was going to spend a lifetime regretting the years he'd never spend with Amy, never seeing that he could still salvage an equally valuable parent–child relationship, not to mention the relationship he could have had with Laurel.

"You take care of yourself, Mrs. Grainger," she insisted sadly. "If Derek doesn't return this call, feel free to keep trying until he does."

"Goodbye, Laurel dear. I feel better already, knowing Derek has you to look out for him."

Not for long, she wanted to reveal, but instead she said a simple goodbye and hung up the receiver just moments before Derek reentered the office area and crossed to join her on the couch. "Any progress?" he inquired smoothly.

He looked good and smelled great. *Too bad he's such a jerk,* Laurel mourned. Aloud, she murmured, "Your mom just called. How long has it been since you talked to her?"

"I'll call her right now if you want."

"Whatever. I've got work to do. Do I need to go to my office to get it done?"

"I won't bother you," he promised. "Have you had breakfast? I could order quiche again. I know, I know," he added teasingly. "'Whatever'—right?"

Stifling a yawn, Laurel turned her attention back to the prosecutor's skillful examination.

◑ ● ◐

They had "whatever" for breakfast and "whatever" for lunch, accompanied by a fragrant bouquet of long-stemmed red roses that Laurel decided to find annoying and insulting. The truth was, her mood was darkening as the day wore on and the transcript continued to resist her assaults. And Derek's total confidence wasn't making things any easier! He clearly believed he was within spitting range of vengeance, and while she found his obsession distasteful, she still couldn't bear to fail. Not after the outrageous guarantee she had so foolishly made the night before.

When she glanced at the clock and saw that it was almost three, she officially started to panic. Where *was* it? It was *always* in there, waiting to be found. The hook. The Achilles' heel. The twist of logic that could make an iron-clad case begin to rust from the inside out.

To make matters worse, she was beginning to think maybe Derek wasn't the only person who couldn't be professional about this case. She herself was seeing red every time she encountered one of Veronica Perry's sanctimonious accusations or tearful outbursts against George.

"Laurel?"

"What is it now?" she asked coolly.

Derek shook his head in weary resignation. "I know you're still angry, but I really think it's time we talked this out."

"You promised me ten uninterrupted—"

"That can wait one more day. For now, I want to tell you something. Something amazing. You said yesterday I've been lying to you, and you were right. I've been lying to you because the truth was dangerous, for a number of reasons—"

"Save your secret, Derek. I already resent knowing the ones I know."

"You're angry," he repeated stubbornly. "But when all of this is over, you'll see things more clearly." Drawing closer, he sat on the edge of her desk and murmured huskily, "I have a beach house in Monterey—"

"Are you for real?" she demanded. "Don't kid yourself, Grainger. When this is over, it's over."

"If I believed that—"

"Believe it!" She stood and glared right into his deep blue eyes. "You should have seen the look on your face last night when I told you I'd find ironclad grounds for reversal today. You'd have thought I was telling you I'd bring Amy back from the grave!"

"In a way, that's exactly what it *did* mean to me—"

"Don't!" She covered her ears with her hands and pleaded, "Are you listening to yourself? This isn't just self-destructive, Derek, it's downright sick! You've allowed your anger and hatred toward Veronica Perry to twist you so completely, you can't even have a genuine emotion. And *don't* tell me you're doing all this out of love for Amy, or justice, because I'm not buying it. This is a vendetta against Veronica, for being such a monster, and for stealing your sperm—"

"You *know* about that?" he interrupted sharply.

"Of course I do. It took me a little while, because you're such a good liar, but eventually . . ." She bit her lip and forced herself to look again into his eyes, this time with the compassion she'd been longing to share. "I'm so sorry about Amy, Derek. She had your eyes, and your smile, and I'll loathe that bitch Veronica until the day I die for depriving that girl of a wonderful daddy like you, but *you have to let it go!* You have to grieve—my sister May can help you, I swear she can—and you have to forgive. Not Veronica, but yourself. Nothing you do can bring your little girl back. If you ever want to have any kind of life, you have to start accepting that."

"I love you, Laurel," he whispered hoarsely. "Can we start from there? Because I have so much to tell you—"

"Don't." She turned her face away, unwilling to allow him to see how much those words had affected her. He loved her, in his own warped-by-vengeance way, and a part of her was trying to believe that could be enough. But she knew better, and so, when she turned back to him, her tone was sad but firm. "I won't put myself through this, Derek. I know it sounds selfish, but—"

He grasped her hands in his own and insisted wildly, "Five minutes! Give me just five minutes, and I'll turn this into a day you'll cherish for the rest of your life."

He was covering her hands with kisses, while his eyes shone with such incredible confidence that an answering glimmer of hope ignited deep within Laurel's heart. "I want that, Derek," she confessed helplessly. "I want to trust you—oh, no . . ." She stared in dismay toward the sound of knocking on the door. May? Joe? Seaton? She couldn't bear to face any of them right now, and so she begged him, "Send them away."

"I will," he promised, relinquishing her hands and bestowing one last kiss, this time on her trembling lips. "Don't move. I'll be right back."

She watched with wonder as he strode toward the door and pulled it open. Could she trust this man again? Could she forgive herself if she didn't? What was she supposed to do in the face of this unpredictable, unquenchable love she felt for him?

Then she realized he was staring. Speechless. His gaze traveling down, and then up, as though he were a teenage boy soaking up every inch of an incredibly voluptuous woman. And Laurel knew, before the throaty voice began to speak, who had come to further ruin any chance for their happiness.

"Derek, darling! Look at you. If anyone had told me you could be handsomer with age, I would have called them a liar."

"Veronica?" he countered lamely. "You're here?"

"Of course! Aren't you going to invite me in?" Without waiting, she stepped into the office and stopped short at the sight of Laurel, whom she sized up expertly before cooing, "I should have known a sexy man like you wouldn't be sleeping alone! Should I come back when your little friend has had a chance to make a graceful exit?"

Derek's scowl was dark and ominous. "This is Laurel Banyon. An attorney I'm working with. We're not sleeping together—"

"Don't be silly. Of course you are." Veronica grinned. "Why else would she be looking at me that way?"

It was true up to a point and Laurel knew it. Her hatred of Veronica was based in her unforgivable treatment of Amy, and to a lesser extent, of George and Derek. But she was also seething with jealousy over this woman's incredible

appearance. Veronica Keyes Perry—so astonishingly, unfor-
givably gorgeous, from her waist-length mane of soft, wavy
hair to her centerfold figure, that it almost made Laurel
physically ill. But it was Veronica's face that was her most
flawless asset, with its perfectly chiseled features, porcelain
skin, and eyes more arresting than the huge, sparkling
emeralds they resembled. The photos hadn't done her justice. She was every man's downfall, and every woman's
nightmare, and she was standing within inches of the man
Laurel couldn't help but love.

And so she gathered her wits and insisted, "Listen, Ms.
Perry—"

"Keyes."

"Fine. Ms. *Keyes.* You're going to have to leave. Derek
and I have a lot of work to do—"

"Who are *you* to tell *me* to leave?" Veronica demanded. "If
anything, *you're* the one who should take a hike. Derek and
I are old friends—or, didn't he mention that?"

"Laurel's right," Derek interceded firmly. "It's not
appropriate for you to be here."

"Appropriate?" Veronica sighed. "How can you say that,
Derek? You're trying to free the man who murdered *my* little girl. How much more appropriate can it get? When I
heard you of all people were going to represent George, I
was devastated, and—"

"I'm sorry if you don't approve of my arrangement with
George, but—"

"Your 'arrangement'?" Veronica cooed. "I know more
about that 'arrangement' than you'd ever guess. It's the rea-

son I'm here, in fact." The smile faded into a pout. "Please, darling? Send your little playmate away so we can talk."

Laurel waited for Derek to refuse, and when he didn't, she turned to him and was startled by his confused expression. Was he having doubts? Was he *insane*? "Derek?" She eyed him uneasily. "We have to get back to work. Remember? We were right in the middle of something important." *Five minutes that would transform this day into one I'd cherish forever,* she reminded him silently. *Please?*

"Laurel, would you mind if Veronica and I . . . ?"

"I beg your pardon? Am I co-counsel on this case or not? Our client's ex-wife—the prosecution's star witness!— shouldn't even *be* here, but if she's staying, I should definitely—"

"Send her away, Derek," Veronica advised, slithering closer to him, as though to seduce him with the heat that was undoubtedly emanating from her incredible body. "I guarantee you, you'll be sorry if you don't."

And Derek didn't even try to move away. He simply turned pleading eyes to Laurel and murmured, "As a personal favor to me, could you give us five minutes?"

"Five minutes?" She stared in disbelief, then turned and grabbed for her purse. "Take all the time you need. I'll have the desk clerk ring before I come back up, so feel free to do whatever it is you two do." The sound of Veronica snickering made her turn at the doorway to add sharply, "You're a disgrace to our profession, Derek Grainger."

He nodded curtly, as though he didn't care anymore about his profession, or his career, or his future at all. He didn't care about anything or anyone, except the bizarre sexual tragedy that had begun one weekend in Sausalito, years earlier, and would apparently never end. Revenge? Lust? Grief? None of these words seemed to fit and, after Laurel found the strength to slam the door in his face, her knees buckled and she had to lean against the wall, heartsick and drained of all semblance of pride or hope, before she managed to begin the lonely walk to the elevator.

The sound of the door slamming—of his relationship with Laurel ending—reverberated in Derek's ears, but he couldn't afford to care. Nothing mattered now, with Veronica's threat hanging in the air. She claimed to know about his arrangement with George, and if that meant she knew Amy was still alive, then all was lost. Taking a deep breath, he ordered, with a sternness he could only feign, "Make it quick, Veronica."

"You're such a grouch today, darling. Isn't your little friend satisfying you?" When he glared, she added sharply, "Have you told her about Amy?"

"What *about* Amy?"

"Don't pretend with me, Derek. I know George told you you were the father. And I know you're probably upset with me for keeping her birth a secret, but we have to put that behind us now, don't you see? *I'm* not your enemy. George Perry is the one you should despise, and in my heart, I know you do. But at first—"she pursed her red lips thoughtfully "—I was a little confused. And hurt, to think you were siding with George against me. I thought maybe you believed his ridiculous stories about my fitness for motherhood. And I thought you were representing him to get back at me, for keeping Amy a secret from you. You'd get that heartless bastard released, just to make me miserable. But that just didn't sound like you, Derek. My noble lover. And then it hit me. The only possible explanation."

Derek forced himself to remain expressionless. "And what is that?"

"It's so devious." Her voice was a purr. "So utterly devious. Make love to me, Derek. I'm halfway there already—"

Grabbing her by the shoulders, Derek roared, "Tell me what it is you think you know!"

"Ow! You're so strong," she whimpered playfully. "Such a bully. You should have tried this years ago, darling. We might still be together. Ow! Fine! We'll talk first." Pulling free, she pouted again, then moved a few feet away to perch on the edge of his desk. And from the suggestive way she eyed the desktop, he knew she'd seen the damned movie.

"Anyway . . ." She sighed with exaggerated disappointment. "I imagine George told you I was a bad mother, but nothing could have been further from the truth. I adored that girl, for all her faults. Do you know," she added, studying him intently as she spoke, "I chose you as her father because you're so big and strong, but *she* really wasn't. Not at all. She was delicate. Tiny. At first I thought it was just because she was a baby, but when she started school, I realized she was smaller than most of the other girls. Isn't it strange? She wasn't going to have my advantages, or yours, and I felt so sorry for her. It made me love her all the more."

"Veronica, just get on with it."

185

"Well," she said with a sniff, "the point is, Amy was a lot like George. Wimpy. And I knew that's what you saw when you met him—a poor, pitiful man. And you knew that the right attorney might be able to get him released, and you couldn't bear the thought of our baby's murderer walking the streets while her ashes laid cold in the grave, and so *you* took his case. To be sure he'd never, *never* go free."

Flooded with relief—*she didn't know Amy was still alive!*—Derek's smile was actually genuine when he protested softly, "You think I'd actually take a case just to intentionally mishandle it?"

Veronica giggled and slid off the desk, approaching him confidently. "I'm so grateful to you. I've had nightmares about that man being released." Curling her arms around Derek's neck she added sincerely, "I'm glad he told you about Amy. I wanted to tell you a thousand times myself, but at first, I wanted her to bond with George, and after that, when the movie came out, I thought you'd see me as some kind of gold digger."

"You have to leave now, Veronica," he insisted quietly. "Don't you see how bad this looks? If word got out that we were meeting like this, I might be forced to withdraw from the case."

"Make love to me, Derek—"

"Laurel's probably right outside, waiting. She won't tolerate this for long—"

"Her? She'll tolerate anything you ask her to tolerate. She's madly in love with you. I could see that in her eyes—those are contact lenses by the way, so don't be too impressed by that phony blue." She grinned with malicious delight before continuing. "Bringing her in on the case was a brilliant move, Derek. It makes it seem as though you're doing everything you can, yet she's just your little pet—"

"Don't underestimate her. If she thought you and I were conspiring against George, she'd report it to the court. I guarantee you that."

"I detest her," Veronica insisted. "But I can see she's useful, so I'll let you enjoy her for a little while. You know," she added provocatively, "I still have some of your sperm stored away safely—"

"What?" Derek took a deep breath and forced himself to speak more calmly. "In a sperm bank?"

"Where else? You should be flattered, darling. I went to elaborate lengths to ensure your immortality."

"It is flattering, in a way," he lied. "How exactly did you do it?"

Veronica shrugged. "It was all set up before you even came to the house. Once I interviewed you in your office that first day, and you were everything I hoped you'd be, I made the necessary preparations. Think back, Derek. We played a lot of games that weekend, but there was one in particular that went very well. Do you remember how much fun you had, lying naked and perfectly still under a sheet, like a freshly dead body in a morgue, while I collected my nice, warm sample? You were such an obedient and accommodating corpse."

He grimaced. That particular game *had* provided a perfect opportunity for collecting a sperm sample. And at the time, he had found it erotic!

"I've always thought about having another baby, but maybe . . ." She brushed her lips across his. "Maybe this time, we could do it the old-fashioned way? But not too old-fashioned," she added with a wink. "I still love my games, you know."

Derek nodded. "George told me about all that. He was perfect for you, wasn't he?"

"He's so talented," she admitted wistfully. "When he did my makeup, I was the most heartbreakingly beautiful corpse you could ever imagine. I wish you could see me that way. Then I think you'd finally understand." She brushed invisible tears from her emerald eyes and murmured, "I'm grateful to you, Derek. More than you'll ever know. We have to see that George gets what he deserves for murdering our baby. He always pretended to love her, but the truth is, he hated her. He resented the fact that I chose you over him, and no matter how often I tried to explain that it wasn't about love, it was about superior genes, he just couldn't accept it, and so he murdered her. Make sure he pays."

"I'll make sure justice is done," Derek agreed, pulling free of her arms and striding toward the door. "Don't contact me again, Veronica. Once this is all settled, I'll get in touch with you and we'll talk about . . . about a second child."

She beamed with vengeful delight, then pecked at his cheek, ogled him openly, and departed, leaving a perfumed cloud behind that made Derek want to retch.

He needed to check

She still had his sperm. The thought left him weak with disgust and concern. But the immediate danger had been averted. She didn't know Amy was still alive. For all her cunning and experience with men, she had somehow blessedly missed the staggering truth.

When she'd claimed to have figured it out, a part of him had almost died. Even now his imagination was reeling at the close call, and he sank into a chair, desperate to drive her image from his mind. How he hated that woman! She had violated his privacy so completely; had used him so insanely; had kept his child from him, subjecting the poor, innocent girl to unimaginable dangers . . .

But now it seemed that for once, at least, Veronica's amoral depravity had worked to his advantage. She simply couldn't conceive of the fact that he was taking George's appeal for reasons other than hate and vengeance. She didn't know that love could motivate a man in a way no negative emotion could ever do. And she couldn't appreciate people like George Perry, who would gladly risk their liberty for the sake of a child. Or people like Laurel Banyon, who selflessly defended the weak against bullies as though it were the most natural and comfortable of instincts.

Laurel . . . He needed her now, more than ever. His priceless, wonderful Laurel. She could banish the taste of Veronica's depravity with one sweet, warm kiss. Just as Veronica had been his downfall, Laurel was his salvation, and all he could do now was throw himself on her mercy and pray that some spark of love still lingered in her heart. With that, they could rekindle the rest and this time, he'd will-ingly allow it to consume him.

◐ ● ◑

Laurel walked for hours, heartsick but knowing that all her usual cures would have no effect. Talking to May, gazing out over the river, dancing, eating chocolate . . . Sleeping with Joe. It was the ultimate irony—that he had chosen *this* week to get over her, just when she might have finally been will-ing to run back into his arms. To just "drive up to Tahoe and get hitched," as he'd suggested so many times. And she'd always told him true love—the kind with fireworks and sleepless nights and searing passion—would be worth wait-ing for. But she had been wrong. So, so wrong.

It was almost time for her six o'clock dance class, and she knew her body could use the workout, but Jessie and Amber would be there, with questions and sympathetic glances, and so she headed for her office instead. There would be mail and messages, and maybe she could do a lit-tle stretching. She might even have a good cry, although no tears had appeared thus far. She was too angry. Too dis-gusted. Too demoralized.

And she needed so desperately to be alone that she almost turned on her heels and ran when she saw Oso Morales, her most persistent non-client, camped on her doorstep. But he'd caught sight of her too, and was grinning with anticipation, and she decided maybe a little of his silly flirting wouldn't feel so bad after all, so she walked up to him and smiled a weary smile. "Don't you ever give up?"

"*Merienda!* You look beautiful, as always. But something is different. Your eyes?"

"I'm wearing blue contact lenses."

"Your heart is broken," he corrected firmly. "Come and sit with me and tell me all about it. Then I'll kill him for you, and you can represent me."

"I love that plan," she admitted, sinking down onto the step and allowing him to put his huge, muscular arm around her shoulders. He really was a bearlike man, in the most fascinating of senses, and she wondered how she would have reacted if she'd met him under different circumstances. If he'd been a little older, and she'd been a little younger, and he hadn't been involved with drugs. Just a sexy flirt in a black leather jacket . . .

Then she shook herself out of the nonsensical mood and edged away from him, just a bit. "My niece told me you came by last week, so I called you at your house. Did your wife give you my message?"

"She's not my wife," he insisted smoothly. "Just a friend. Like you, only not nearly as beautiful."

"Cut it out." Laurel sighed, pulling completely free of his arm. "She's been with you ever since I met you. Have some respect for her."

"Anita is my true love," he agreed with a grin. "But when I'm around *you*, I forget all about her. And then I go home, and she reminds me. Do you see?"

"I see that you're hopeless," she chided. "Why are you here?"

"The truth?" His dark eyes clouded. "It's time to say *adiós, merienda*. Anita and I are leaving Sacramento, and I may never see you again. But I'll always remember how you saved me from prison—"

"Where are you going? What's wrong?" She eyed him sternly. "What have you done, Oso?"

"Nothing! I swear it. But I've attracted the wrong kind of attention—don't ask me how—and now I can't drive two blocks without being pulled over. And our apartment has been searched twice in the last three days—"

"What?" Laurel remembered Joe's threat to have his buddies start hassling Oso as a means of impressing Melissa. It wasn't like him to actually do it, but she'd learned first-hand lately how misguided a person in love could be. "You don't have to leave town, Oso. If you haven't done anything wrong, I'm pretty sure I can get the cops to lighten up on you."

"*Verdad?* You would help me again? Just like old times?" He beamed with relief. "I'm flattered, *merienda*. I thought you might be relieved to see me go, but instead, you're going to fight for me."

"Just give me a few days," she insisted. "I'll call you, and we can meet—" Her gaze was distracted by a black sedan, cruising by them as though studying them, and she winced slightly. The perfect ending to a perfect day—a drive-by shooting.

But it was Matthew Seaton who pulled up to the curb and shrugged out of the driver's seat, and she exhaled with relief while patting Oso's muscular forearm briskly. "I'll be in touch, I promise. Just stay out of trouble in the mean-time, please?"

"For you? Anything." He smiled as he mischievously kissed her hand. "But first, tell me your visitor isn't the lover who hurt you."

She grinned and pulled her hand free, scolding, "Go away," before she turned her attention to Seaton. "This is a pleasant surprise, Your Honor. Come on in."

But Seaton had moved into Oso's path and now boomed, "Morales, right?"

"That's right."

"I have a piece of advice for you—"

"Hey, hey!" Laurel stepped between and instructed sharply, "Oso, go home. Judge Seaton, come inside. Now! Honestly . . ." She corralled the older man up the steps and into her waiting room. "Sometimes you drive me crazy, Your Honor."

"I thought Derek was going to talk to you about that hoodlum."

"I don't take orders from Derek Grainger!"

"Not orders," he agreed hastily. "Advice. From a concerned colleague. And potential partner, if what he tells me is accurate."

"We toyed with the idea," she admitted quietly. "But it turns out we have very different ideas about how to run a practice, so . . ."

"It should have worked," Seaton insisted. "But the stress you've been under—from your involvement with that hoodlum Morales and that pervert George Perry—has been too much for you. I've been worried sick over it, Laurel. Thinking of your brilliant career going up in flames. And Derek! He's been such a beacon of talent and integrity—"

"Integrity?" Laurel almost laughed aloud, but knew it would further disturb the old jurist, and so she decided to soothe him instead. "You spend too much time worrying about Derek—"

"Not just him. All of you. You've inherited a system that's hell-bent on destroying you, when you should be honored and respected for the work you do. Sometimes I think the world's gone mad."

Laurel winced at the realization that it was probably Seaton himself who was headed in that direction, and she patted his arm anxiously. "You scare me when you're like this. Don't you know you're supposed to mellow with age?" When he didn't smile, she added softly, "My sister's a psychologist. Did you know that? And she's such a good listener—"

"There's been too much talk already," the old man grumbled. "I've spent my life talking, but no one listens, and things keep getting worse. Drugs everywhere! Little girls burning to death in cabins—"

"Please don't judge George so harshly," Laurel begged, and then to her surprise as well as Seaton's, she buried her face against his shirtfront, consumed by a rush of hurt and confusion. "He may be the only one who really does have integrity in all this. He put his life, liberty, and happiness on the line, just to rescue that innocent child. If only . . ." *If only Derek's motives could be half so noble . . .*

"There, there." Seaton patted her back tenderly. "It's not as bad as all that, is it?"

"You don't understand what George was up against," Laurel insisted, gasping for measured breath as she spoke. "His ex-wife is so awful. I know her now—all about her—and he just couldn't take a chance on her being even a small part of Amy's life."

"That's fine then," the old man murmured. "Maybe I did misjudge him after all. Help him if you think it's the right thing to do. He's lucky to have you."

"I can't let him down," she agreed as she slowly brought her emotions under control. "After all he's been through . . ."

"Help him," the judge repeated. "But not Morales. I know I'm right about him, Laurel. He's brazen, showing up here the way he does. Hounding you . . ." He cupped her chin in his hands and instructed firmly, "Go home and take a hot bath. Forget about all this for now. Leave everything to me. I'll find a way to make it all better."

"That's so sweet." Laurel sighed. "I'm so glad you came by here today. It helped me remember that George is the one at risk here. Not me. Not Derek." She hugged the judge gratefully, then turned and pulled open a desk drawer, where she located one of May's business cards. "Please?" she cajoled as she handed it to Seaton. "You helped me, and now let May help you."

"I'll consider it," he grumbled, stuffing the card into his pocket. "If you'll promise to have no further contact with Morales."

"I can't promise that. But I can promise to be careful."

195

She took his hand and squeezed it. "Take care of yourself, Your Honor. Please?"

"Don't worry about me." He smiled grimly. "Can I offer you one last piece of advice?"

"Sure. What is it?"

"Trust Derek. He's the finest man I know."

"He says the same thing about you," Laurel assured him wistfully, but her thoughts had again turned to George Perry. Because in her heart she knew that the finest of *all* these so-called fine men was the one who would do anything for the sake of his only child.

Ten

When Laurel reentered the suite, Derek sprang at her as though she were a lifeline. "Thank God! I was beginning to think—"

"You thought I'd quit?" She pushed him away and reminded him briskly, "George Perry didn't screw me, *you* did."

"Geez, Laurel!"

"We both know *you're* the one who should resign from this case, but since we also know you won't, because of your sick need for revenge, I have to insist that you *back off* and let me do my job. *I'll* be lead counsel from now on. Any attempt by you to alter that will send me straight to the State Bar. I'm sure they'd love to hear this story."

"I didn't sleep with her."

"I never said you did. And I couldn't care less. I can't *afford* to care until I've done everything possible to help my client, so please, just shut up for once and let me work."

"She still has some of my sperm."

"*What?*" Laurel stared in stunned dismay as the words registered, then she stumbled to the couch and eased herself down on the cushions. She couldn't take any more of this, and yet it kept coming and coming and coming! Her brain was screaming for a break, but instead she had to think harder than ever, because *this* was pure madness, and couldn't be allowed.

Derek knelt before her and took her hands in his own. "I'm so sorry, darling. I'd do anything to make this easier on you—"

"Forget about me," she commanded. "We have to act right now, before it's too late. That bitch might do it again, Derek. We have to call Joe—he'll know the fastest, most discreet way to get some sort of search team in there to find and seize—"

"No, Laurel. Not yet. I've got her lulled into trusting me, for the moment, and I don't dare—"

"Don't dare what?" she wailed. "Jeopardize your precious plan for revenge? You'd risk allowing her to impregnate herself again?" She sandwiched his face between her hands. "I don't know you at all, do I?"

"You know me," he assured her tenderly. "That's why you keep coming back."

"No! I come back because of George. Because in this whole crazy mess, he's the one who tried to do something positive. Something brave and wonderful."

"Making sure Amy was safe?" Derek smiled gently. "And making sure Veronica played no part in her upbringing? I agree. That was a worthy goal. It's the same goal I have—"

"Don't compare yourself to him! Not ever! He's motivated by love. You don't even know the meaning of the word."

"I didn't really know it, until I met you," he agreed, his

dark eyes shining with admiration and commitment. "I thought I loved Amy, and in my heart I do, but I didn't know what it meant—how truly life-altering it could be—until you walked into my life."

"Derek, don't. If you have any respect for me at all . . ."

"Do you remember the day you told me why you broke up with Harrington?" he persisted. "You said you wanted a love that was born like this—from fire and conflict."

"Fire," Laurel agreed sadly. "The fire of love, not the cold flame of revenge. I never wanted *this*."

"I'm so sorry," he repeated, gathering her into his arms and reassuring softly, "I love you so much. I've put you through so much, and you keep coming back for more. It's unbelievable, Laurel. I don't deserve you, but thank God I have you, because we have an incredible task ahead of us."

"Don't talk," she whispered, wanting to pull free of his embrace but unable to convince her body to cooperate. His arms felt so good. So strong. So safe, despite all the hurt and confusion. Maybe it was true. Maybe *he* was the reason she kept coming back. She couldn't resist him, despite his flaws. Veronica Perry had warped him, and maybe it would take the love of a decent woman to banish all that.

Laurel had read Derek's book, filled with insightful observations, lofty goals, and noble instincts. She had spent hours listening to him think aloud—she *knew* how his mind and heart worked!—and aside from his tragic reaction to the loss of his child, he was all she could ever want in a man, and so she repeated, more forcefully, "Don't talk. Just hold me for a while."

"My pleasure."

The phone began to ring, but neither made a move toward it, and finally the machine clicked on and Melissa's hesitant voice was pleading, "Laurel, are you there? I'm at your office, and Anita Morales is with me and . . . and she's been beaten up pretty bad. I tried calling Mom but she's not back from work yet—"

"Melissa!" Laurel had lunged for the phone and now caught her breath before instructing quietly, "Don't worry about anything. I'll be there in five minutes."

"Thanks, Laurel. I didn't know what to say to her. He—he always seemed so harmless . . ."

"You mean Oso? That's who hurt her? Are you sure?"

"She wants a divorce, and she said you're the only lawyer she knows."

"Does she need an ambulance?"

"No. She's just—well, just a mess."

"Tell her to lie down. And keep trying to get your mother, okay? I'll be right there, and as soon as I get there, you can leave. I'm sorry you got caught up in this."

"I'm okay. But—hurry, okay?"

"I'm on my way." Laurel placed the receiver back into its cradle, then informed Derek softly, "I have to go. Right away."

"I'll come with you."

"No! You're the last person I should be with right now. I don't know you, and I'm not even sure I like you. This is *so* nuts. This day . . ." She was trembling from the rush of suppressed rage and despair that now engulfed her. "I have to go, and you have to stay here. Work on the transcript. Concentrate on Veronica's testimony. Try not to think about anything else, and I'll call you in the morning."

"Laurel . . ."

"Goodbye, Derek." She backed away slowly, then turned and sprinted desperately for the door.

◐ ● ◑

While May calmly prepared a pot of tea, Laurel peeked through the kitchen door and into the living room, where Anita Morales was watching a game show. She was a tall, pretty girl of eighteen, but looked like a child now, all curled up on the couch, still wearing Oso Morales's black leather jacket and Sacramento Kings cap. No bones were broken, but her shoulders, where he'd grabbed her to shake her, were bruised, as was one cheek. It could have been worse, and Laurel had no doubt but that the next time it would be.

"She says it's the first time he's done more than just grab her or shove her," she reported quietly to May. "She says they fought over *me*, if you can believe it. Because she was jealous of the way Oso teases her—by bragging about my education and the way I quote-unquote saved him from prison."

"And yet she came to you for help?"

"Right. Because Oso says I'm the best lawyer in the world. If you knew anything about the past forty-eight hours of my life, you'd know that makes complete sense in

201

Laurel-land." She turned to her big sister and tried to smile. "I couldn't just send her to a shelter. And I thought Oso might come looking for her at my office—"

"This is fine, Laurel. I'll fix her a bed on the sofa, and maybe later, she'll talk to me a little. And tomorrow, the three of us can decide where she goes from here."

"Do you want me to stay too?"

"I want you to go home, run a hot bath, have a glass of wine, and try to pamper yourself a little. Tomorrow, after we've decided what Anita should do, we'll get to work on you."

"I'm in love with Derek."

"Yes. I know."

"I'm in love with him," she repeated stubbornly, "and he's completely warped. So what does that make me?"

"Poor Laurel," May said fondly. "I almost wish I could turn back the clock, and meet you again in that bar at the Plaza. I'd tell you not to get involved with the Perry appeal. But of course, you'd do it anyway, so . . ."

"You're right. I was hooked the moment I met him. He even said that to me today—that I wanted a hot, unpredictable love affair, and boy did I get it! And I wanted to work on a really dramatic, high-profile, complex case. It just proves that old saying: be careful what you wish for."

"Right now, I wish a little peace and quiet for you." May smiled. "I know you, Laurel. With a good night's sleep under your belt, you can handle almost anything. Provided nothing else goes wrong, of course."

The younger sister loved the flicker of concern in the

elder's eyes, and assured her gently, "There's nothing else that *can* go wrong. Believe me. Veronica, Oso, George, Derek, Anita, Judge Seaton . . ." She was counting them off on her fingers as she spoke. "Yep, that's all of them. Everything's officially as bad as it can get. I just hope my jinx doesn't go to work on my family next."

May grinned. "We're immune. How else could we have survived you this long?" Her face softened with love as she handed Laurel her purse and gestured toward the door. "Take care, honey. I'll be in touch first thing in the morning."

◗ ● ◖

Too weary to think, Laurel concentrated on driving to her condominium, parking her car, and climbing the flight of stairs that led to her door. Whenever a face tried to invade that simple mind-set—whether it was Derek's, Amy's, or Anita's—she firmly rebuffed it. Tomorrow would be time enough for that. Tonight she was going to pamper herself, like May and Seaton had suggested. But not because it would feel good or help anything. She would take the bath, drink the wine, and forget her problems because she was simply too discouraged to come up with a better plan.

The message light was blinking, and she suspected it was from Derek—the last person on earth she should be talking to—but she didn't dare ignore it. Not with the series of crises that had plagued her lately. Joe could be lying in a ditch; Clay could have broken Jessie's heart; someone's cat could have died. She knew only one thing: this couldn't possibly be good news. It just wasn't that kind of a day.

"Hi, honey, it's May. I'm sorry to have to tell you this—it's the last thing you need right now, but I knew you'd want to know. Anita decided to go back to Oso. I did what I could, but she was determined. I gave her my card—I'm sure she's going to need it, and maybe next time, she'll be ready to face the truth about that relationship, but for now . . . She's responsible for her own decisions, so please don't let this torture you. Just remember you did your best, and let yourself off the hook. Good night, Laurie, and sleep tight. And remember that we all love you . . ."

"Perfect," Laurel announced to the empty room. "The perfect ending to a perfect day." Raising her voice, she informed the universe stridently, "I'm taking my bath now! Any objections?" With a melodramatic flourish, she grabbed a thick towel from the linen closet and headed for the bathroom.

An hour later, she was wrapped in a thirsty white robe, listening wistfully to a taped collection of waltzes while staring into a glass of shimmery gold champagne. She hadn't stayed at the wedding long enough to toast Elaine and Jonathan, and so she toasted them now, then raised the glass to her lips just as her door bell started to ring.

She growled under her breath. *"Perfect.* At least now I'm clean. And—" She took a quick gulp of champagne. "I'm ready for round forty-four, or whatever this is." Hoping that it was Oso, so that at least she could punch *somebody* in the nose, she sashed her robe more securely and yanked open the door without even bothering to check through the peephole.

Flowers . . . champagne . . . candy. He had come armed and dangerous, with the true danger coming from those midnight blue eyes and the smile that had melted her heart right from the beginning. And she knew instinctively that this was the moment for which she had lived her entire life thus far. It was a staggering thought, and he was a staggeringly handsome man, and she needed to either send him away forever or throw herself into his arms and never let go. There was no middle ground anymore.

"Laurel? Can I come in?"

"Are those for me?"

He nodded, his eyes twinkling with relief at the encouragement. "Did I forget anything?"

"Did you call your mom?"

"Yeah. I called her this morning."

"Well, then . . ." She stepped into him and wrapped her arms around his neck. "I've decided to let you live."

"Thanks." He stretched to put his peace offerings on the entryway table, then cradled her gratefully in his arms. "I have so much to tell you—"

"No. I want you to dance with me. I can listen later. Right now, I just want to *feel*."

"That sounds great," he admitted, his voice husky with relief as he maneuvered her back into the living room. "You're playing our song?"

"Mmm . . ." She swayed with him, desperate to ignore everything but the feel of his body against hers. But the last vestiges of hurt were too strong, and so she murmured finally, "You said she still has your sperm. What else did you and she talk about?"

"She thinks I took the case with an ulterior motive: to guarantee that George doesn't get a retrial, by sabotaging the appeal process."

"She doesn't know you at all," Laurel said with a sigh. "Of course, neither do I."

"Laurel . . ."

She pulled free slightly, then looked him in the eye. "She believes I'd sabotage George too?"

He nodded warily.

"Because she could see I had feelings for you?"

"Yeah. She has no idea that women like you exist."

Laurel moistened her lips. "Go on."

"Huh? Oh . . ." He grinned as he rested his hands on her hips. "Intelligent women of principle, who fight for justice, and defend the weak, and do it all with such style that guys like me can't help falling in love. And begging for forgiveness."

She stroked his cheek. "Begging is good. Kissing too." To prove it, she pulled his head down toward hers, and in an instant they were devouring one another with heated thoroughness. Dancing, loving, petting—wallowing in their mutual need with both appreciation and desperation. Then he swept her up into his arms and carried her to the bed, lowering her and pulling open her robe with one gentle, masterful movement.

"Smooth." She laughed in musical delight as his lips

explored her breasts, then traveled amorously down her torso. "I'd like sixty hours of foreplay again, please."

"You're lucky I'm even able to survive *this* much." He chuckled darkly. "I've been going crazy over you, Laurel, and I don't just mean emotionally. I'm a wreck in every possible sense."

"Come here, then." When he'd complied, she moved her fingers to his shirt buttons and admitted shyly, "I'm dying for this too. To feel you, inside me . . ."

His eyes flashed with desire and he rolled off her, divested himself of his clothing, and was back in record time, mounting her and nuzzling her, savoring the moment before entry while clearly unable to resist much longer. Fortunately for him, Laurel had no intention of making him wait.

◐ ● ◑

He no longer wanted to keep anything from her, but was sheepishly glad she kept forbidding any talk beyond lustful entreaties and grateful cooing. Once he told her about Amy, she'd be completely distracted from lovemaking, and while he was as anxious as ever to find the little girl, he wanted this—this precious, amorous abandon—for just a few hours longer. It was so blissfully perfect. So innocently hedonistic. So absolutely Laurel.

Still, he needed to tell her soon and, when her phone began to ring at two in the morning, while they were half-dozing, half-cuddling in one another's arms, he cursed aloud with frustration. And when Joe Harrington's voice came booming in from the living room, he bristled with vestigial jealousy and pulled her possessively closer, pleased when she muttered softly, "I *hate* answering machines."

"Hey, Laurel, pick up the phone. It's me. I know it's late, and I know you're asleep, but wake up and pick up the phone because I've got a mess on my hands and you're right in the middle of it. Oso Morales's wife was shot about an hour ago—"

Reluctantly, Derek released her, and she dove for the phone to wail, *"Joe?* Are you there? How badly is she hurt? Oh, no!" She raised pleading eyes to Derek, as though he could somehow prove to her that Joe was mistaken, then she murmured softly, "Have they arrested Oso? Oh, no. He's just going to have to find someone else. I can't possibly—What? . . . Oh, no . . ."

"Laurel!" Derek interrupted sternly. "Tell him to call the public defender. This isn't your problem."

She sighed and nodded, but into the phone she promised, "I'll be there in twenty minutes. Just don't let him say anything else, or I swear I'll get the charges thrown out with the confession. I'm counting on you, Joseph Harrington. Okay, bye."

"Laurel . . ."

"I know, I know." She dragged her fingers through her tousled hair. "I tried to get out of it. But Joe says Oso's going berserk. He keeps shouting for me, and saying I'm his attorney—"

"Tough! He beat up his wife and then killed her—"

"I know, I know. But I don't think the cops know anything about the spousal abuse yet, and I wasn't about to be the one to tell them."

"You can't represent Morales in this even if you wanted to," Derek reminded her. "His wife came to *you* tonight all busted up, which means you're a potential witness *against* him."

"I know." She stretched her nude body, then slid out of the bed and walked toward the closet. "I'll try to be back before you wake up—"

"You're kidding, right?" He shook his head and strode across the room to pull her into his arms. "We're in this—this, and everything else—together. From now on. Believe me," he murmured ruefully into her hair, "this is nothing compared to the messes I'll be dragging *you* into before the end of the week."

"Thanks, Derek." She hugged him tightly, then pushed him away just as forcefully. "Hired guns, right? So let's get this over with, shall we?"

◐ ● ◑

"Hi, Joe." She hugged her bleary-eyed friend warmly. "Thanks for being here. Has he settled down yet?"

"A little. But he swears he doesn't know anything about the shooting. He's screaming for revenge, and either he's one terrific actor or he really didn't do it. She was shot outside their building, and claims he was inside, sound asleep, when it happened. She was supposedly going for cigarettes."

Resisting an urge to fill him in about the beating Oso had inflicted only hours before the shooting—he wouldn't be so quick to believe Oso's protestations then!—Laurel shrugged out of her trench coat, draped it over her arm, and motioned for the guard to open the door to the interrogation room.

She was grateful when Derek, who had insisted upon accompanying her, stayed back near the door while she approached Oso's seated form with a no-nonsense expression on her face. Then the arrestee raised his anguished eyes to her, and she forgot her prejudice and moved quickly to kneel before him and take him into her arms.

"They shot my Anita." He sobbed angrily against her chest. "I'll *kill* them for this! I'll rip them to shreds! You have to get me out of here, *merienda*. I have to find the bastards who did this—"

"Oso, don't. Shh, calm down, okay? Look at me now—am I your lawyer or not?" When he'd raised his eyes again, she said finally, "You have to tell me everything. Where were you when it happened? After you—after you had that fight with her, did she come back? Did you see her between the fight and the shooting?"

"They were trying to waste *me*," he explained mournfully. "No one would want to kill Anita. She was wearing my jacket—"

"Oh! Oh, I see what you mean. You're probably right." Her heart ached for the trusting, misguided young girl, whose lifestyle had doomed her so cruelly. "Look me in the eye, Oso, and swear to me that you didn't do this."

"I swear it!"

"Okay, good. Now I'm going to talk to the D.A. about this—about looking for whoever wanted to get you. I need names, Oso. Don't fool around about this."

"There's no one," he insisted softly. "I don't hurt people, *merienda.*"

"You hurt Anita. I saw the bruises."

"That was nothing—"

"Don't say that!" She caught her temper and insisted more evenly, "We'll talk again in the morning. But I can't represent you on this, Oso— No, wait! Don't argue, just listen." She waited for his sullen nod, then explained. "I *can't* represent you. I can't do a good job of that, for a lot of reasons, one of which is, I'm a witness to her bruised and battered condition. But I can help you find someone good, and I'll make sure they do a good job. I'll watch them every step of the way. Do you see?"

He nodded again, this time with resignation in his eyes. "At least you came. I didn't want to talk to anyone else."

"Once you're rested, and the police have done some more checking, things won't look so hopeless."

"Anita will still be gone."

"I know, and I'm sorry, Oso. When you're rested, we'll talk about that too, okay? But don't talk to anyone else, about anything, until you see me again or I send an attorney for you. Is that clear?"

He nodded, suddenly stoic. "No problem."

She sighed and embraced him again, then turned to Derek and shrugged helplessly. Stepping forward immediately, he took her arm and led her back to the outer room, where Joe was waiting for them.

"He didn't do it, Joe."

"Maybe not," the prosecutor agreed. "Does he have any idea who did?"

"He thinks they were shooting at *him*, which makes sense. She was wearing his jacket and hat."

"Right."

"I'm surprised anyone could get near either of them, with all the police protection you've been providing him lately," Laurel added, her tone softly accusatory.

"Huh?"

"He told me your buddies have been hassling him for the last few days. Ever since our lunch at the hotel?"

"I didn't put them up to it," Joe assured her. "But maybe something's going on I don't know about. I'll do my best to find out for you."

"Thanks." She raised up on tiptoe and kissed his cheek. "You're a good friend."

"Yeah, thanks, Harrington," Derek interrupted, offering his hand to the prosecutor. "Keep us posted on this mess."

"Sure. Just get Laurel home safely, and I'll stick around here for a while. This is the last thing you two need, with it coming down to the wire for you on the Perry appeal."

"We still have plenty of time," Laurel protested. "By this time tomorrow, we'll have it done."

"By this time tomorrow, it'll be the day *after* tomorrow," Joe reminded her. "So go home and rest."

Laurel nodded, then turned to Derek and repeated reassuringly, "There's still plenty of time. Right?"

His eyes were clouded, but he managed a cheerful "Absolutely" as he ushered her toward the door.

ELEVEN

"I can't believe you're suggesting *that*, Laurel!"

"Don't be such a prude." She eyed him mischievously. "Come on. It'll be fun. I'll go first."

He watched in fascinated frustration as she flopped back against the pillows—limp, nude, and motionless—staring into space like a beautiful violet-eyed zombie.

"I'm not doing this," he assured her. "It's perverse." When she remained eerily lifeless, he chuckled and stretched along side her, then whispered to her that he loved her and began to kiss her. Her arms curled around his neck almost immediately, while she complained, "That's cheating."

"I love you, Laurel."

"Fine! If you're going to be warm and tender, forget it. I'm going back to work."

He chuckled again as she pulled a heavy transcript into her naked lap. "We're supposed to be having our talk first. I have the ultimate in gelescent facts for you."

"'Gelescent'?" she scoffed. "There's no such word. And even if there were, I don't have time to waste on conversation. I've got to focus on these two little tattletales for a while. Why don't you take a shower or something?"

"Tattletales?" It confused him momentarily, then he

burst into laughter. "Are you referring to those two cute kids who testified for the prosecution?"

"Cute? They're finks! Stoolies! Picking on a nice guy like George, when they should have been in school or something."

"You're not going to be able to attack *their* testimony, Laurel. They're just kids."

"Bad seeds," she countered with an indignant toss of her hair. "Why should we go easy on them, just because they're a little younger than us? If they're going to put a man in prison, they have to follow the rules just like anyone else."

He laughed again and settled back to watch her work. She was so colorful, he noted fondly. Even nude, with only a white sheet around her, she lit up his world with a myriad of brilliant hues—russet, violet, and pink; ivory and tan—while her amazing spirit lit up his heart with unconditional love and acceptance.

She had forgiven him completely, without even knowing the amazing truth about Amy. That simple fact humbled him, and spurred him to want to confide everything to her, but she had resisted all such efforts, and he thought he knew why. For all her resilience and strength, she was instinctively protecting herself from any more stress, even stress that might emanate from good news.

He'd seen an example of that when, during breakfast, Joe Harrington had called with an update on Oso, who had been released, based on interviews with eyewitnesses who insisted the gunshot that killed Anita had come from a passing car. Laurel had been pleased, of course, but only in a subdued, tentative way, as though even this was interfering with her ability to concentrate on her job. She didn't want *any* news until they'd found the error that had eluded them thus far. And Derek had to admit that he too was growing concerned over the likelihood of finding it in time.

"What's this about?" she muttered, half to herself. "What's he *doing*?"

"Who?"

She motioned for Derek to be quiet as her eyes wildly scanned the page, then she glared. "Did you *read* this? Did you *see* what this judge did?"

Derek tried to catch a look at the page, but Laurel was waving it angrily. "He got down from the bench and escorted the little tattletales to the witness stand! Did you know that?"

"I guess so. I mean, I noticed it, but . . ." Derek studied her anxiously. "He was just being solicitous—"

"*Solicitous?* Since when is it *his* job to be solicitous? Isn't he supposed to be neutral?"

"They're children—"

"They're witnesses! It's bad enough that we all naturally assume they'll tell the truth, but for the judge to go out of his way—to get down from the bench!—to put his stamp of approval on them . . ." She jumped from the bed and grabbed for a robe. "Are you getting any of this?"

"He thought they'd be intimidated—"

"They're *supposed* to be intimidated! That's the whole point! That's why he sits up there and wears black robes! Since when is he allowed to decide that a particular witness, child or otherwise, is so inherently honest that they don't need to be intimidated."

"Okay, so 'intimidated' was the wrong word. He just didn't want them to be scared—"

"Oh, right," she drawled. "And it made them feel so much better to have a strange man in a black robe come down from on high and take them by the arm? Don't kid yourself, Derek. It was a pompous, self-absorbed, prejudicial gesture. If he really wanted to make them feel more comfortable, he could have let a parent or social worker walk them up and hover nearby. He could have let them bring a stuffed animal, or suck their thumb—anything but act like their goddamned grandfather!"

Planting herself directly in front of Derek, she demanded, "Have you ever seen a judge *come down from the bench* for any reason when the jury's in the room? *No!* And do you know why? Because he's supposed to be impartial and detached. He might as well have told the jury that he could personally vouch for these kids, and that he believed they were being traumatized by big, bad George Perry! It wasn't his place. It was wrong. It was"—she grabbed his face between her hands and assured him—"it was really, *really* wrong. Do you see what I'm saying?"

Derek nodded soberly. "You think this is it?"

"Don't you?"

"Yeah, I think maybe it is. But, trial counsel didn't object—"

"They were caught off guard. Who wouldn't be? And we all know how futile it is to challenge things like this on the spot. But the real beauty is, this error was inherently pre-judicial to the entire case. The kids' testimony was pivotal—if the jury hadn't believed them, George would have had a real shot at an acquittal. The appellate court won't let this go, Derek. It's too fundamental."

He was stunned, not so much by the success as by his reaction to it. His heart was literally thundering in his chest at the prospect of meeting his little girl at last, just when he'd almost given up hope of that ever happening without a long, drawn-out battle with George. He had dreaded ever having to take such a course, knowing it would subject Amy to the glare of rabid publicity, not to mention the more dreadful horror of a reunion with Veronica Keyes Perry.

"Are you okay?" Laurel whispered tenderly. "Are you thinking about Amy? I know you wanted this, for her, and I'm glad we found it. But now, I want something from you. In fact, I insist on it."

"Anything," he vowed as he pulled her into his arms and nuzzled her gratefully. "Ask anything, and it's yours."

"I want you to see a grief counselor. My sister can recommend a good one. Because, as much as this retrial means to you right now, darling, I don't think it's going to matter in the long run."

"Laurel—"

"You promised," she reminded him firmly. "I won't take no for an answer. We'll write the brief, and after that, we'll talk this through. I want to hear it all. How George told you; how you reacted. I know you well enough to know you resisted the truth."

Derek nodded. "It's not exactly the kind of thing you take a stranger's word for. I was a detail guy right down to the end."

"And you were devastated, and furious, and powerless to change it. So you focused on helping George. That was the right move then, Derek, but it's not going to be enough."

"That's true." He flashed her an exuberant smile. "How about this? How about if I told you . . . ?"

"Told me what?"

He stared into her trusting eyes and knew he had to be careful. This news, while purely good, was also staggering, and to someone with Laurel's tender heart it would be doubly overwhelming. "First, I want you to sit down here with me and take a deep breath."

She moistened her lips nervously. "You can say anything to me, Derek. You know that. But you don't *have* to. If this is painful for you—"

"She's alive, Laurel," he blurted softly. "George faked her death. He used the ashes of another dead child from his parents' mortuary, and he rigged the stove to explode, and he hid Amy somewhere safe, *but I don't know where*. I've been desperate to find her, and winning the appeal has been George's price. He'll tell me now, and then . . ." He hugged her close and buried his face in her hair. "We'll go get her. Right away. Maybe even today!"

Laurel pulled free and scanned his face warily. "What?"

"I couldn't tell you at the beginning, sweetheart. And I tried to tell you yesterday, and last night—"

"Amy?" Laurel murmured, as though permanently dazed, then she stood and wandered out of the room.

Following apprehensively, Derek watched as she retrieved the file—the Amy file—and sorted carefully through the various photographs. Settling on one, she curled up on the couch and began to trace her finger gently over the child's features while whispering in an unfamiliar, singsong tone.

"Laurel? Are you okay?" He joined her and slipped his arm around her shoulders while studying the photograph himself. "I know it's a lot to absorb, and I know you're probably feeling like I exploited you. And let's face it, I did. At first, I didn't know you well enough to trust you with this. Then I was worried about your career—I didn't want to ask you to participate in deceiving the court. And I was afraid you'd think that Veronica, as 'the mom,' had a right to know, and so . . . Laurel?"

When she turned her face to his, her confused eyes were sparkling through tears of joy, and so he continued more confidently. "Do you see why I had to humor Veronica? And why I did all those background checks? And why I kept insisting that winning the appeal was more important than *us*?"

"Do you think George will let us raise her?"

"Huh?"

Laurel's face was shining with innocent hope. "If we get him out of prison permanently, will he still let us have her? I mean, he can visit, of course, but . . ."

Derek cupped her chin in his hand and nodded. "He'll

know we'll have better luck keeping her away from Veronica. We *are* going to keep her away from Veronica, aren't we?"

"Yes, Derek. We'll keep her safe. We'll hug her, and kiss her, and spoil her, and love her—oh, Derek!" She threw herself into his lap and covered his face with kisses. "She's alive! It's a miracle! Your little baby girl."

He wasn't sure if the dampness on his cheeks came from Laurel's tears or his own as he grasped her anxiously and insisted, "I should have told you—"

"You couldn't take the chance! I might have blabbed it to the court! You were right not to trust me. You couldn't afford to care about anyone or anything else until you found her."

"Why does that sound familiar?"

She laughed and cuddled happily against him. "I kept thinking about George—about the kind of man who could be so unselfish that he'd sacrifice anything to ensure his little girl's happiness. And all along, it was *you*."

"*And* George. Mostly George."

"You and George," she agreed proudly. "What a genius he was to fake her death! And what a genius *you* were to hire *me*!"

He laughed and shrugged to his feet, still holding her in his arms. "Shall we go tell George the news?"

"I'll come, but I'll stay outside. We can't afford to spook him now, Derek. Don't breathe a word about me. You were right about that. You were right about *everything*," she added wistfully. "I would have been too impatient to handle this

221

secret. I probably would have run screaming to that prison and tried to choke Amy's location out of him."

"I thought of that myself a couple of times," Derek admitted, "but now I'm glad I waited. Happily ever after, right?"

"Why are we still here?" she interrupted. "Give me a kiss—*a really good one*—and then let's go!"

◗ ● ◖

The temptation to make love had been strong, but the prospect of finding Amy won out, and they dressed in record time, then headed for the lobby, where Derek sent for his car. While they waited, they nuzzled one another until Derek observed cheerfully, "Isn't that your niece? Melissa, right?"

"Ooohh . . ." Laurel was enchanted by her niece's seductively innocent blue sundress, only belatedly noticing her unhappy expression. Then she waved brightly and called out, "Melissa? Over here!"

"Laurel!" The girl was quick to join them, and greeted Derek before explaining, hesitantly, "I'm meeting Joe. At least, that was the plan. But . . ."

"He's late?" Laurel sympathized. "When he sees you in that dress, he'll be sorry he wasn't early."

"He's not just late. I think he's not coming at all, and I don't know whether to be annoyed or worried. I mean"— she sent Laurel an oblique message with her expressive blue eyes—"this was a *very* important lunch date. That's why we were meeting here. At the hotel."

Laurel winced, remembering *her* first time with Joe. He'd gotten a room at the Plaza that time too, filling it with flowers for the occasion. Joe would have crawled on his belly to make that appointment on time, and she was fairly certain he was even more psyched for this one. "Did you call his office?"

"They said he left hours ago, for an eleven o'clock meeting with Judge Seaton, and then . . ." She flushed and glanced self-consciously toward Derek. "They said he was taking the rest of the afternoon off, which is what I thought too."

"We talked to him briefly this morning, about Oso—"

"Oh, that's right," Melissa interrupted. "I meant to tell you, I'm so sorry about that girl Anita. She seemed so nice."

"I know. It's awful. But I'm glad, at least, that Oso wasn't involved." She saw the worry return to her niece's face and offered quickly, "I can try calling the judge. Maybe they got so absorbed in their meeting . . ."

Shifting her gaze to the lobby clock, Laurel almost groaned. Two and a half hours—no one could stand talking to Seaton that long without a break, especially when it meant keeping a lover waiting. Joe Harrington, among his many fine qualities, was a perfect gentleman, not to mention a voracious lover.

"I called over there already," Melissa admitted sheepishly. "I didn't want to embarrass him, but I'm missing class for this, so . . . Anyway, no one answered. And I tried Joe's cell phone, and his house, and now I'm worried, because he just wouldn't have missed this without calling me."

"I agree," Laurel announced briskly. "Let's go find him. Derek? Do you mind? It'll only take a few minutes."

"It's fine," he assured her. "But do you know where to look?"

"Seaton lives ten minutes from here, and Joe's house is right on the way. We'll just cruise both places, and keep trying him on the car phone, and when we find him, we'll embarrass him to death. Right, Melissa?"

The distraught girl sighed. "I just hope he's okay."

Derek left word for Joe at the desk, then escorted Melissa to the car while Laurel trailed him with admiring eyes. He was so kind and gentle, and infinitely patient, saving his temper and passion for the moments that counted—the moments that had made their love blaze, as she had dreamed it could.

And she had wanted that for Joe too, and it was beginning to seem as though he'd found it. But where *was* he? This just wasn't like him, and while she joked about him as they drove the streets, she could feel her throat tightening with apprehension over his complete disappearance.

When she spied his Mustang, tucked almost completely behind Seaton's stately residence, she let out an exaggerated sigh of relief. Then, almost immediately, new questions arose. Why stay so long? Why not call? What could be going on? "I'll go in alone. You two wait—"

"No way," Derek protested. "They're not answering their phones and he's been here for almost three hours. Anything could have happened."

Melissa gasped. "You think they're *dead*?"

"Smooth, Derek. Any more horror stories before we go ring the bell and discover a perfectly normal explanation?"

His gaze caught hers, and she knew he was trying to prepare her for something *ab*normal. But she was miles ahead of him. This just didn't feel right, and it was all she could do to smile blandly toward her niece as they made their way up onto the porch.

TWELVE

Derek pounded firmly on the front door and, when there was no response, rattled the handle, but without success. Laurel had already started toward the back and didn't know whether to be pleased or more concerned than ever when she saw the judge's black sedan in the space next to Joe's. A quick peek into each car confirmed that there were no bodies, a concept that seemed morbid but that she could see had definitely occurred to Derek, who conducted the same ritual when he caught up with her.

At the back door, he didn't hesitate long between knocking and twisting the handle, which this time was unlocked, and soon the three were standing in the judge's kitchen, where nothing seemed amiss. In fact, everything was spotless.

From a distance, they could hear a television or radio, and as they made their way toward the sound, Derek called out cheerfully—first for the judge, and then for Joe—then motioned for the women to stay behind while he investigated further. But Laurel had no intention of letting him go alone, and Melissa clearly had no intention of staying behind either, and so they followed him closely despite his frown of displeasure.

There was no one in the living room when they arrived there, but at least they had now pinpointed the noise, which was coming from behind closed double doors. "That's the judge's study," Derek explained in a terse whisper. "Let *me* go in alone this time."

Laurel rolled her eyes. "Just open it, he-man. When you hear what a great screamer I am, you'll be glad I'm right behind you."

"I already know what a great screamer you are," he reminded her with a wink. "Now stay back."

She watched him pull open the doors, and for a moment his body blocked her view. Then he growled "damn" and burst ahead to pull the gag from the mouth of a securely tied Joe Harrington, who was staring up at them from the floor with a sheepish grimace on his face.

"Oh, Joe!" Melissa wailed, dropping to her knees and throwing her arms around his neck before Derek could go to work on the ropes. "I knew you were in danger! I knew you wouldn't just miss our—"

"Shh, honey, I'm fine. Don't cry like that."

"Is the judge hurt?" Laurel asked anxiously as Derek located his pocket knife and began slitting the bonds. "What happened? Look at the bump on his head, Derek. Poor Joe!"

"I'm fine," Joe repeated grimly. "And so is the judge, at least for the moment. He's the one who knocked me out and tied me up."

"*What?*" Derek demanded. "What are you talking about?"

"Don't make him talk," Melissa interrupted. "He's been

through a lot, and he needs a doctor. We're lucky he's still alive."

"It's not that bad," Joe protested, although it was clear he was enjoying Melissa's comforting. As soon as the last rope was cut, he shook his arms, then stood and pulled the distraught girl into a warm embrace, explaining over her head, "You guys aren't going to believe this, but it's true. I checked around, Laurel, and the reason the cops have been leaning on Morales is because Seaton arranged for it—unofficially, of course. He's got a lot of friends downtown. And in the meantime, two witnesses to the shooting mentioned seeing a black sedan—"

Laurel gasped. "You're not saying . . . ?"

"It was looking pretty bad, but I wanted to give the old guy a chance to turn himself in. So I called him, and told him I needed to talk to him, and when I got here, he blindsided me."

"This is crazy," Derek murmured.

"Tell me about it." Joe was rubbing his head ruefully. "To the old guy's credit, he tied me up, but waited around until he knew I wasn't seriously injured. Then he told me he never intended to shoot anyone—just to scare Morales into leaving town by sending a bullet whizzing by his head. And I believe him. He's really broken up over killing an innocent girl. I'm afraid he'll do something to himself. We have to find him right away. He left about an hour ago."

"His car's right outside," Laurel corrected softly. "Are you sure he's gone?"

Joe exchanged worried glances with Derek. "I just assumed he'd left, but—"

228

"But I didn't," came a tired voice from behind them. "Where would I go?"

Laurel spun and, when she saw the pistol in the old man's hand, shrieked softly. Not that she feared for herself or her companions. The weapon was aimed directly at Seaton's own temple, and the anguished look on his face told them he had every intention of firing it.

Joe groaned. "Oh, man . . . Put that thing away, Your Honor."

"That's right," Derek insisted, edging toward the judge as he spoke. "Let me have it, sir, before someone gets hurt."

Seaton smiled sadly. "I'm glad to see you're able to walk and talk, Joe. Take the women outside, won't you? I need a word alone with Derek, and then . . ."

"We're not going anywhere," Laurel assured him. "And you're not going to do something like this in front of my niece, so just listen to Derek and Joe and put the gun down."

"You don't understand, Laurel—"

"Of course I do. You tried to scare Oso away, because you thought he was stressing me out and jeopardizing my career. You told me yesterday you'd take care of everything for me, right? I understand—"

"I murdered an innocent girl."

"Murdered?" She shrugged. "I don't think so. Manslaughter, maybe. We'll see. There are a lot of extenuating circumstances here, and it'll take a little while to sort it out, but . . ." She pursed her lips, then shook her head as though finally certain. "Murder's definitely out."

"She's trying the case," Seaton grumbled. "Right here, while I have a loaded gun in my hand. Didn't I tell you she wasn't normal?"

"We all know you aren't the kind of man who'd run away from your problems," Laurel chided him lovingly. "It would make a mockery of everything you stand for."

"And what do I stand for?"

"Pride, professionalism, justice—"

"Intelligence and compassion," Joe added.

"And honor," Derek finished sternly. "Put the gun down, sir. Things aren't as bad as they seem. Laurel and I will represent you—"

"I won't drag the two of you through this. You've been through too much already with the Perry case."

"You fired that gun to scare Oso away from me," Laurel reminded him softly. "It was wrong, but your motive was unselfish. You're a lot like George Perry—don't you see? And Derek and I are proud to be your attorneys. *And* your friends."

Tears were streaming down the judge's face and, when Derek stepped forward and wrapped his fingers around the pistol, the old man relinquished it easily. Then Laurel was embracing him, while Joe picked up the phone and began to dial for assistance.

"I don't want special treatment," Seaton was protesting over Laurel's shoulder. "Just call 911."

"Don't be silly," Laurel scolded. "You're hardly a common criminal."

"I killed that girl—"

"I'm not minimizing that. She was an innocent human being whose life was every bit as important and valuable as yours or mine. But I'm going to tell you what I tell *all* my clients, and I want you to listen carefully."

"What's that?"

"*You're* my concern right now. No one and nothing else. The prosecution can worry about the victim. That's not *my* job. Cooperate with me—*trust* me and do exactly what I say—and I promise you we'll get through this."

"Laurel?" Melissa interrupted. "Isn't that George Perry on TV?"

"*What?*" She whirled just in time to see the picture of George, and to note the grim face of the anchor person in the foreground. Derek quickly adjusted the volume control as a solemn voice announced, "In a bizarre finish to the notorious case of George Perry, we've just learned that earlier today, the convicted child murderer was stabbed to death in his cell—"

"No!" Laurel buried her face in her hands and repeated softly, "Oh, no . . . Derek . . ." She temporarily abandoned the judge and moved to wrap her arms around her shaken co-counsel's neck. "Derek, don't worry. We'll just— Oh, Derek. This can't be happening."

"Not now," he whispered haltingly. "Not when we were so close."

The newscaster continued solemnly. "Authorities say it's common for other prisoners to target inmates who have committed crimes against children. Special precautions were taken for Perry, but repeating the story, he has been stabbed to death by an unidentified fellow prisoner."

It was Seaton's turn to offer comfort, and he did so without hesitation. "I know you both learned to admire that man—to know him and care for him—and I'm sorry. You've worked so hard—"

"I have to call my office," Derek interrupted. "Excuse me."

"Use this phone," Joe offered, but Derek continued out of the room without a backward glance.

"He needs to use his car phone, because he needs to be alone," Laurel explained sadly. "This case meant more to him than any of us knew—"

"Go with him," Joe urged. "Everything's under control here, right, Judge?"

"Yes, of course. They'll want to observe me for a few days, I'd imagine," he added with a rueful smile. "Go and grieve with Derek, Laurel. There'll be plenty of time to mount my defense next week."

"Joe? Are you sure? Don't you want us to wait for the squad car?"

"There won't be any squad car," Joe assured her. "Just a couple of friends of mine, bringing him to a hospital for observation. Don't worry about him, Laurel. Just go help your partner. And take it easy. This is rough on you, too."

"You're such a wonderful friend." She sighed, then hugged him with all her might. "You helped Oso out, when I know you can't stand him. And"—she lowered her voice to a whisper—"you're being so sweet to the judge, even though he hit you over the head. Are you sure you don't need a doctor?"

"I'm fine for now. But after I wrap all this up, I'm taking the rest of the week off." He too lowered his voice before adding, "I'm hoping maybe Melissa and I can head up to Tahoe and do a little gambling or something."

"Or something?" Laurel studied him wistfully. "Are you going to get married without me there to kiss the groom?"

"Who knows? I had a lot of time to think, while I was tied up there, and all I could think about was her."

"That's sweet. She's a lucky girl. I just wish . . ." She pictured Derek, alone in his car, and shook her head. "I've got to go. Melissa?" She turned and beckoned to her niece, who had been standing by the window, keeping a sympathetic watch on Derek. "Can you take over now?"

"Sure." The girl smiled and moved forward confidently. "Don't worry about anything here. I'll take good care of everyone. You go help Derek. He looks like he just lost his best friend."

◐ ● ◑

"Derek?"

"Hi." He allowed her to hug him, although he seemed too listless to actually be taking any comfort in it. "I called the office. I was hoping maybe George left a note for me, or made a dying statement, or something."

"Nothing?" she guessed sympathetically.

"He died instantly. From multiple stab wounds. He should never have been in there, Laurel—"

"I know, I know. But if he'd been out here, Veronica

would have killed him herself, or hired some thug to do it for her. She made that very clear to him—without witnesses of course. We both know that, and George knew it too. I just wish . . ." She struggled against tears of both frustration and grief. "If only he had called you right after the fire. To represent him at trial—"

"He was so sure he'd get off easy," Derek reminded her woodenly. "He didn't want to have to tell me about Amy. Not ever. It was only desperation that made him send for me after the verdict, and it was already too late. We just didn't know it."

"Too late for George," Laurel agreed. "But not for Amy. She has us, remember?"

"We don't know where she is!"

"I know, I know." She cradled him gently as she promised, "We'll find her, Derek. We found error, right? And now we'll find Amy. I guarantee it."

"I appreciate the sentiment, Laurel, but it honestly may be hopeless. Our one chance is that he told her caretaker about me, and he or she will contact me now that George is dead. But I have a sinking feeling he didn't want anyone to know about my role in this prematurely, and so—"

"I'm not saying it's going to be easy, but it's definitely not hopeless. All we have to do is think like George. Poor, mixed-up George." She allowed a wave of grief to wash over her for a moment—George deserved that and more, she told herself sadly. Then she steadied herself and wondered aloud, "Who would he turn to? Who would have understood, besides you?"

"You saw those background reports, Laurel. There's no one. His parents loved him, but they were equivocal when it came to Veronica. I doubt he ever told them the perverse details, and so they clung to the idea that a mother was the natural person to have custody of a child. Even their grandchild."

Laurel noticed an official-looking car headed their way and suggested, "Let's get out of here before this place becomes Grand Central Station. We can talk at one of the coffee shops on the way to the Bay Area. And we need to go see George's parents, right? So why don't we head over there and get some lunch."

"I already called George's parents," Derek informed her wearily. "He didn't leave any kind of message for me there."

Laurel's heart sank, but she insisted firmly, "We were his friends. We should pay our respects to his parents. And I want to talk to them—"

"To ask them about people George was close to? Believe me, I've been through all that. I hired investigators. I looked into every crack and crevice of his life. I did everything humanly possible, short of asking *Veronica* where George would hide a child. Our hands are tied—don't you see?— by the need to keep this from her. If we go public, or attract any attention whatsoever, she'll figure it out. And then," he predicted knowingly, "*she'll* know exactly where to look."

"Humor me."

Derek shook his head as he grumbled, "It's a dead end, but since I ran out of ideas weeks ago, I'm willing to drive you anywhere you want to go."

She hugged him again, then watched with quiet concern as he slipped behind the wheel and followed her instructions to the restaurant. He was shell-shocked, and needed her to back off, and so, when they found a quiet booth in a remote corner, she cuddled with him in melancholy silence until the waitress arrived to take their order.

When they were alone again, Laurel couldn't restrain herself. "Tell me everything George told you. Word for word. Maybe he subconsciously gave you a clue."

Derek shrugged. "We spent less than an hour together. And he spent most of that time assuring me I'd *never* find Amy unless I came through for him on the appeal."

"Humor me again."

"Fine," he grumbled. "He told me about Veronica having my sperm frozen or preserved, or whatever—he didn't know the details. He only knew she had herself impregnated. Then he told me about Amy—how sweet she is, and how much he loved her. And he told me they were a fairly happy family for the first few years. He and Veronica had their little games, and Amy was a joy. But then Veronica grew jealous, especially when outsiders complimented Amy's looks. And it became clearer and clearer that there wasn't much resemblance between them beyond hair color and skin tone. Size; face shape; smile—it was all new. All fresh and threatening. And George began to worry, and carefully monitored the mother–child relationship. And as time went on, the details began to be more and more chilling."

"And the more solicitous he became of Amy, the more

jealous of her Veronica became?" Laurel guessed. "And that led to the divorce and the custody battles?"

"Exactly. Then all the business about the plastic surgery came up, and George understandably panicked. His first thought was to contact me, but he didn't trust me to respect his right to custody of Amy, so he came up with his harebrained scheme."

"Describe that, just the way George did."

Derek took a deep breath. "He waited for a dead child's body to come into the mortuary, then he did the cremation himself, and intentionally did a lousy job. Then he stole the burned remains, rented the cabin, and set everything up to make it look like an accidental fire. Then on his regular visitation day, he drugged Veronica, turned Amy over to a trusted caretaker, and drove up to the mountains to start the fire."

"What do you know about the other child?"

"What other child?"

"The one whose ashes George used."

Derek shrugged. "The family used the Perrys' mortuary, and George stole the ashes."

"They lost a child right around the time George made his plan," Laurel mused.

"Right. What's your point?"

"I was just thinking about what you said earlier—that there was no one in George's life who could understand his fear for his child's safety. And I was thinking—"

"You think *they'd* understand? The family of the dead child?" He shook his head and almost smiled. "That's a stretch, but it's a sweet one. Except, I suppose they'd be the *last* people in the world who would want to help George, considering that he stole their child's ashes. Right?" When she didn't agree, he glared. "Right?"

"Maybe. Maybe not. It's like organ donors, Derek. Death is always a tragedy, especially the death of a child, but if some good can come out of it—if some other life can be saved or improved, then . . ." She coughed and took a cautious sip of her water, wondering if she was wrong to be badgering him like this. Still, it made sense to her, and so—

"Did George use the word 'stole'? Did he say 'I *stole* a child's ashes,' or did he say 'I *used* the ashes of a dead child'? Because this morning, when you were telling me the wonderful news about Amy, I think you said—"

"I said 'used,'" Derek recalled quickly. "And I think that's what George said too. I just assumed he stole them, because I assumed no grieving parents would just hand over such a precious thing to a stranger."

"But it depends on how the child died," Laurel insisted, wishing her voice didn't sound so naively hopeful. "And on the impression George made—"

"He didn't say he stole them," Derek confirmed again, his voice beginning to resonate with hope. "I'm positive now. He said something like 'I took the buried remains and brought them with me to the cabin.'"

His expression was so confused that Laurel hastened to admit, "It's a long shot. It's probably nothing."

"No," he countered softly. "It's right. It's *exactly* what George would do. Because Veronica would never be able to figure it out, even if she guessed Amy was still alive. Because this kind of compassion—of selfless giving—is rare. George had it. The parents of the dead child have it. And *you* have it."

"Don't get your hopes up—"

He smiled a shaky smile and put his finger to her lips. "My hopes soar whenever I'm with you, because you're the most creative, imaginative, gutsy person I've ever known. You found that damned error, but that wasn't enough, and so you found my daughter for me—"

"Derek—"

"I'm not through," he insisted, his eyes glistening with love and appreciation. "I want you to marry me. To be my wife and my lover and my partner. I want you in my arms, and in my bed, and in my practice, and in my heart, making every day exciting and unpredictable and filled with love. Forever."

"Okay."

"Okay?" His laugh was tempered, as though he didn't believe he deserved the happiness that was flooding through him at that moment.

Laurel's own eyes were welling up with tears. "In your arms, in your bed, in your practice, and in your heart. I can't imagine anything more perfect."

"Well, then . . ." He cleared his throat, then took her hand in his own and asked softly, "Will you marry me?"

"Mmm . . ." She wrapped her arms around his neck and brushed her lips across his.

"Is that a yes?"

"Yes. On one condition."

"What's that?"

"We get our sandwiches to go, so we can get out of here and *find your daughter.*"

⊙ ● ◐

"It was so considerate of you two to drive all the way down here, just to offer your condolences."

Derek smiled solemnly. "Your son was a very special client."

"That's right," Laurel offered tearfully. "He was the most unselfish, pure-hearted client I've ever had. I'm so, so sorry he's gone. The world was a better place when he was here."

George's mother dabbed at her eyes and admitted, "We loved him, in spite of his flaws. It's nice to know he had people like you in his life. People who didn't just judge him for what he did to my granddaughter. There was more to George than that."

"Much more," Laurel agreed.

"He was always a strange little boy," the mother continued with a weary sigh. "So clumsy and shy. Afraid of his own shadow. You could have knocked me over with a feather when a classy woman like Veronica Keyes fell in love with him."

"Classy?" Laurel stared in disbelief. "Didn't George ever tell you about any of *her* little flaws?"

"That business about her being a bad mother? Don't you believe it. She adored that little girl. We all did. Our Amy

"Veronica warned everyone to keep George away from
Amy, and she was right."

"What he did, he did out of love, you know," Laurel
declared, ignoring Derek's warning glance. "In a sense, he
gave his life to help your granddaughter. *His* daughter. I
should think that would be a source of pride and comfort
for you over the years to come."

"It's sweet of you to defend him that way. But really, it's
Veronica I'm worried about." Mrs. Perry sighed again.
"Losing Amy, and now George. She loved my son, for all his
faults."

Laurel scowled. "You keep saying he had faults! What
about his strengths? What about—?"

"Laurel!" Derek flashed Mrs. Perry a reassuring smile.
"There's no need to get into that now. The bottom line is,
we all cared for George."

"And that means so much. And I'm sure you're busy, but
if you wouldn't mind waiting for just a few minutes."

"Waiting?"

"My husband is making arrangements to have George's
body brought here," Mrs. Perry explained. "But I'm sure
he'd want to meet you. He saw your movie," she added hesitantly. "I only watch comedies, but my husband loves
courtroom drama. He didn't miss a day of George's trial,
you know. He said those lawyers were just wonderful."

"Which ones?" Laurel drawled.

Derek sent her a second, more threatening warning

41

glance and insisted, "I'd very much like to meet him. And in the meantime, there's some information we need to get from you, if you're up to it."

"What kind of information? Now that George is dead, isn't your job finished?"

Laurel intervened briskly. "There are documents we have to file. Very technical legal documents. Substantiating some of the allegations in the depositions that verify our conclusory suppositions and negate any adverse inferences in connection with George's past affirmations." She smiled sweetly, ignoring Derek's widened eyes. "I suppose that doesn't make very much sense, does it?"

"Oh, I understand perfectly. We're required by law to keep those records, you know. Feel free to look through any of our files. Maybe you'll see an idea for your next movie!"

"Wouldn't that be something," Laurel agreed, arching an eyebrow to warn Derek to play along.

Mrs. Perry beamed. "In the meantime, couldn't I at least offer you some coffee? Or tea?"

"Tea sounds delicious."

Derek waited until the woman had departed, then playfully grabbed Laurel's shoulders. "What in blazes was that? Conclusory suppositions and past affirmations?"

"Do you want to look in those files or don't you? We need to keep this to ourselves, right? The last thing we need is for her to tell her beloved daughter-in-law what we're up to."

"Here I was worried about dragging you into something dishonest, and you were *born* for it!"

"Trained for it. There's a difference. Just because you can't do it— Oh, wait. I just remembered: you're a *wonderful* liar."

"Touché." He chuckled, then turned toward the file cabinet with a hopeful gleam in his eye. "If these are organized by date, we may still be able to find Amy before she falls asleep tonight."

"And if we have to wait until tomorrow," Laurel sympathized mischievously, "I'll try to find some way to make it up to you before *you* fall asleep tonight."

"Come here."

She loved his dazzling, seductive smile and went to him easily, warmed and comforted by the feel of his arms around her. If only they could surrender completely to this incredible chemistry between them. But that would mean they didn't have a daughter waiting patiently somewhere for them, and she would never trade that miracle for anything. On the other hand . . .

"My nieces will love Amy," she informed Derek with a devilish smile. "They'll want to baby-sit her, and play with her. And they'll want us to go on a long, long honeymoon, so they can have her all to themselves."

"You read my mind," he groaned. "Part of me never wants to let her out of my sight, once we find her, but you are *so* sexy . . ." Growling wolfishly into her hair, he assured her, "I'm going to learn to do one of those juggling acts you told me about."

"Hmmm?"

"Juggling fatherhood and career. But in this case, my career is going to be making love to you."

"Office romance? I frown on that, you know. But in your case—" she moved against him suggestively "—I'll make an exception. I'll even consider doing the desktop tango, like in the movie."

"That damned movie is sounding better by the minute," he began, then broke off hastily as the doorknob began to turn, announcing the return of their hostess. Insisting sternly that Laurel "Behave," he yanked open one of the file drawers and innocently pretended to be engrossed in its contents.

◐ ● ◑

"Malcolm Dunn—what a beautiful name."

Derek nodded pensively. "Do you think we should call him? His number's right here—"

"And give him a chance to run away with *our* kid? Not likely," Laurel scolded. "We have to sneak up on him. Who knows what George told him."

"Assuming he even *has* Amy."

"That again? You don't have any faith in me, Derek Grainger. It's really getting on my nerves." Abandoning the teasing tone, she said gently, "Look at this file. Dunn lost his whole family in a single, hideous automobile accident. His daughter, his son-in-law, and his only granddaughter, killed by a drunk driver. It's excruciating. He's the perfect caretaker for Amy. I'll bet his soul literally cries out for some sort of justice in this world."

"It's true," Derek murmured. "I've only been a father—or rather, I've only *known* I was a father—for a short time, and already I feel so bound up in her life and well-being."

"And Dunn's a widower, according to this, so who knows what other anguish the poor man has endured? I'm so glad George chose this particular guy, Derek. I'm sure he's taking good care of her, and reassuring her, and promising her George will come for her soon."

"But instead, I'll show up," he finished. "I hope she isn't too disappointed."

"She's a Grainger," Laurel reminded him. "She'll put you through your paces, and make sure you're worthy of her, and then she'll accept you. I've been there."

"Did I do that?"

"Yep. On the plus side," she added, "once a Grainger accepts you, they make life so sinfully perfect, you wonder how you existed before you met them. And then the fun begins, and," she eyed him amorously, "with any luck, it never ends."

"You're making it very hard to think about making the long trip to Los Angeles instead of the short trip to my place," he warned. "But I suppose I'd better call the airline. Right?"

"Right. If they don't have a flight for us, right away, I'll just die."

"If they don't have a flight for us," he assured her, "I'll call Carson Barrow. Do you know about him?"

"Your client from *False Pretenses*? Of course I know!" She

eyed him mischievously. "He gave you that gorgeous Jaguar, and pledged himself—body, soul, fortune, and empire—to you, for saving his life. That scene, at the very end of the movie, was incredibly moving. It's the reason my nieces are so sure there's going to be a sequel."

Derek chuckled ruefully. "I guess I'm going to have to break down and see that movie, just so I know what people think I'm all about. Anyway," he continued more sincerely, "Carson really was grateful—not Jag grateful, but grateful. And he's made it clear a number of times that he'd like to do me a favor. He's got a personal jet, not to mention several corporate ones, so we'll get to Los Angeles one way or the other."

"A commercial flight is less complicated," Laurel mused. "But a private jet is so . . . private. I mean, we'd be all alone, right? Clothing optional?"

"If you don't cut it out—" He pulled her into another amorous embrace and she surrendered completely, allowing the Dunn file to slip to the ground and spill out over the floor. And she was more than willing to join it, and to let Derek lock the door and make love to her, when the ill-timed Mrs. Perry again decided to visit them.

This time, George's mother couldn't help but witness the embrace, and blushed in earnest apology. "I should have knocked."

"Don't be silly," Laurel reassured her. "Derek and I were just—well, just consoling one another." She bent hastily to recover the file and Mrs. Perry, still blushing, stooped to help her. Once it was all back together, Derek offered a final series of condolences and thanks, and the couple dashed for the door, anxious to call the airport from the car, and to close the distance between themselves and Amy at long last.

THIRTEEN

It wasn't quite clothing optional, but the commercial airliner proved romantic in its own way, as Laurel and Derek snuggled in one another's arms on the half-empty flight, making elaborate plans, both for parenthood and for their honeymoon. Derek had definite ideas on the latter—Tahiti, nudity, decadence, and passion. And who was Laurel to disagree?

On parenthood, he seemed much less confident, and she found herself telling him story after story of her own father's experiences with his four daughters and seven nieces—and no son or grandson to offer male solace.

"When he gets together with my brothers-in-law, that's what they fantasize about. Having a boy kid. It's hilarious."

"I don't blame him for retiring to Arizona as soon as you left for college. It must have been nerve-racking for him," Derek said with clear sympathy. "Watching girl after girl go off on dates, wondering if the boy would behave. Ugh." He shook himself in pure disgust. "Amy's not dating until college."

"There you go!" Laurel beamed. "That's exactly what Dad always said."

"And?"

"And we started at fifteen, of course. And believe me, even *that* was conservative. But we were taught to respect ourselves. That's the key, right?"

"What good does respect do when some oversexed jock is pinning down a helpless girl—"

"You're really good at this! My dad's going to love you. You'll fit right in."

"Fifteen?"

"If you're lucky. Who knows how old she'll be when she meets some boy at a football game, when she's supposed to be with her girlfriend—"

"Did *you* do that? How old were you then?"

"Fourteen," she admitted, enjoying his groan of disbelief. "I was madly in love with a boy Dad couldn't stand. A *senior*, with the neatest car—"

"Stop," he pleaded. "You're killing me here. She's not going to any football games unless *I* take her. And if she wants to get together with girlfriends, they can play at our house."

Laurel giggled wickedly. "This is fun. Next you'll be saying she can't wear makeup—"

"Makeup? Why would she want to do that? She's pretty just the way she is. Too pretty," he added mournfully. "I'm not going to survive this, am I?"

"You're going to be wonderful at it. All your instincts are right on target. Luckily, so are mine. For example, when you look handsome like this, my instinct is to run my hand inside your shirt, like this."

"I like that," he admitted. "Anything else?"

"Mmm." She ran her hand mischievously down his torso. "This is where your instincts and my instincts join forces."

Derek groaned. "I should have gotten Carson's jet. This feels *too* good."

"Some day," Laurel whispered sweetly in his ear, "Amy and *her* fiancé are going to—"

"Laurel!" He shook his head, then raised her impish hand to his lips and kissed it. "I can see I'm going to need a lot of advice from your father. How soon do you think I can meet him?"

"We'll take Amy to their ranch the first chance we get. My parents will adore you both. But, Derek?" She smiled sweetly. "You're not going to tell Dad that football game story, are you? I mean, I was just kidding—"

"Revenge"—he grinned malevolently—"is going to be very, very sweet."

◗ ● ◖

Derek eased the rental car up to the curb in front of Malcolm Dunn's neatly groomed two-bedroom cottage and announced quietly, "This is it. Any last-minute advice?"

Laurel's heart ached for him—for the hopefulness in his face and the hoarseness in his voice. So much was riding on this for him—to find his child, to make a good impression, to find the words to tell her all she'd lost, and found, in this one chaotic day. "I'm starting to wish we'd called first," she confided. "What if we're wrong, Derek? Will you ever forgive me?"

"This is pure George," he reminded her confidently. "And you know we couldn't risk calling first. They might have had some kind of code or something. We couldn't take a chance on alerting him. He's undoubtedly heard about George dying by now, and it's quite possible he's *never* heard of me. And we have to assume that his overriding goal is to keep Amy away from Veronica, so . . ." He gave her a reassuring smile. "Five more minutes, and then we'll know, one way or the other."

"Five minutes that will change our lives forever. Again." She took a deep breath and offered, "Do you want to go in alone?" When panic flickered in his eyes, she reassured him quickly. "I'm *dying* to go with you. So come on. Let's just do it."

He chuckled at the military tone to her suggestion and pushed open the driver's side door. "Here goes nothing— or should I say, everything?"

When he came around to hand her gallantly out of her seat, he paused for one last embrace, whispered "thanks," then hurried her up the pansy-lined walkway that led to the front entrance. Only the screen door was closed, although all the shades and blinds had been pulled. Peering into the darkness, Laurel began to worry. "It's the middle of the day. If he's home, why's it so dark? And if they're out, why leave this door open?"

"Maybe Amy's napping. But . . ."

Laurel nodded. The house wasn't simply dark, it was eerily so, and when she knocked on the doorjamb, she did so softly. Then she glanced at Derek's face, saw the tension

therein, and pushed open the door without further formal-
ity. Two steps into the hall gave her a view of the living
room and she gasped at what she saw.

Candles, everywhere, illuminating and shadowing as
they flickered and burned, emphasizing somehow the
deadly quiet of the plainly furnished room. It was like a
wake, she decided, although she didn't dare give voice to
that reaction for fear of further straining Derek's compo-
sure.

"What in the hell?" Abandoning all restraint, he strode
toward a window, ripped open the blind, then turned and
blanched all in one move as his eyes fixed on the sofa that
now faced him. "Laurel . . ."

She hurried around to the front of the couch and
groaned at the sight of an elderly man lying on his back, his
hands folded across his chest, his features still and lifeless
despite the garish pink blusher and dark lipstick that had
been applied in an attempt to simulate robust health. The
stories came rushing back—stories of morbid rituals and
perverse enjoyment . . .

"Veronica," Derek whispered in disgusted disbelief.

"How did you know?" a cheerful voice demanded from
behind them and they spun to see her, eyeing them with
angry amusement, a pistol pointed solidly in Laurel's direction.

She was dressed in jeans and a baggy T-shirt in an obvious attempt to mute her eye-catching proportions on this
particular mission. Her hair was twisted and braided tightly
against her head and she wore little makeup, although the

scent of her perfume was characteristically overpowering. Still, it was the gun that stole the show, at least from Laurel's perspective. And unlike Matthew Seaton's display only hours earlier, this time, the danger was definitely to Laurel and Derek.

"Where's Amy?" Derek demanded, stepping between the two women and shielding Laurel with his towering form.

"Good question," Veronica said coolly. "I was hoping *you'd* know. This old man wouldn't tell me."

"And so you killed him."

"Of course not. He was the only one who could tell me where my little girl is," Veronica reminded him sharply. "Unfortunately, he had a heart attack—almost the instant he saw the gun, in fact. But no one could ever blame this on me—I never touched him."

"A heart attack?" Laurel moved swiftly toward the couch to check the poor man's pulse, but his skin was so cold, she shrank away quickly despite the rush of tenderness she felt for his soul at that moment.

Veronica laughed. "I know a dead man when I see one. Just ask Derek. And take my word for it, this one looks better dead than he ever did alive. Didn't I pretty him up well? George would be so proud of me."

"Put the gun away, Veronica. We're calling the police."

"Don't be a fool." Again she leveled the weapon expertly in Laurel's direction. "We have to get out of here and find Amy. If we leave now, no one will ever be able to connect us with this. George is dead now, and we have a fresh

253

start—the three of us. Or should I say, the four of us?" She grimaced meaningfully. "I don't *think* so."

"Forget about Laurel!" he advised sharply. "She's irrelevant now. The case is over, and she'll keep her mouth shut about Amy if I pay her well, which I will. Right now"—he moved again between the pistol and the woman he loved—"we have to figure out where Amy is. That has to be our priority. How did you find out about Mr. Dunn?"

"*You* told me," Veronica admitted, studying him cautiously. "When I heard the news about George on the radio, I ran to his parents' mortuary to find out what they intended to do about his body. If there was any chance we could still view it . . ." She shivered slightly, and Laurel was fairly certain it was with delight rather than dread. "As I pulled up, I saw the two of you getting into your car. I went in to interrogate Donna, and she was sobbing, and there was a file in her hand, and she told me you'd been looking at it, and it took me about thirty seconds to realize what my fool husband had done. He was such an idiot, but you! You were so clever and resourceful to have figured it out."

"So you rushed here?" Derek nodded. "But Mr. Dunn didn't say anything at all?"

"He said he gave Amy to the next person on the list." Veronica's eyes flashed with disgust. "Can you believe that idiot George actually made a *list*? I've been looking for it, but Dunn must have destroyed it. Or he passed it on to the next person for safekeeping. There were instructions too, he said. I can't believe George was so perverse! Hiding her with strangers—"

"And there's no trace of Amy here anywhere?"

"No clothes, no toys, nothing. But I can feel she's been here. A mother knows these things, Derek. My baby was here, crying for her mommy. You just *have* to reunite us!"

Derek nodded. "I can see now how much you really love her. It's too bad things have gotten so far out of control. All of this could have been worked out. Especially now that you've been getting some counseling. That's what it said in your deposition, right?"

"Yes, Derek," she insisted breathlessly. "You were right to tell me I needed help all those years ago. It's made such a difference. I swear it."

"I'm sure it has." He pursed his lips and studied her openly. "I always believed that, with a little help, you could be—well, frankly, the perfect woman."

"That's so true!" Veronica brightened with relief. "I'm ready to be a better mother now, Derek. It was never right when George was alive, because he was jealous."

Derek was nodding again. "I could see that when I visited him in prison. He needed me, but he still hated me for being Amy's real father."

"That's true too." She moved now until she and Derek were staring deep into one another's eyes. "He hated you because he knew I never forgot you. I chose you for Amy's father because you were the most attractive, satisfying man I'd ever had. That's why George was so jealous."

Laurel watched, fascinated, as Derek deftly handled the unbalanced woman, luring and seducing her with his

255

strength and sex appeal. *He could have been an actor,* she realized proudly. *He's saving my life . . .*

"If we find our daughter," Derek was insisting, "you have to promise to continue with your therapy. At the beginning, I'll have custody, but we'll work toward a time when we can live in the same house, for Amy's sake, and sleep in the same bed." He rested one hand on Veronica's waist while his second traveled up to stroke her breast. "I've been thinking about you, ever since you came to the hotel. And I've been thinking about what you said, about giving me more children. Stronger ones, this time."

Her lips had curled into a tell-tale smile of triumph, and now she wrapped her arms around his neck, breathing his name as though they were about to make love right there in front of Laurel. Or perhaps she had forgotten Laurel completely. Either way, she was now only halfheartedly gripping the gun, as the handsome father of her child lowered his head to kiss her deeply and passionately.

When the pistol clanked to the floor, Laurel dove for it, but her effort proved unnecessary. At the first possible instant, Derek had jerked himself free of the kiss, yanking Veronica's arm behind her almost viciously and pinning her against the wall while coolly requesting that Laurel call 911.

$$\textbf{0} \quad \bullet \quad \textbf{0}$$

The police response was quick, and Derek was fairly certain it was because of Laurel's message—something about a wild-eyed Amazon with a gun and a corpse painted up like a clown. Veronica shrieked, threatened, wheedled and pouted, but was still led away with her wrists handcuffed behind her back, all the while protesting her innocence and warning Derek that his plans for a relationship with Amy were futile.

"I'm her mother, and George was her father!" she screamed moments before being sternly pushed into the backseat of a patrol car. "The whole country knows that! And I didn't kill that stupid old man—he had a heart attack! I didn't lay a finger on him!"

Laurel seemed to enjoy explaining the felony-murder rule to her, and suggesting to her that she get a good lawyer fast, finishing with, "You have the right to remain silent, Veronica, like these nice policemen just told you. So I suggest you shut up and get into the squad car before the press arrives to take photographs of you in jeans with no makeup."

But when things finally settled down, and a detective had finished taking their statements, Derek was surprised to see his usually resilient co-counsel trudge to the rental car and slump into the passenger seat as though defeated. She'd been such a source of energy and hope for him, and now it was time to repay some of that, so he joined her, insisting cheerfully, "I gave that detective my mother's address and phone number. He wants us available for the next day or so, so why don't we just go over there for dinner, and she can show you my baby pictures."

Laurel studied him wistfully. "She lives here in Los

257

Angeles? Did you grow up here?" When he nodded, she sighed. "I want to meet her, of course, but—what about Amy? We have to find her. And we have funerals to go to. Anita, George, Mr. Dunn—three innocent people, dead. And I'm worried about the judge. And Oso—"

"Everyone will be fine for a few days more. And we'll try to make the funerals, but we can only do our best, right? And as for Amy . . ." He tilted her chin upwards with his finger. "When news of Veronica's arrest hits the papers, the second caretaker on the list will know it's time to contact me. George is gone, Veronica's out of the way—it's logical to assume that the instructions cover this, right?"

Laurel shook her head. "We lucked into finding Mr. Dunn, but with this second person, the connection to George might be so attenuated we can't figure it out. And in the meantime, what if they just decide to keep her? Or what if they don't know about you? You said yourself, George wouldn't want anyone knowing about that prematurely. What if George told them to keep her forever if anything happened to him?"

"They may not know I'm the father, but when they hear George and Veronica are dead, they'll definitely contact the authorities. They won't want the responsibility of keeping her for too long with no clear legal right to custody, even if George did give them informal permission. Right?"

"I guess so."

"Come on, Laurel. Snap out of it. Our happy ending's right around the corner. I'll admit, I don't like waiting, or picturing Amy in the custody of social services while this thing is hashed out. And I'd rather she learned about George and her mother from someone who loved her . . ." He winced, realizing he was depressing himself without making any appreciable dent in Laurel's mood. "The bottom line is, we're better off than we were an hour ago, when Veronica was pointing a gun at our heads and planning on finding Amy herself."

"And having another Grainger baby," Laurel agreed softly. "We can stop that now at least, Derek. With everything out in the open, and irrefutable proof of how nuts she is, we can do whatever it takes to retrieve your specimen and see that it's disposed of. That's *such* a relief."

He nodded and started the engine. "As soon as we get to my mother's, I'll call my office and have them get an investigator on that. I imagine Veronica must have used a sperm bank somewhere in the Bay Area, right? The cops can get a warrant to go through the records until they find the right one and we can recover the specimen and have it destroyed."

"Right. A sperm bank. That's probably exactly where it is. What was I thinking?" Reaching down for her purse, she pulled out an elasticized hairband and pulled her mane into a tight ponytail. "There. That's better."

"Do you have any idea how many times a day you do that?" Derek asked fondly.

"What? Put my hair up?" She shrugged and admitted, "I can't concentrate when anything's on my neck. You'll never see me wearing a turtleneck or a choker—"

"And it explains why you go so crazy when I nibble at you?"

Her violet eyes began to sparkle again at last. "I also can't concentrate when you look at me like that, so just keep your eyes on the road and let me try to think like George again. I'm *not* letting Amy spend one more night with strangers, and that's that."

He wanted to tell her to let herself off the hook, but couldn't, because he too was impatient to wrap things up— to cradle the child in his arms at long last. And he'd learned that Laurel could make things happen. What was it the judge had called her? A renegade who didn't know her place? "She doesn't play by the rules," he'd said. "She makes them up as she goes along."

Give it your best shot, Laurel darling, he encouraged silently as he watched her from the corner of his eye. *And if it doesn't work this time, we'll still be just fine. Because we have each other—and eventually we'll have Amy—and that's so much more than I ever thought I'd have.*

FOURTEEN

"Thinking like George" wasn't easy for someone like Laurel, who was accustomed to having family and friends nearby to offer unconditional support and love. For George it had been so different. Five minutes with his mother had told Laurel *that*. And so he had turned to Malcolm Dunn, a virtual stranger, in his time of need. It was sad. And it was frustrating, because she knew that the infamous second caretaker was probably even more remote from George's life than Dunn, and thus even more difficult to track down.

Think, Laurel, she pleaded with herself. *It has to be someone George trusted to treasure a child—this particular child, or children in general. But not a relative, or anyone Derek might investigate while working the appeal. Someone who would be willing to do something this unusual and imposing. Maybe someone who owed George a favor? A really, really huge favor . . .*

That didn't seem likely. George was sweet, but semireclusive—not the type to be gaining influential support or earning anyone's boundless allegiance. While she was sure he'd done a fine job in the mortuary, and had brought a strange sort of comfort to the bereaved families who shuffled sadly past his work, he hadn't exactly been doing reconstructive surgery. And outside the mortuary, he'd been strictly a homebody, devoted to his daughter and dabbling in watercolors, but not really socializing, even with his neighbors.

Dunn and Derek. Those were the only two persons Laurel could imagine as candidates for a favor of this magnitude—Dunn, because of his loss, and Derek because he was the biological father and so, in his case, it wouldn't be a favor at all. It would be an honor. A duty. A heartfelt pleasure. Derek Grainger wouldn't just be willing—he'd be *grateful* for the chance to do this enormous favor for George.

Why did that sound so familiar? Being grateful for the chance to do a favor—to repay a monumental debt that could never really be repaid. She racked her brain and then, like a bolt of lightning, it hit her. In fact, she could see his face with startling clarity, although she knew it was actually just the face of the actor who had been chosen to portray him—as the grateful client in the film *False Pretenses*.

If George Perry had seen that movie's emotionally charged ending—and Laurel suspected jubilantly that he'd watched it again and again—then he had known *exactly* who would be willing to shelter Amy Grainger without question or hesitation should Malcolm Dunn ever need to step down.

Carson Barrow, ready and able to hand over the keys to a shiny new Jag, or to lend a private jet at a moment's notice, or to put an empire on the line—an empire that probably boasted half a dozen remote island homes, far away from the prying eyes of reporters and psychotic

Amazons. The chance to play hero to a little child and repay an old debt at the same time had probably been so intoxicating.

"Give your poor brain a rest, Laurel." Derek was smiling gently. "My mother's house is just around the corner. We'll have a nice leisurely dinner, then we'll break into a bottle of cognac and figure out who else George would have trusted."

She was determined to keep her face expressionless for fear of raising his hopes prematurely, but in her heart she had no doubt that she was right. Carson Barrow had Amy, and was undoubtedly following George's instructions with manic devotion, whisking her off to a fairy-tale location and lavishing her with toys and reassurance. He wouldn't have had advance warning of this—George would never have taken that kind of risk, for fear Barrow might tell Derek prematurely. George would have hoped Dunn would carry through to the end, but if not . . .

Contact a man named Carson Barrow, she could hear George explaining tersely to Dunn. *His headquarters is in New York. If you call him and tell him he's in a position to do a valuable service for Derek Grainger, provided he follows your instructions to the letter, he'll be on your doorstep within hours, and he'll do just like we ask.*

Of course, after the initial shock, Barrow would have been dying to contact Derek, but would he risk it? Wouldn't he find some melodramatic pleasure in doing all this, sight unseen, until the moment of revelation arrived? Who knew what threats or misleading dangers George had outlined in his 'instructions'? If nothing else, the danger from Veronica would have been easily verifiable.

Barrow would soon hear about Veronica's arrest, but if he was in another country, or on an island paradise, it might be hours, or even days, before that happened. And so Laurel would short-circuit that time frame. She'd call him from Ellen Grainger's house, without telling Derek, and if she was right—

"We're here. Are you ready to meet your future mother-in-law?"

"Yes, Derek. I can hardly wait."

She knew her cheeks were flushed and her eyes sparkling, and hoped he'd attribute it to nerves or anticipation over this first encounter. But she didn't have time to feel nervous or concerned about making a good impression. All she cared about was getting to a phone!

Still, she took a deep breath while Derek found his key, opened the door, and boomed, "Mother? Are you here?"

"Derek?" The voice was as cultured and gracious as it had been on the phone, but this time, it was laced with surprise and delight. And when Ellen Grainger came through a swinging door and approached them, the sheer joy in the woman's face left Laurel almost speechless. Had it been *that* long since they'd seen one another? Was a visit—planned or otherwise—from her only son such a novelty in this poor woman's life?

"This is just the most amazing surprise! And you must be Laurel! Oh, please come in and make yourself comfortable." She hesitated, then grabbed Derek and hugged him warmly. "I've missed you so much."

Derek hugged her in return, then announced briskly, "You won't believe why we're in Los Angeles, Mother. In fact, you'd better sit down somewhere before we fill you in."

"First things first." Ellen beckoned for Laurel to approach her, then took both her hands and squeezed them gently. "It's so nice to meet you, Laurel dear."

Laurel smiled at the hesitant gesture. "I'm a hugger, I'm afraid. So?"

Ellen's face lit up and they embraced fondly. "You're as lovely and warm as your voice. I was afraid Derek wouldn't notice, but of course, he couldn't help but be drawn to you. I see that clearly now."

"She's going to marry me, Mother, believe it or not. What do you think of that?"

Ellen laughed. "I think it's wonderful! And maybe I really should sit down. From the looks on your faces, you're bursting with even more news than that."

"Believe it." Derek gestured toward the living room. "After you, ladies."

When they had settled down, with Laurel and Derek on the gray velvet sofa and his mother in an elegant wing chair, Derek explained. "This is going to be a shock, but under the circumstances, you probably need to hear it all at once. Let's start by saying—"

"Let's start by saying Derek and I want to have children right away," Laurel interrupted cheerfully. "Does that bother you?"

"On the contrary. I've dreamed of having grandchildren to spoil and love. I have the time now, and . . ." She smiled sheepishly toward her son. "Well, let's just say, there are things I'd do differently if I could live my life over again. But since that's not possible, I'd consider grandchildren a sort of reprieve, as well as a blessing."

Derek seemed surprised and touched by the words. "You did your best. In fact . . ." He gestured around the room, indicating the expensive artwork and tasteful furnishings. "You did all this, without help. It's impressive, don't you think, Laurel?"

"Absolutely. I barely manage to pay my rent each month," she explained to Ellen with a cheerful smile. "I don't know how you did it."

"Laurel works hard," Derek intervened hastily. "But her clients are poor—"

"And she's too tenderhearted to insist that they pay her what she's worth?" Ellen smiled. "You need a business manager, dear. If I weren't retired, I'd offer my own services."

Derek grinned. "She's got me now. When it comes to managing a business, I take after you, remember? Anyway . . ." He sent Laurel a stern glance, as though warning her not cushion his announcement again. "Like Laurel said, we're going to have kids right away. In fact, we already have one. Because it turns out I fathered a little girl, six years ago, without even knowing it, and now, we're planning on raising her. It's a long story, and we'll fill you in later, but for now—what do you think?"

"I think she'll be lucky to have the two of you in her life."

"The three of us," Laurel murmured. "And all my family too. It's really a miracle, isn't it?"

"Yes, Laurel. It's wonderful news."

Derek eyed her with wary appreciation. "You're taking it well. I thought you'd be shocked."

"Well, I don't know all the details, so perhaps you can still shock me," Ellen said with a smile. "You might start by telling me where she is right now."

"She's safe," Laurel insisted quickly. "But her stepfather left her in the care of a series of trusted friends, and we need to track them down. If it sounds bizarre, that's because it is. But she's perfectly safe. Her name's Amy. Derek, do you have a picture . . . ?"

He pulled out his wallet and exhibited a snapshot proudly. "What do you think, Mother?"

"I think she has your eyes."

Laurel felt a lump rising in her throat and had to steady herself before she suggested, softly, "Derek mentioned you might show me his baby pictures, and I'd really love that. When you have a minute—"

"He was an adorable boy," Ellen confirmed. "Why don't we have a light meal, and then we can all look at them together. Derek? Go along to the kitchen and fix us some sandwiches while Laurel and I get better acquainted."

"Sure. Whatever." He shot Laurel a look that loosely translated as *See? Didn't I tell you she wasn't maternal?* then headed down the hall.

The moment he was out of earshot, Laurel whispered, "I have a theory about Amy. About where she is, I mean. I didn't want to get Derek's hopes up—he's been through so much already!—but I'm almost sure I'm right."

"Oh?"

"Do you know who Carson Barrow is?"

"Certainly. The man Derek saved from the gas chamber."

"A wealthy man, who pledged himself to Derek, and would just love to do him a favor like this! And he'd have the means—a remote hideaway, a private jet, et cetera, et cetera. I'd like to use a phone to contact him, right away. It would make Derek so relieved, and so deliriously happy, if we could give him good news. And if I'm wrong, he never has to know. Will you help me?"

"Of course. In fact"—Ellen's blue eyes twinkled with conspiratorial delight—"I have a theory or two of my own about possible hiding places for Derek's little girl."

"Really?" Laurel grinned. "I knew from the moment I saw you that we could be allies. And maybe even friends?"

◗ ● ◖

Derek paused in the hall and listened to the faint sounds of the two women discussing him. Their camaraderie pleased him, and so he decided to concentrate on *that* and to ignore such details as his mother's asking *him* to make sandwiches—not only was she lacking in maternal instinct, but she was a lousy hostess to boot! She'd probably be a lousy grandmother too, but if she was successful in the mother-in-law department he could forgive her the rest. With that in mind he pushed open the kitchen door and as he did, all of the righteousness and judgment disappeared from his jaw and it sagged open in disbelief.

From her seat at the table, a blond angel beamed in his direction, waved cheerfully, and greeted him. "Hi."

Derek tried to speak but couldn't. His eyes were filled with the sight of his daughter—her huge blue eyes, chin-length golden hair, and tiny, perfect hands. Ten fingers—he could see that. And as she swung her tiny feet under the table he imagined ten toes under the black patent leather, and his chest ached with a rush of pure relief. His daughter, his firstborn, was healthy. Glowing, in fact! And she was waiting for him to respond, or move, or at least to breathe, so he moved shakily toward the table. "Hi, Amy."

"Do you want a sandwich? The grandma lady made them for me."

"The grandma lady?" His gaze swept over the plate of fancy sandwiches between them on the table. Perfect little triangles, with the edges cut off, and filled with some dainty, unfathomable filling. His mother had made these? For this child? His child?

"She let me play with your toys."

"My toys?"

"In your room. In the closet. The trucks and stuff."

"Oh." He shook his head in awed amazement. "Do you mind if I sit down here with you, Amy? I'm a little shaky at the moment."

"It's okay." She watched him intently as he settled into his chair, then turned her attention back to her dinner.

"How are you doing, Amy? Are you okay?" He wanted to

pat her hand but didn't dare. "Do you feel safe here?"

"It's neat here, 'cept there are too many boy toys. But I like the doctor kit, cause the grandma lady said that's a girl toy too."

"She's absolutely right." He cleared his throat, then dared to ask, "Did she tell you who I am?"

Amy nodded. "You're my other daddy."

It almost knocked the wind out of him—that innocent summary of her chaotic little life, pronounced in that sweet, trusting voice. "Is that okay with you? That I'm your daddy, I mean?"

The girl nodded again. "My first daddy went to heaven, so I need a other one."

"I'll do my best." He studied her warily, surprised that she could have adjusted so easily to news of her beloved father's passing. Then he remembered that it had been more than six months since Amy last saw George. Apparently, Malcolm Dunn had taken good care of her, as she grieved for the loss of her parent. Or rather, parents—because after all, she had undoubtedly loved and missed Veronica . . .

"Did the grandma lady tell you about your mommy?"

The blue eyes clouded slightly. "She has to go away to get better, and it'll take a long, long time. Almost forever. Daddy already 'splained it to me. But the grandma lady said not to worry about it, cause it'll be okay, so . . ." She shrugged, then smiled sweetly.

"Well, I agree. There's nothing to worry about. Everything's going to be fine. You'll be spending lots of time with us. With me, and with the—with your grandmother.

And with a lady named Laurel, whom I'm going to marry right away. Then she's going to help me take care of you. You'll love Laurel," he added, calmed just by the act of repeating her name. "She has beautiful auburn hair, and huge violet eyes, and the most loving heart in the world."

"Is that her?" Amy pointed behind him and he turned sheepishly toward the two women. Laurel's eyes were swimming with tears of amazement and happiness and, as he stood to lead her toward the table, he wondered how it all could have come to so miraculous a conclusion.

"Yes, Amy, this is Laurel."

"Hi, Amy." Laurel was on her knees beside the child's chair, hugging her with the abandon Derek had come to adore. "You can't believe how happy we are to finally meet you. I think you and I are going to be wonderful friends."

"If you marry my other daddy," Amy observed quietly, "you'll be my other mommy."

"I'd love that. I love your daddy—*this* daddy standing right here. In fact, I love him so much I have to grab him and hug him right now. Want to help me?"

"No, I'll just watch you."

"Okay, but it's a lot of fun," Laurel said, clearly trying to entice the child. "If you change your mind, feel free to join in." Jumping to her feet, she held open arms toward Derek and his sobbing mother. "Come here, you two. We don't have a minute to lose."

He felt their arms—his mother's, his bride's, and then, most wondrously, his daughter's—and the moment became a rebirth for him. A rebirth of hope, and trust, and commitment to a style of life he had believed denied to him forever. It had seemed impossible, but there was *always* a hook—Laurel in all her mischief had taught him that!—and together they would teach it to Amy, and then to the other children that would follow from their lovemaking.

Stroking Laurel's tear-streaked face, first with his eyes, and then with his thumb, he whispered his thanks to her and then, without losing that priceless contact, reached down with his free hand to scoop up his firstborn—into his arms and into their hearts forever.